I0682865

A-Sides

&

B-Sides

A-Sides

&

B-Sides

EVAN BROWN

Columbus, Ohio

A-SIDES & B-SIDES

Published by Gatekeeper Press

2167 Stringtown Rd, Suite 109

Columbus, OH 43123

www.GatekeeperPress.com

ISBN: 9781732010109

Printed in the United States of America

Contents

CHAPTER 1

I can't put my finger on it

IT'S ABOUT TIME I told more people what happened to me in London, as I've been sitting on this story for almost twenty years now. Only one other person heard it before and that's my friend Brian. And the reason he heard it was, like it or not, he enabled it.

Some twenty years ago I was hanging out at Brian's house as I pretty much did every week from junior high into college. I'd go over there and we'd listen to music pretty much all day long. Funk, Indie, Punk, Classic Rock, Free Jazz, Metal, Prog and Kraut Rock—we absorbed it all.

When we weren't listening to music at Brian's house, we were making music in mine. My parents had a soundproof basement where my drums bothered no one. Brian was free to turn up his guitar amp and record on his beat up four-track. The music we made was just as crude as the four-track recording, but we did show some potential here and there.

The spring we graduated from college left me with a stomach-churning feeling called What Now? I was working five days a week in a coffeehouse, making good money in tips and saving up for a rainy day.

Brian on the other hand, was racing toward middle age. He had a job as a salesman for the Pirates, making twenty-two thousand a year plus bonuses selling people season tickets to see a mediocre baseball team. At twenty-one, he was already engaged to a very nice girl named Janis who was going to cosmetology school. She planned on becoming a hair and makeup stylist.

Brian was not just content to stay put in Pittsburgh—he welcomed it with open arms. He once told me "I hope my mom lives a long time. But if she passes away and she left me the house, it would be ideal. All I need is this house, my guitar, my dog and Janis."

To me, the idea of staying put in the house where I grew up or settling down before I'd seen any part of the world sounded like one long complacent nightmare. Even though I wasn't yet sure what I really wanted to do with my life beyond something having to do with writing or music, I sure as hell knew I didn't want to put down roots at twenty-one, least of all in the city where I grew up. It was more or less all I'd ever known. That had to change.

I was filling in for the assistant manager Karen one weekend when I decided to go to Europe. Like a last fling kind of trip before I tackled bigger life goals, like careers. I'd been working at the coffeehouse for a few years and was getting bored.

It was six-thirty in the morning and the Bicycle Gang was arriving one by one. The Bicycle Gang, as I called them, were a group of forty and fifty-something males, who met every Saturday to take long rides on bikes that cost as much as my first used car. They were all nice, funny, rich and great tippers. Each week a different one would buy drinks for the others, plunk down forty dollars and say something like: "keep the rest, it's still cheaper than buying a round at a bar."

This particular morning, Mister Fitzsimmons was the first to arrive. I was already pouring his usual medium coffee in a large cup so he would have lots of room for cream before he'd even entered the store.

"How's it going, Evan?"

"Fantastic. I've decided I'm going to go Europe

"That's great!" Mister Fitzsimmons said. "When?"

"August."

"You'll love it. You need to go to Malta. My wife and I lived there back in the 70's for two years. You will love it."

I knew I wanted to go to Paris and Rome and London but I wanted other destinations beyond the obvious. I didn't know anything about Malta, but I liked Mister Fitzsimmons and his recommendation was enough for me. Malta fit the bill.

On one of my off days I booked an appointment with a travel agent who was a friend's mom. We sat for an hour while she helped book the flights in and out of the main cities so I would have some fixed dates. She also got me a decent price on a rail pass that covered almost all the countries I wanted to see. My itinerary was fixed.

I would arrive in Prague in the middle of August and make my way west, through Austria, France, and Italy. Then I'd fly down to Malta. After four months, I'd finish up my vacation in Wales and London.

When the travel agent finished printing up the tickets she said, "People usually start in the most western country and make their way to more foreign places."

"I know. But at the end of four months I'm going to be tired. I'd rather be disoriented first and end on familiar ground."

That took care of transportation part. Through guidebooks and online research I came to the conclusion that bed and breakfasts would be preferable to hostels. For one thing, I wouldn't have to share a room. And for the incremental extra price, I'd have one meal thrown in. Malta and Paris were the only places where I'd stay in a regular hotel unless I faced an emergency situation. That would be taken care of courtesy of my parents.

Throughout my month of planning, Brian and Janis were having difficulties. While he had assumed she was happy with putting down roots and settling in for the rest of their lives, it didn't turn out to be the case. Janis was nineteen. She wanted to experience more than just their zip code. When the three of us would get together, there was an uneasy tension hanging about them. Janis kept asking questions about my upcoming trip. I got the sense she wished she were coming along. Her digs about Brian never taking her anywhere were far from subtle.

Brian became more desperate to fix the relationship. He surprised Janis with a spontaneous trip to Myrtle Beach for the weekend. The result was like putting a Band-Aid on a ruptured artery.

Brian wasn't going to change. He had his small map laid out in front of him and he planned on following it. I don't knock that. All these years later I still haven't found my map or put down roots. At the time though, it seemed odd. I thought Brian was too scared to change or just set in his ways. He was twenty-one, going on seventy. It was only a matter of time before Janis left.

One night, Brian and I were jamming in my parents' basement. Whatever personal problems we went through, music was still the ultimate escape. Whether listening to music, or trying to make it, we left our issues at the front door.

Our current favorite genre was psychedelic blues. Brian's guitar playing had improved that summer. He was now able to play the solo to Cream's "White Room," and even improvise the solo in a way that didn't sound like a mistake.

While we were taking a break, Brian said: "You know what I really need? A Theremin."

Brian was the king of effects pedals. Flangers. Phasers. Wah-Wahs. Delays. Reverbs. Samplers. He'd tried dozens. He even had a Talk Box for the one week he got into Peter Frampton. These flirtations wouldn't last long. After a few weeks, he'd get bored with tinkering and sell them back to the guitar store.

In addition to being one of the oldest electronic instruments, the Theremin was unique because it is the only one you play without touching it. They used it to make UFO sound effects in 1950's B-movies. We saw some concert footage of Jimmy Page playing it in The Song Remains The Same. He looked like a magician, coaxing these soundscapes out of air.

"Where are you going to get a Theremin? They don't sell those at the guitar store."

Brian opened his backpack. "I found a guy in England who makes one." He handed me a printout of an email thread.

"He does this as a hobby. He says they aren't that complicated to make. You just need the right components."

"How much does it cost?"

"Forty pounds. I don't know how much that is."

"Around fifty or sixty bucks."

"Not too bad," Brian said. "He said he has to add shipping though, which might be another ten. He said it takes a while to make and it'll take a while to arrive, but that will give me a chance to get 'Whole Lotta Love' down." Brian mimicked Jimmy Page playing guitar.

I pointed to the paper. "His email address. It's from a school in London."

"So?"

"I could pick this up for you. You'll save a few bucks. And you'll know it'll make it over in one piece."

"Man, that would be great. It won't take up a lot of room. It's not that big."

"Of course. Besides, it'll give me a chance to meet someone.

Some science student." I spoke in a really bad cockney accent. "A British bloke. Why not, then?"

Later that night, I jumped into the email thread, introduced myself to Tony Bassett, and told him I'd be able to pick it up in November. Not even ten minutes later he sent a response with his number, telling me to ring him when I arrived.

Until I got to London my European trip was as profound as it was mundane. I saw some amazing sites. I was propositioned by prostitutes in foreign languages in every train station on the continent. I like to think if they didn't know how to pronounce "no," in English, they learned. I also met other locals who didn't want to have sex with me for money. In Strasbourg there was a Pakistani waiter who DJ'd in Germany and invited me to one of his gigs. In Paris I met an incredibly French looking girl on the train who taught me how to conjugate the verb "to rain," which I still remember. *Il pleut. Il pleuvra. Il pleuvait.* Once again on a train this time to Rome, two nuns fed me chocolate and gave me a large can of some of the worst beer I'd ever tasted.

Whenever the language barrier got me down, I'd join a museum tour and look for someone wearing a Canadian flag and then I'd have an English-speaking friend for the day. Most people think Americans are the obvious tourists. I saw more Canadian flags in Europe on my trip than I ever saw Canada.

I spent most of my time seeing the sights but also just observing people and collecting impressionist memories for later: A mother taking her shy four year old to a small merry-go-round in the middle of Strasbourg. An old man with a violin busking on the Charles Bridge in Prague, like a Chagall painting come to life. Eating a too-sweet cake. Drinking *Kaffee mit Schlag* in Vienna's oldest café. Sleeping homeless men with chiseled wrinkles being roused by police in Roma Termini central station. Fat British tourists with loud voices and loud matching bathing suits complaining about the food in Nice.

I spent an hour in an unofficial cat sanctuary in Malta, where whole streets were dedicated to protecting the four-legged fur balls, who in turn ate the island rats and rubbed up against you as thanks.

Once or twice a week, I'd check in with my parents to let them know I was okay. Somewhere in France, mom told me Janis broke up with Brian. It happened two weeks after I left. Brian was now calling my mom to cry about it and worry about me. I owed him a call; I'd get to it sooner or later.

I sent stacks of postcards including one from Malta to Mister Fitzsimmons. I had various drinks for the first time like Absinthe and Campari. The former made my eyes see fuzzy and my ears buzz. The latter was just bitter. I picked up a stomach bug in Malta but it only lasted a day. A British expat who owned a health-food store sold me a sour yogurt drink, instructing me to drink it all in one day. That did the trick.

August turned to September. The weather got cooler and it rained more in Austria and Germany. October in Nice, Rome and Malta were warm. On October thirty-first I said goodbye to the bright multi-colored fishing boats in the Maltese harbor and boarded an Alitalia flight to Heathrow feeling drained.

My east-to-west theory proved correct. In London, I boarded a train for Cardiff and spent a few days in the city, staying at a lovely bed and breakfast with charming hosts who played amateur genealogists. Based on my grandmother's maiden name, they assured me I was indeed Welsh. Despite the grittiness and rain, or perhaps because of it, it was the first time I'd felt at home in months.

By the time I got to London I felt relaxed. No more pantomime to make myself understood. No more flipping through the language translators. No more restaurants that looked good but might be tourist traps because I couldn't read the menu. No body language I didn't understand. I checked

into my bed and breakfast in Bloomsbury, washed up and
headed out for the nearest red telephone booth.

"Hello." The voice on the other end of the phone sounded
rough, like it had just woken up.

"Is this Tony Bassett?"

"No, he's out at the moment. Who is this?" the voice sounded
older.

"My name is Evan. A friend of mine ordered a Theremin
from Tony and George. Are you George?"

"Ah" the voice brightened. "Yes. And you are the American.
We've been expecting you. Can you come tomorrow, around
half three?"

"Sure."

The voice on the other end of the phone gave me directions
to Belsize Park from the station nearest me. It was simple.
Goodge Street Station to Belsize Park would take about twenty
minutes. After that it was a short ten-minute walk to the house.

I spent the rest of the day taking a walk and doing some mild
sight seeing. At that point in the trip it was all I could manage.
I'd take a good look at the outside of a museum or landmark or
church or government building I was supposed to care about,
and then keep walking. If I felt motivated, I'd take a photo.
After so many months, I'd had my fill of culture. It wasn't fair
to London, but I promised I'd go back and put forth more of an
effort next time. I'd been over-stimulated for months now. For
this last leg of the trip, I wanted to do as little as possible and
just calm down.

My first night in London I had a very late French dinner at
Pierre Victoire. I strolled back to my bed and breakfast, flopped
on the bed and planned my itinerary for the week. After I picked
up the Theremin, I would be doing the following. No more, and
no less:

Go to easyEverything/internet café to write emails.
Call Brian.
People watch.
See Parliament.
Buy Doc Martens.
Read.
Postcards.
Buy some new music.

The next day I got up early, had a giant English breakfast and went for a long walk. I lost track of time wandering through Borough Market. It was two-thirty when I left, and three by the time I made it to Goodge street station.

The trip to Belsize Park took fifteen minutes. The walk to the flat on Aspern Grove took five minutes at most. I found the address, knocked on the door and waited.

An older man opened the door. He had a trimmed grey beard and short grey hair. He was wearing a drab sweater over a drab shirt, grey slacks and sandals with socks.

"The American," he said, pumping my hand. "Tony's upstairs. Come in." He didn't tell me his name. I assumed he was George.

He led me up a narrow staircase that emptied out into a cluttered room filled with electronics parts that were stacked from floor to ceiling. It looked more like I'd stepped into a strange lab rather than a flat.

Tony came over and introduced himself, pumping my hand in the same vigorous manner. Despite his email address, he wasn't a student, or at least not one anywhere near my age. He was a full-grown man, also with a grey beard, but fuller. His grey hair was thin, long, and messy. Both he and his friend were flashing grins at each other. Was it a secret sign? Perhaps this is what they meant by British eccentrics.

"So you're on holiday," George said. He giggled for no reason I could see.

"That's right, I've been away for a few months now and I'm going back this week."

"And you're here for the Theremin. For your friend," Tony said.

He walked over to a metal bookcase covered with all kinds of electronics and picked up a metal rectangular machine with an antenna taped to it. He took the tape off, and placed the antenna upright in the machine. He fished around for a quarter inch jack, plugged it into the Theremin and plugged the other end of the jack into an amplifier.

"Right," Tony said. He flicked the Theremin switch, and it hummed. He moved his hand towards the antenna and that familiar UFO sound came through the amp. He moved his fingers back and forth, controlling both the sound and the volume.

Tony looked at me and nodded towards the Theremin. I stuck out my hand. After a few seconds of fiddling with it, I knew Brian was going to love this for about two weeks before getting tired of it. They aren't like guitars where you could play by ear. It would take serious trial and error to get correct sounds from it, never mind a proper key.

"So you see it works then," Tony said. "I didn't want you thinking you're spending forty pounds for nothing."

"Oh it definitely works," I said. There was a pause where no one spoke. That's when it dawned on me. He was asking for the money in a roundabout way. I reached into my pocket and handed him the cash.

"Yes these things have come back into fashion. For a while I was only building a few a year. Now with the new music exploring old sounds, I'm quite busy again," he laughed. "I'm one of the few who knows how to make them still. It's not all that difficult you see, but it's not like you can go to your local Radio Shack and pick up everything you need. Not any more, anyway."

George came over. "Would you like some tea?"

"Sure, that would be lovely."

"How do you take it?"

"No cream, no sugar."

George walked into the small kitchen and put the kettle on the stove.

"Sit down," Tony said. He led me over to the small living room area. I sat on the sofa, while he flopped down sideways on an old recliner. George came back with tea for us. I sipped mine. It had cream and sugar in it.

"We have some other machines we are working on," George said. "Would you like to see one?"

"Sure."

He looked at Tony who in turn gave him an enthusiastic nod. While Tony sat and smiled and nodded, George fetched another machine from the big metal bookcase. It was smaller and thinner than the Theremin.

He presented it to me with a broad smile. "This," he paused. "*This* is the A'hu Machine."

He placed it on the coffee table and sat down next to me, so close our thighs almost touched. The machine was flat with a quarter inch jack on either side of it. On the top was a small hole, and beneath it was a flat rectangular indentation.

George turned and sat half-sideways to better face me. When he spoke, his voice was pleasant, even-toned like a hypnotist. "You see, it is called the A'hu Machine because I thought of it while I was lying down listening to the way we breathe." He inhaled. "When we breathe in, the sound is 'ah.'" He exhaled. "And when we breathe out, the sound is 'hu.'"

"I see."

"And so this machine, the A'hu Machine, runs on our breathing. Do you know what it does?"

I get a feeling of wanting to laugh when I'm nervous. In school when a teacher had said something with a double entendre, for instance. Or when I'm in trouble with my parents. I had that feeling now. I swallowed hard, resisting the urge.

"If it's a machine that runs on our breathing, it must have something to do with us, right? That's as far as I can deduce."

George touched my knee with a fingertip to emphasize his words. "It solves problems. Big and small," the man finished. "Would you like to try it?"

I drank some more tea. My cheeks felt warm. The two men were staring at each other, the same placid smiles on their faces.

George put up his hands, protesting his innocence. 'There is nothing to be afraid of, I assure you. This machine helps you." His eyes darted at Tony. "You see, we invented it for humanity."

In my brain, curiosity and dread wrestled. Curiosity won. "Okay, why not?"

"Great," George said. He got up from the couch and went into the kitchen with his back stooped over, like Groucho Marx.

Without taking his eyes off me, Tony leaned his head toward the kitchen and said to George: "I think he has potential."

George popped his head out. "You do, too? Marvelous."

He returned to the area walking with deliberate steps, hands behind his back. His eyes were shining. He stammered when he spoke.

"Do you think I might, that is to say, is it okay if I—"

He brought out a pair of scissors from behind his back. They came towards me in slow motion. I thought—here's where it ends. My life comes to an end in a tiny flat in North London. My death will be the senseless inexplicable kind that makes headlines across the world. Young Man Stabbed By Elderly Scientists. American Tourist Slain In Bizarre Ritual.

Before I could scream or put my hands up, he snipped off a lock of my hair.

From his same spot on the recliner, Tony laughed in great gulps like a baby who'd been tickled too much.

George took my hair strands and put them into a small Ziploc baggie, the kind drug dealers use. "Sorry! I'm sorry. Truly I am," he said through tears of laughter. "It's just if we had told you, you would have said no. But this is absolutely necessary." His laughter stopped. He was serious again. "Now watch."

He took the baggie with my hair in it and stuffed it into the A'hu Machine. Then he took a small blank piece of paper and handed it to me along with a pencil.

"Now without showing us, I want you to write down your problem. And then fold the piece of paper into thirds. Go on, then."

He got up and disappeared into the kitchen. Tony's eyes were heavy like he might doze off at any moment. I sat there, trying to figure out what my problem was. Aside from the person who just took a locket of my hair and stuffed it into a machine that wasn't plugged in to anything, I didn't have any problems at that moment. I was on vacation. I loved my family. I didn't have a girlfriend, but that wasn't a pressing issue. When I got back home, the manager of the coffee house where I worked said I could have my old job back. But I didn't want it.

For a moment I considered writing down "I don't want to die at the hands of these crazy people." Despite the strangeness though, I really didn't feel threatened. Perhaps that's what it feels like when people joined cults. What at first seems disturbing becomes normal. And then you're wearing robes and Nike's and drinking Kool-Aid or stuffing your hair into a metal machine that—

What I really wanted was to be a full-time writer. I wanted

that more than being in a band. Don't get me wrong, if Brian and I managed to make a few great songs that led to a record contract and touring and groupies galore, I wouldn't have complained. But Brian wasn't passionate enough. He wasn't serious about making music a career. Besides, how could he tour if he never wanted to leave Pittsburgh? It was already a dead end. I wanted to write. I just didn't know how I could become a professional.

I ended up writing "I want to be a writer for a living." And then for whatever reason, I added: "I want the right job," underneath. I made sure to cover my answer with my right hand as I wrote. I then folded the paper into thirds as I was instructed and turned back to the machine. The paper was too thick to see through. There was no way they could read it.

George returned holding a small bottle with an eyedropper on top. He appraised my folds. "Perfect." I tried to hand him the paper but he shook his head. "No, you must be the one to put it in the machine, otherwise it won't work."

He told me to put it in the same hole where my hair was. Once I did that, he took the small bottle and squirted some of the contents onto the rectangular indentation.

Still focused on what he was doing, he said "Clove oil. It's a proper conductor."

He then sat down sideways to face me. He placed his hands on his knees and stared in my eyes. He gestured for me to sit the same way. It was awkward, but I did so.

"Now before we begin, we must relax," he said in that same hypnotic voice. "We must inhale and exhale slowly, five times. Are you ready?"

I nodded.

"Okay. So. Like this." "He inhaled. "Ah," and exhaled "Hu."

We breathed in tandem. Once. We breathed in tandem a second time.

"Ah. Hu. Yes that's it."

I heard a noise. Out of the corner of my eye, I saw a small Indian girl coming up the steps. She was dressed in a school outfit, couldn't have been older than twelve. She was carrying a backpack by one hand, letting it dangle on the floor. I turned to face her. My eyes felt heavy. She looked back. Her face didn't register surprise or shock. Nor did she laugh. It was much worse than that. She looked disappointed, as if she'd turned on TV to watch her favorite show, only to find out it was a rerun.

Without changing the tone of his voice, George spoke to her. "You are fifteen minutes early for your maths lesson. Please wait downstairs."

She left without saying a word.

"Ah. Hu. And again. Ah. Hu. Yes. There is so much goodness in you. Ah. Hu. One last time: Ah. Hu."

Once our breathing exercises finished, I turned back to the A'hu Machine.

"Now, put your index fingers into the clove oil and move your hands in circles," George said. "Just like that. Yes. Close your eyes, if you think it helps. Concentrate."

I didn't close my eyes all the way. I half-closed them. If they were planning to murder me, I wanted to see it and react in time. I sat there and let my mind wander.

The smell of clove was strong. My index fingers were moving in circles in clove oil that was working as a conductor to a machine that ran on breathing. Or something. This machine would solve my problems. A machine powered by my hair and a problem written on a folded up note. Like it was a cheap magic trick. Two people who made electronics for a living made this machine. It seemed as if they made their living that way. And those electronics worked. Was there something to this machine? Also, who was that schoolgirl? Why was she here? And what the fuck was I still doing here?"

After what seemed like an appropriate time, I opened my eyes. Tony had changed positions on the recliner and was watching me like I was the final five minutes of a championship soccer game. George was doing the same.

"So?" Tony said? "Did you get an answer?"

I felt bad telling the truth but part of me didn't want to lie. "No. I'm sorry."

"Oh." They hung their heads in unison.

"I mean it could be me," I said. "I've been traveling a lot. I came here from Malta just recently. It's only an hour difference, but maybe it's jet lag?"

"Mm," Tony said. His voice was noncommittal.

Hope flashed in George's eyes. He looked at Tony. "Do you think? That is to say, could we, Tony?"

"We shouldn't" Tony said.

"You're right," George said. He slumped back in defeat. "Look. This may all seem—" he waved his hands. "But the machine has never been wrong. It always provides an answer to the problem." He looked at Tony. "We were hoping. That is to say, I was wondering if, well," he frowned, and began again. "We would like to keep working on your problem. Would you mind? That is, would you please allow us to think about you?"

I looked back and forth between them. Please don't let me laugh in their face.

"Well of course you can keep thinking about me," I smiled. "You didn't even need to ask."

They both came back to life. "Sometimes it just takes some time," Tony said. "You'll see."

I took the pencil and another piece of paper and wrote my email down. "Let's keep in touch."

"Oh," George said. 'We would very much like that. Very much, indeed."

"There's just one thing," I said. "And I do hate to ask."

"Yes?" Tony said.

"Do you mind very much if I take my hair back?"

They broke out in laughing fits.

"Of course not," George said. "You must have thought we were right nutters at first," he said. He gestured to the machine. "And take the problem note, too. Keep it folded." George averted his eyes as I removed both from the machine.

He smiled. "The machine remembers, you know. Who you are. What problem it needs to solve. It remembers everyone. That way it's easy for us to monitor."

I took the hair and folded up piece of paper and shoved them in my pocket. My master plan was to fly home and then when I saw Brian and he asked for the Theremin, I would give him my Ziploc bag of hair first and then tell him the story.

"Thank you both for giving these back. I was worried I would offend you," I said.

"Not at all," Tony said. "We're glad you gave the machine a go."

I stood up, wiped my fingertips on my jeans and grabbed Brian's Theremin "My friend will love this."

I shook both of their hands. Tony said, "I hope he enjoys it. But if he has any trouble at all with it tell him please don't hesitate to email us and we'll see if we can't sort it out."

We went downstairs. I opened the door and stepped outside, surprised it was still light. My watch said it was only four. It felt like I had been there for six hours. The little girl was nowhere in sight. My cheeks were still warm.

"You know how to get back, right?" George asked.

"Oh yes. I just make a left and Belsize Park station's there. Then it's straight on the black line, for a few stops. It's quite close."

I shook their hands once more. "Take care," I added.

"You too," George said. "The answer may not have come

today, but don't worry about writing. You'll find the right job soon enough.

CHAPTER 2

The Dark Is Rising

THE SUN DIDN'T set so much as drop all at once like a heavy orange weight below the horizon. Katia was still in the forest with another three kilometers before she'd reach the creek and small wooden footbridge that led to their farm just outside the main village.

Her mother was sure to give her an earful for being late once again. She couldn't help it. The forest held its charms and no tall tales or warnings could dissuade her from playing there.

When she was younger, Katia's father told her scary bedtime stories. Witches lived in giant hollow trees. Ghosts of lost souls rustled the leaves. Under every twig an evil demon lay in wait for young girls. The stories never scared her.

She knew the forest better than any grown man. Knew the death caps mushrooms to avoid. The fresh dung and paw prints announcing predators more scary than ghosts. Where to find fresh water, which fern shoots were edible. How to make bilberry tincture for coughs. She'd fashion miniature bouquets out of tiny white flowers that grew by moss out of sight from most eyes. She loved the smell of decaying trees, moist earth, damp rocks.

Katia ran panting under the roof of trees, past tall shadows of trunks, the shining stars peeking out through the occasional clearing. She ran to avoid the lecture of being late. Ran to avoid the disapproving look. Her parents meant to best for her, she knew. But she'd grown so much in the past few years. She was no longer the wild child with bedraggled hair and dresses stained with grass and mud. The skinned knees were gone. The rough and tumble tomboy had changed into a young lady,

Katia stopped by a tree stump to catch her breath and tie her brown shoes tighter. In the distance, her mother called. She called out in response. She was just about to take off running again when she saw something out of the corner of her eye.

The tree stump glowed. She bent down to look closer, holding her knees, and squinting her eyes. Lightning bugs, she thought at first. And then—no, it couldn't be. Lightning bugs didn't gather in clusters. When did they ever land on anything? Yet here were twelve glowing balls of light, still and quiet as night itself.

Katia ran her hand over the stump. As if reacting to her movement, the yellow orbs flattened themselves, embedding into the wood. Her mother's voice called again. Katia took one last look at the lights, and then forced herself to run home. She was only five minutes late.

"What were you getting up to in the woods this evening?" Her mother eyed her. "At least your dress is still clean."

"Mother," Katia said, still breathless. "I saw something I've never seen before."

"Tell us at the table after you've washed up."

Katia did as she was told, washing her hands and face in the basin before sitting down at the table. She folded her hands and said grace. They ate their simple meal of pork and boiled potatoes with mustard and dill.

"Mother tells me you saw something tonight?" her father asked with a bright voice. "A buck, perhaps?"

"Oh no," Katia said. She frowned. "I don't know hat it was, Papa."

"Not fireflies? Honey fungus?

"No, Papa."

She told him what she saw.

"I must see these for myself. On Saturday we shall look together. In the meantime, perhaps you should draw me a picture of what you saw, so it stays in your mind until the week's end. And be sure to make a map so we can find it again."

Katia cleared the dishes, kissed her father on the cheek and ran to her room.

It was getting close to bedtime. Katia's father sat in his favorite chair, smoking his pipe. His wife sat nearby, knitting a new sweater for him. It was halfway finished.

"I don't know why you encourage her," she said. "Artistic pursuits and roaming are for idle hands."

Her father sighed. "She is the first one up in the morning. Griselda's milked before I've risen. She tends to the chickens and has made them strong. The eggs fetch a great price in the market. The way she has helped work the field, come harvest time we'll have no trouble getting through even the worst winter. I would hardly say she's idle."

"She is good around the house and farm," her mother agreed. "And well educated," she said. "I just wish she'd spend less time in the forest and do something more productive."

"Katia is a bit of a dreamer."

"Dreams are for those who are asleep."

They sat in silence for a time. Katia came out in her bedclothes. She leaned over to kiss them both good night.

"Papa," she said, her eyes bright. "I finished the drawing. Come and look."

He went into her room. She pointed to the drawing on the bed.

"These are the tree rings?"

"I counted them. I'm sure it is the right number."

He counted twenty-five rings. That spring there was a terrible rainstorm such as their village had never known. Thunder and lightning raged for days. They feared for their harvests, animals and homes. On the last night of the storm, lightning struck the forest three times. The first time was deep in the woods. The second and third times fell within sight of their home. Katia's father was tending the chickens when he saw the giant bolts flash in the sky, heard the sound of cracking timber, and saw the wood catch fire. After all that rain, there was no danger of fire. The forest was safe.

After nine day's time, Providence showed mercy. The storm gave way to a strong hot sun that made the soil rich.

"This tree was young?"

"Yes." She yawned. " I only saw the stump. Perhaps the rest had decayed. Perhaps someone took it."

He pointed to the small circles on the rings. "And these were glowing?"

She nodded. "I didn't add a color yet but they were a faint yellow. When I touched them they had no shape. It was as if they were part of the tree somehow. Papa, you must believe me. Please let me show it to you."

He stared at the circles in the rings. They were familiar, somehow. He couldn't say why.

"Finish your studies and chores. Put in a good work during the market. And Saturday evening we will see this magic tree together."

Katia smiled and fell asleep.

The weekdays passed. Katia did her studies and chores. The money earned from market day proved to be a windfall. At long last her father had enough to buy a new plow. It was second-hand, but the farmer assured him it was well looked after.

Come four o'clock, Katia's energy was so great her mother chased her out of the house to check on the barn cat. Luisa just had a small litter of kittens. She found the cat nestled in the hay, her kittens suckling with their eyes closed. All looked healthy. Katia hoped they could keep one of the boy cats. They could use an extra hunter to keep the mice from eating the grain.

When Katia went back inside, her mother sent her right back out to fetch water from the well. It would be dinnertime soon. Then at long last they could set out for the forest.

"The trees can wait," her mother said. "Patience, child."

It was a little after six when they left the house, Katia running in quick steps to keep up with her father's long strides. She clutched her drawing. On the back she'd drawn a map of the location.

"You sure you know the way?"

"We shall reach it just before sunset."

For perhaps the first time, Katia walked through the forest without lingering. She ignored the babbling brook, turned deaf to the flock of starlings coming home to roost. The tree stump was a beacon. She walked in a hurried trance towards it.

"There." She ran, pointing toward the small clearing.

Her father continued his stride. He felt proud of his daughter for knowing the forest as well as she did. In a few short years she'd be a woman. She'd make a fine wife, he thought. And no lesser man would do for a husband. They weren't rich, but they were far from being poor. He would not settle for just any man for his daughter. Ah but let that time be a way down the road still, he thought.

By the time he reached the stump, she was sitting on her knees before it. She reached out a hand. With an effort he got down on his haunches. The sky was still light pink. He counted the tree rings. Twenty-five. He could see the outline of the circles. They were not glowing.

As if sensing his thoughts, Katia said: "It's not dark yet. Wait till the sun has set. You will see."

Ten minutes passed. Pink went to black. Her father gasped. As if waking from slumber, the circles started glowing.

She held her drawing to the stump, frowning. "I saw them clearly. I drew them that evening. I could not have been wrong."

Her father reassured her. "And you weren't wrong at all, Katia. These little orbs are glowing, just as you said."

"But they're different tonight." She compared the paper to the stump. The orbs were in different positions. She was sure she drew them as she saw them. For the entire week when she closed her eyes at night she could see their position. How could she have been wrong? And if she wasn't wrong, it meant they'd moved of their own accord.

The orbs looked raised, as if they were bugs or insects. He reached out to touch the stump. They melted into the wood. When he removed his hand, he grabbed Katia by the arm.

"I know what it is."

Her heart pounded.

He began walking round the stump. His steps were slow and deliberate, like that of a diviner. But instead of looking at the ground for water, his eyes stared toward the heavens.

"There," he pointed. "Do you see?"

Above them, the gnarled trees gave way to a clear night sky awash with stars. She stared at them, uncomprehending.

Her father stepped behind her, put a hand on her shoulder, and pointed to an open star cluster. "There. Beside Cassiopeia."

He felt her shoulder stiffen.

"Papa, what does it mean?"

"I've no idea," he said.

"What should we do?" Her voice was anxious.

"We'll just have to keep watch and see."

They walked back home, the stars lighting their way past the sleeping chickens and sheep. Both father and daughter carried a sense of excitement and dread. They made plans to check every few days. Once home, he praised Katia for her keen eye. His wife dismissed the story.

"Nothing more than fantasy. Why must you encourage her?" she asked.

"I saw what she saw," he said. "With my own eyes."

He pulled the almanac from the desk. He flipped through the pages, searching. His face was distracted.

She sat next to him. "You mean to say what Katia saw is real?"

He told her how Katia had sworn they moved position on the stump. How they seemed to correspond to the night sky. The skepticism never left her face. It only softened.

The harvest moon passed. No comets were due for arrival. Nor was this the month for meteor showers. The only clues the almanac offered were a forecast of impending winds later in the month, and a new moon on the equinox. These weren't real connections. Nothing was tangible. He closed the almanac with a sigh.

They lay in bed that night, unable to sleep.

"Even if this make believe turns out to be true, what does it mean?" his wife asked.

"One way or another, the answer will come."

Monday turned cold. Soon there would be frost. He put aside questions of the unknown to focus on the immediate task: reaping the rest of harvest. Despite Katia's preoccupations, she was still practical. The root cellar was full. She'd put up the last of the apples. Some of the fields would lie fallow. In the others, they'd plant the crops for spring. Katia stored the firewood her father had chopped. Her mother finished knitting.

Strong rains fell, and with it a damp thick fog crept in, casting the land with a heaviness that lasted ten days. With the bulk of their chores complete, Katia became listless. Most afternoons she sat looking out the window toward the forest.

One night, a chill wind blew in from the north leaving the house so damp not even the hearth could warm them. At least the wind blew the rains and fog away.

After Friday's lunch, her mother cleared the plates, and then returned to the table looking at them in turns. "Now that the sky is clear, I want to see this tree stump." Katia's eyes were bright.

When sundown approached, the three wrapped themselves in wool and their heaviest jackets and headed out. The ground was muddy, the air chill. Katia led the way. The stump was as they left it. So were the glowing orbs.

"They've moved again," Katia marveled.

Her mother gasped when she saw them. Just like her husband, she reached out a tentative hand to touch. This time, the orbs stayed raised.

"Strange," Katia said. "The rings have vanished."

Her father looked at the ring-less stump and then at the sky. A faint umbra shone around the new moon.

"Papa, why are the orbs still raised?"

At the sound of her voice, they glowed brighter. Her father remained silent, ill at ease.

"I am sorry I doubted you," her mother whispered. "It was as you said."

"But something is wrong," Katia said. She crossed her arms as if feeling a chill. "I don't like it."

Her father nodded. "For every sleeping deer, a predator hides in the shadows. We told you stories as a young child to make this point known. The forest contains beauty to behold. And dangers, too."

He fell silent. After a time, Katia's mother spoke. "That is true as you say, but I've not heard tell a forest fairy tale whose warning signs point to the sky."

Katia stood up, never taking her eyes from the glow. "I've grown up in this forest. I know the way the brook babbles in spring and is silent in winter and the way the bird songs come and go with the season's change. The crunch of my feet under leaves is as distinct as the crunch of my feet upon snow. The smell of rotting wood, mushrooms moss and flowers are unchanging. Nature is dependable. It moves like clockwork."

"Indeed, child," her father said.

She pointed to the stump. "It has rained for ten days, yet no mushrooms have grown here. There are no signs of rot. The wood has no insects on it." She knocked on the side of the stump. Its sound was thick. "You see? It's not even soft."

Without another word, they left. What once was a wondrous mystery was now an unfathomable sign. They walked back with deliberate steps, moving neither fast nor slow. They reached their home in time for a low-hanging fog to obscure the sky and cover them with dread.

That night, Katia decided she wouldn't visit the forest for a very long time, and wouldn't look for the trunk again. Whatever she found, she was determined to forget.

The winter was harsh and bitter. Day after day the snow fell, until the village was buried in white. Night after night, the dark would rise in contrast to the blinding white snow. Katia would lie in bed under her heavy patchwork quilt, listening to the jagged icicles that hung on their farmhouse snap off the gutters, landing in snowy silence.

Despite the promise she made to herself, Katia couldn't forget what she'd seen. In the darkest of the hours when her sleep was deepest, the orbs would appear behind her closed eyes, as bright as if she stood over them in the forest. She watched their positions move with the stars each night. And as winter grew darker, they shined ever brighter in her mind. Soon she could make out corresponding shapes coming from the sky. Come they must. Like all the things in the forest, she knew everything had a season.

CHAPTER 3
Land of Laughs

The car drove down a winding state road, its streets slicked with rain. It was a white Lexus. Its aggressive headlights looking like the face of an angry metallic snake. The soundtrack tried and failed to be 1980'a techno, as if the filters creating the angular crunch and gated snares were smoothed out, like an industrial factory turned into lofts. The camera cut to a profile of the car. It was gleaming. They must have polished it for hours to get it like that. The car passed by an old time billboard touting the virtues of train travel.

"Sit back...Relax...," the voice over said.

The camera then cut to inside to the car. No one was in it. The steering wheel moved back and forth as the car hugged the winding road.

"...And leave the driving to us. The all-new, self-driving Lexus HZ."

Cut back to the billboard of the train, now covered in dust.

Cut to the car stopping on the street in three-quarter profile.

"The future of driving," the voiceover told me, "is now."

"The future is shit," I answered.

I was sitting at home slurping a bong on my futon and watching TV as I did every Saturday night when Jackie came bouncing through the door, her dreadlocks smelling of fresh henna made from cinnamon, cloves and lord knows what else.

It was seven thirty. Dinner would be here soon. It had been a minute since we last ordered sushi, so I figured now was as good a time as any. Last time, I ordered too much sushi, and even though we were stoned it was like the munchies didn't kick in or something and we ended up just leaving a bunch of it on a plate. I remember long after our hunger had wound down and the stuff was just sitting there congealing or whatever it is sushi does when it's sitting out too long, Jackie picked up a chopstick and poked her spicy tuna roll and I looked at her and said "Pushing sushi." We laughed at that phrase until we were gasping for air.

"You know what?" she asked between laughs. "That sounds like something you'd hear in a Blaxploitation film. It's like describing a pimp who specializes in Asian women."

"Yeah, and they're either underage, or all over fifty." I said. "Half and half." Then I acted like I was in a movie from the mid-seventies. "Hey, Super Girl," I said. "You hear what Big Willie was getting' up to?"

"Shit," she said drawing out the word. "I know what he's been up to, Muffin Man. He got busted for pushin' sushi."

Who knew where sushi would take us tonight? Jackie and I were best friends. At school they called us yin and yang. She was African American and really tall and I was neither.

Despite our different backgrounds, we'd grown up watching the same cartoons and movies. We had so much in common it defied logic.

Jackie was engaged. Her fiancé worked Saturday nights so she'd come over to my place to hang out then. She never told him about me, but it didn't matter because shit, all we ever did was study together, get high and watch TV. We were grad students. We'd met in art class.

And now that she was here and Saturday could really begin, I laid the bong next to a glass pipe and a joint.

"What is your weapon of choice, warrior?"

Before she could answer, there was a knock on the door and I got up startled, trying to remember who else was coming before I realized no one else was coming and it was the sushi delivery guy. This thought took all of two seconds but felt like five minutes and I must have been higher than I realized which happens quite a lot on Saturdays.

I paid the delivery guy and then slammed the door shut and locked it. When it's August in Atlanta the weather is beyond hot. You tend to shower six times a day or stay in the air conditioning. I didn't want to let the AC out so that door stayed open for the bare amount of time. The lock was just routine procedure. Car doors, regular doors, if it has a lock, I lock it.

I got some plates from the kitchen. Jackie opened her bag and brought out her own stash. When that happens, it means she has some good shit to share. I could see her licking the wrapping paper of a wound up joint all ready to go.

She picked out some leaf from her tongue. "When are you gonna get a real TV, Sean?"

My TV was a flat screen thirty-inch LCD. "What're you talking about? This works fine. Had it since before I was an undergrad."

"That's what I mean," she said. "It's what, seven, or eight years old? We just got a smart TV and the resolution is insane. Shit, you don't even have cable."

"Which is why I still get channel 53 and you don't. They haven't switched over to HD or whatever, and that means you can't get it on your new-fangled TV, which is why you come over here. You need me for my TV."

"Among other reasons." Jackie lit the jay, inhaled and passed it to me. "But you know Channel 53 is shutting down in a few months. They're getting bought out."

"All the more reason to spend every last moment with Uncle Bob," I said, exhaling a long stream of smoke. "What's so special about this new TV of yours, anyway?"

"I've got a menu where I can watch whatever I want, on demand. There's a bunch of apps where I can shop or order food. I never have to take my eyes off the screen. And you're still ordering dinner by calling somebody. It's got hundreds of apps, all these a la carte TV channels and dozens of video games, too."

"You sound like an ad," I said. "You know it also has the capability to spy on you, all the time. You know that, right?"

She picked up a spicy tuna roll and popped it in her mouth. "There you go again. Mister Analog Man."

"That sounds like a song by Rush." I played air bass and sang in falsetto. "Analog Man, he does what he can, to keep it unpreserved in a world that's canned." I put my hand out to play air keyboard. "This is where Geddy would come in with a synth riff."

I sat back down, winded. "Mock me all you want, but you know it's true. You heard about the Komong TV? They were collecting data on their consumers' viewing habits without telling them. Then they sold that data to advertisers so they could tailor-make ads to you. There's a class-action lawsuit going on now because Komong didn't tell anyone they were doing it. A lot of consumers were pissed about it."

"Who cares, though?"

"I do."

"But what's the big deal?"

I took the joint back and held it. "There was a story a few months ago. This guy found out his girlfriend was pregnant based on the ads on her computer. He was surfing and every browser kept showing an ad for baby clothes and shit like that. He checked her history, right? She'd been searching for an obstetrician. Thing is, she told him she couldn't have kids. Turned out she was lying. She was cheating on him. That's how he found out."

"Shit's fucked up," Jackie said. She held out her hand for the joint. I kept holding it.

"In exchange for a free email service from Diddle or some bullshit social media account, they get to know everything about you. Your shopping habits. Your politics. Religion. Your health. Even the porn you like. It's none of their business. But we've made it their business." I gave back the joint without inhaling again. I didn't need it.

"Diddle owns the ad network as well as the email. They read your emails for keywords. They monitor your searches in their browser and place ads accordingly. Those shitty ads that follow you on all the sites you visit. Fuck that. I like my privacy. I have extensions on my browsers to block all that advertising shit. I don't want to be tracked by anybody. No ads. No cookies."

Jackie looked at me. "Cookies? Do I want cookies right now? I don't, do I? Do you have any cookies?" She looked at the coffee table and the giant plate of sushi in front of her. She took a few edamame, dunked them in soy sauce and popped them in her mouth, one by one. "Never mind. I'm high."

"All I'm saying is today it's your viewing habits, tomorrow it's everything else. If something is free it means you are the product."

Jackie stacked a cut up sushi roll, popped the whole thing in her mouth. "You've been smoking too much. It's making you paranoid."

"Just because you're paranoid, it doesn't mean they aren't out to get you."

Jackie shushed me. Our favorite show was about to start: *The*

Land of Laughs, starring Uncle Bob. The show always began with that old black-and-white test pattern, the one with a Native American head on top and those five propeller-looking things. I kept meaning to look up what those patterns represented but never got around to it.

The test pattern appeared and this cheesy 1950's horror music started playing, just like always. Then the test pattern was replaced by a cheap set piece made to resemble something like Dracula's lair on a B-movie budget, like they'd spent less than a hundred dollars on it.

After a moment, *The Land of Laughs* appeared in a sickly green typeface resembling ooze. Meanwhile, a man dressed in a black suit, white shirt, and black tie appeared from nowhere. He looked like an undertaker. It was Uncle Bob. When he spoke, his voice was theatrical and silly, like a cross between Bela Lugosi and a campy version of Mister Rogers.

"Good evening, girls and boys of all ages. This is your friendly host, Uncle Bob. And since it's almost our final months of broadcasting, we're making every episode really special. Boy, do we have a treat for you tonight." Uncle Bob walked over to a giant coffin with a metal box on top of it. "My groovy ghouls. Tonight, our friends Bugs Bunny and Woody Woodpecker will drop by to pay us a visit. We also have a special anime imported from Japan." Uncle Bob pointed to a safe that was made out of cardboard and spay-painted black. "But first, we shall begin by going into the vault."

"The Vault," Jackie and I said in unison. We clapped our hands like school kids. It was going to be one hell of a fantastic night for two space cadets. Whenever Uncle Bob brought something out from the vault it meant there was some extra weird shit from bygone days that may have once appeared on the TV screens of our youth but more often than not came from a different country. There might have been a good chance whatever it was had never aired before. We had no idea how he got them.

The Land Of Laughs was a weird show to say the least. It was not mainstream by any stretch of the imagination. But it did have a significant cult following that had kept it on the air for a decade and a half. It was one of those shows you'd get into as a kid, forget about for a few years, and then rediscover the joys of watching it years later.

The best part about it was the show never changed. Uncle Bob didn't look like he aged one day. He was thin, had slicked back black hair in a ponytail and still looked like he was in his mid-forties. If he'd worn tinted granny glasses he might have been a Geddy Lee impersonator. Not that I'm obsessed with Rush or anything, I'm just saying if you gave him a bass, he would have made a great stand-in.

To the best of my knowledge, *The Land of Laughs* never once repeated a cartoon. Each week was an hour's worth of animated madness, ready made for kids and stoners alike. I don't think the former was watching much any more but the latter group definitely was. They had to be. *The Land Of Laughs* occupied that TV-watching block before *Saturday Night Live* or *Adult Swim*. While those other shows were more famous, to us Uncle Bob was way better. We identified with him. We wished he were our real uncle. And really, the cartoons were gold.

You couldn't go wrong with Bugs Bunny's carrot-munching sarcasm and social commentary or Woody Woodpecker's screwball antics. What Jackie and I looked forward to was the weird shit Uncle Bob would drop on us from The Vault. Like Soviet-era cartoons, or animated musical shorts from Brazil, or a freaky silent stop-motion animation film from some former Soviet country.

Our favorite game was to try and guess what the hell people were saying in all those languages we didn't speak. When we exhausted the fun of that, we'd just make up our own translations.

Before those foreign segments, Uncle Bob would say: "Remember, boys and girls, these are in different languages. So if you *really* want to know what's going on, turn on your closed-captioning. We've translated it especially for you. And you're in for one heck of an eye-opener!" We never turned on the closed-captioning. It was funnier without knowing.

Uncle Bob had some extra bat shit crazy cartoons in the hopper tonight. First up was a German cartoon starring a bear named Heinrich. Children sang a song called *Heinrich der Bär* for what seemed like a half hour. All the while, Heinrich got up to all kinds of no good, scaring hikers, stealing their food, and in one extended sequence, doing who knows what behind a giant rock.

Jackie got up and went to the fridge to grab some water. She was laughing so hard. "I can't deal. This shit's like Yogi Bear on acid."

"With children singing."

"Man, I'm gonna miss Uncle Bob."

Jackie's phone rang. I put the TV on mute, guessing it was her fiancé. As far as he was concerned, I didn't exist. We were careful to keep it that way. Jackie looked at the phone, rolled her eyes and answered. She never sounded happy to talk to him when he called. Instead, her voice was distant and neutral.

"Hey. Nothing. Getting dinner. Tamica's supposed to meet me. Huh? For real? Okay. I mean I just got here. But I guess I'll let her know and come back. Bye. Love you, too."

She hung up the phone and said: "I gotta go. There was a fire in the restaurant. He's on his way home."

"Everything okay?"

"Yeah, but I gotta jet," she said.

Aw man," I said. "And you missed the ending." I picked

up the remote and put the volume back on but not as loud as before.

"How'd it end?"

"No idea. I spaced out."

I got up to unlock the door.

"Sorry," she said.

"It is what it is," I said. And then started singing in mock German about *Heinrich der Bär*.

She laughed her way out the door. I closed it, locked up and sighed. I grabbed some water from the fridge, and then flopped back on the futon. Jackie left some of her stash for me so I decided I'd pack up the bong. But first I swapped out the water, which was a huge process in my state. Once satisfied with water and package, I slurped one up and exhaled it, watching the smoke leave in a slow cloud.

I turned my attention to the TV again. Uncle Bob was back on camera. So was the closed captioning. I must have turned it on by accident when I was messing with the volume.

Just as well, really. Not to belabor the point, which I'm sometimes guilty of doing, especially on Saturday nights, but I was pretty fucking Scoobied. If I focused, it would be easier to read than listen. I'm one of those people who can read when I'm stoned. I also cook really well, too. I become a fucking Iron Chef when I'm stoned.

I set the bong down and the smoke cleared and I leaned back on my futon thinking at some point I should get a grown-up couch. Then again I was still watching cartoons. It could wait.

Uncle Bob reminisced about the joy of Saturday morning cartoons, something kids today know nothing about because they don't bother showing them on network television any more.

He was talking about getting up early and eating oatmeal or cereal or pancakes and bacon if his mom was in the mood to cook. He would settle in for hours and watch from seven 'till eleven before he'd go out and play for twice as many hours.

Although Uncle Bob was in his forties and I was in my mid-twenties, we both shared that memory. And it was one I'm sad that today's kids don't get to experience. I don't mean to sound all *Catcher In The Rye*, but I am very much against kids growing up too fast and losing the simple pleasures I was lucky enough to experience as a kid. All that shit from my childhood has been uploaded to YouTube so it's there if they really want to see it. But it's just a bummer because there's no collective ritual like there used to be. The Internet made everything fragmented.

My mood soured. The world's a horrible place. We should do everything in our power to keep kids from having to experience that dark side for as long as possible. I think my parents did a good job and I think Jackie's did, too, although I suspect her childhood was harder than mine. Though she never said so, I don't gather she grew up in the greatest of neighborhoods. Whatever her childhood was like, it wasn't all that horrible. It couldn't have been.

My mind was trying to hold on to thoughts like trying to catch soap bubbles with my fingers. I was feeling nostalgic, but also angry. Jackie's fiancé was kind of a dick. It wasn't my place to say anything, but I felt like she deserved someone who wouldn't check up on her every five minutes like a control freak.

I know she was protecting our relationship by not introducing me to him. But it still made me sad sometimes because I don't like the feeling I'm doing something wrong when I'm not. On paper I could see how it might look, but everything looks one way on paper. She wasn't cheating on him with me. I'm nobody's secret and don't like feeling like I am.

I don't know how long my mind wandered around while I stared at the TV. Looking but not watching. It could have been a few seconds or a minute, or fifteen minutes. All I know is at one point I had clarity. And I don't mean stoner clarity where you think everything you say and do is brilliant. I mean clarity as in I snapped out of it and I was sober as a nun. Once my brain figured out there was a technical issue going on in front of my eyes, it decided to overcome the fog and send out a distress signal.

I was watching Uncle Bob speak while the closed-captioning was typing underneath. But the subtitles weren't matching what he was saying in the slightest. At first I thought there was a lag, and it was just out of sync. When I read what was being typed, I realized the words weren't even close to what was coming out of his mouth. There were two different conversations going on.

I heard Uncle Bob say: "Tonight's show is almost coming to a close, boys and girls. Thank you as always for your company. I do love it. Because lately it's been so cold and lonely here in this crypt."

What I was read on screen was this:

...ONLY TWO MONTHS BEFORE OUR LAST BROADCAST, OUR FINAL S.O.S. DON'T LET THEM HEAR YOU. DON'T LET THEM GET TO YOU. TURN OFF YOUR PHONE. TURN OFF YOUR COMPUTER. AND REMEMBER, IF THEY CAN CONTROL YOUR CAR, THEY CAN CONTROL EVERYTHING.

The closed captioning stopped. Uncle Bob was wrapping up the show: "And if you ever want to write me, boys and girls, you know what to do."

An address popped up on screen. I always keep a pen and paper on the table. For some reason, I reached over and scribbled down the address.

"See you next time. Same macabre show. Same dark station," Uncle Bob said. He then put on a cape, hid his face with it, and disappeared in a thick haze of smoke without uttering one more word. The closed-captioning kept going.

TIME IS RUNNING OUT. WE MUST DEFEAT THEM. IF THEY TURN EVERYTHING SMART, WE WILL TURN INTO ZOMBIE SLAVES. JOIN US. AND REMEMBER, IF THEY CAN CONTROL YOUR CAR, THEY CAN CONTROL EVERYTHING.

The show ended and the Channel 53 logo came up. There wouldn't be another show on the station for the night. If you kept watching Channel 53 after *The Land Of Laughs* ended, the logo is all you'd see until morning when the next block of programming started. More than a few times, we forgot to change the channel, wondering why nothing else was coming on. The morning block started at six am and was usually infomercials or old shows like Andy Griffith.

I turned the TV off, got some more water and went over to the computer. I tried searching "Uncle Bob, closed captioning," but nothing came up. Then I tried "Weird closed captioning." Again, nothing came up.

Next I tried searching "Uncle Bob, Land of Laughs." I got tons of hits about the show including a very in-depth site devoted to episode recaps. It hadn't been updated in five years. Elsewhere, I found some interviews with Uncle Bob from back in the day. The most recent was three years ago and that was just a short blurb in our local newspaper with the headline "Uncle Bob's still entertaining kiddies of all ages."

No comments on the closed captioning situation anywhere. No new news on Uncle Bob, despite the fact Channel 53 was going to shutter or be bought out.

In this day and age you can find anything and everything online. Russian Brides, drugs made from toad toxins, camel jerky. You can fall down rabbit holes and get wrapped up on minutiae on every subject under the sun. How was there no info on this closed captioning shit? Was I the only one who saw it? I know I was high, but I wasn't that high. How long it had been going on?

I read somewhere countries like France and Germany were pushing back against some of the major Silicon Valley companies. They demanded there be ways to ensure people could be forgotten online if they so chose to. Like a Right To Privacy kind of thing. But every article I'd read about it said there were big flaws. For instance, the search engines would only honor the right to be forgotten in the country of origin. In other words, skankybaboobass.de wouldn't carry your info because that's in Germany but the browser people use the most which is skankybaboonass.com, would still carry it.

Countries were fighting for the right to privacy and the right to be forgotten online. Here, I was angry that the one thing I wanted to find online didn't exist.

I thought about that for a while and then I started listening to music and an hour or two went by and the next thing I knew, I was surfing on top of the melodies in my head, so to speak. Then I fell asleep on the sofa.

When I woke up the next morning, I saw Uncle Bob's address on the table and thought maybe I should write to the *Land of Laughs* to see what was going on, but then I got distracted and the day slipped by and next thing I knew it was Monday and I was due to work at the copy shop so I didn't have time to think about it after that.

The rest of the week I worked and went to class. Some time on Thursday, I called Jackie to see what was up and if she needed a ride to school. The fact she answered the phone meant she was in a place where she could talk. I suppose I could have texted, but I hate texting.

"Yes, please," she said.

"What about Saturday, or is it too soon to say?"

"He went to see his mom yesterday. He's driving back but not till the weekend sometime. I'm down."

"Cool. I have a favor to ask."

"What's that, Muffin Man?"

I paused, trying to figure out the best way to say "don't get high before you come here" in code. "I don't know if you are going to pre-game before but I would like you to do me a favor and hold off before you get here."

"Uh, okay, Sean, you can count on me not to pre-game," she said, mimicking the tone of my voice. And then: "The fuck's this all about?"

"It's nothing I can explain without my sounding crazy. I have to show you something in person."

"Should I be worried about this?"

"Yes. I mean, no. It's hard to say."

"This doesn't have anything to do with you and me, does it?"

I laughed. "Nope. I need to show you something. I don't need to tell you something."

"Okay," she said. "Because sometimes it's like, you know, when I leave early like that—"

"You wish you didn't have to."

"Right?" She laughed. "I don't want to make it weird, because we're cool, but sometimes it's like, I mean I don't want it to get complicated."

"Jackie. Sometimes I wish you didn't have to leave either. But what I'm talking about right now is more along the lines of an Encyclopedia Brown mystery than *Say Anything*, you know what I mean?"

"Aw man, I love that film. When Cusack is holding up that boom box. What a trip."

"But you know what I mean, right?"

"Yeah," she said. "It's cool. I'll be there. And I'll be alert and trustworthy just like a girl scout. Without the outfit, though. Don't get any ideas, perv."

I laughed. "Believe me," I said. "It'll be weird enough sober."

An hour or so later I picked her up. I could have waited to tell her in person but whenever I have something to say I want to say it right there and then.

We went to class and then I dropped her at the train station and worked again on Friday and went to sleep early and it took all of my being not to try and figure out how to speed up time on Saturday until she arrived. I knew how I could slow it down, but resisted the urge. Good thing I had a month's worth of laundry to do. That took up most of the day.

Jackie arrived early. "Okay, Encyclopedia Brown, what's all this about? Do we need to order something special for dinner? Something to feed our mystery-solving?"

I patted the sofa. "We'll figure out dinner later. For now you need to sit here and watch *The Land Of Laughs*."

She tilted her head like a puppy having trouble figuring out where their chew toy went. "That's it? You tell me to show up straight so we can watch the same thing we always watch when we're high?" She paused. "Are *you* high?"

"This is important."

Jackie kept her head in the same position but sat down on the sofa. "If you say so."

We waited a few minutes and then like clockwork, *The Land of Laughs* green typeface appeared and Uncle Bob started acting goofy as always.

Jackie pointed to the screen. "Uncle Bob." Her voice was flat. "What am I missing?"

"Listen to him."

We sat and listened to Uncle Bob talking about tonight's show being fun-filled and wacky as ever. I picked up the remote and turned on the closed-captioning.

"Now read the subtitles."

Here's what Uncle Bob said:

"Grooves and Ghoulies, tonight's episode is jam-packed with the best cartoons from the madcap master. We're talking an entire show devoted to Tex Avery. That's right, kids. We're going deep into the vault to show you shorts not seen since they premiered during the talkies at the cinema. In the early 1940's!

Here's what the closed captioning read:

DON'T BE FOOLED BY EUROPE'S SO-CALLED WINS AGAINST THE SILICON VALLEY EMPIRE. THEY WILL CONTINUE TO COLLECT DATA ON EVERYONE. THE GOVERNMENTS ARE IN THEIR POCKET. WE ADVISE YOU TO DELETE YOUR SOCIAL MEDIA, INSTALL AD-BLOCKERS ON YOUR TABLET, LAPTOP AND PHONE, AND NEVER EVER USE AN INSTANT MESSAGING DEVICE. REMEMBER—IF IT'S FREE, YOU ARE THE PRODUCT. FIGHT THEM.

I watched Jackie's face process the difference between sight and sound. I'd never seen her look scared before. She turned to me. "What. The. Fuck."

"When you left last week, I accidentally hit the closed-caption button. That's when I saw it."

"It's a joke, right? He's playin'."

"I searched for a few hours online. No one's mentioned this at all. Nobody. Last article on him was a few years ago. There's nothing about this anywhere."

Jackie shook her head. "Bullshit. Someone has to know. We're not the only ones watching. Plenty of people still do. I work with people who do."

"True. But how many people are watching on older TVs like me? And how many watch with closed captioning on?"

"You think that has something to do with it?"

I shrugged. "Figure it's gotta be."

The first of the cartoons came on. Tom and Jerry. Since they were silent, there was no closed-captioning at all. Once we realized, we ignored it.

"What did it say last week?"

"From what I remember it was the same. Warning about technology. It talked a lot about cars. Like they can control your cars."

"Well, no shit," Jackie said. "It's all smart cars now, right? Apps on the dashboard and GPS?" She smiled and dug in my ribs. "Except yours, though. It's older than your TV isn't it?"

My car was twelve years old. "You don't mind getting picked up and dropped off in it. At least I have a car."

"Touchy," she said. Then she started playing with my hair. This was typical. She'd do it at least once whenever we hung out. "'They can control your cars.' Who is they?"

"Good question. Is it everyone who works in Silicon Valley? The government? Terrorists? I sound like a tinfoil fat conspiracy theorist."

"What I want to know—how is Uncle Bob involved? Is he part of it? And who's typing that shit up?"

I sat upright. "That's something I didn't think to check." I reached over and grabbed the remote and started channel surfing. We spent a few minutes checking all of the other stations I could get. In each case, what was being typed matched what was being said.

"So it's only Uncle Bob. But why?"

We flipped back to the *Land of Laughs* and watched some more. While the closed captioned message didn't repeat itself word for word, it kept to a theme. Tonight's topic seemed to revolve around privacy laws, what was happening in Europe. We were giving up our privacy for free stuff. Europe was trying to fight the good fight, but Silicon Valley had so many lobbyists installed it was only a matter of time before they would lose.

THEY WANT TO GIVE WHOLE CITIES, WHOLE
COUNTRIES FREE WI-FI. IF IT'S FREE, YOU ARE THE
PRODUCT. THEY WANT YOUR DATA. THEY WANT
EVERYTHING YOU HAVE TO GIVE AND THEN SOME.
THEY WANT TO ENSLAVE THIRD WORLD NATIONS.
DON'T DO IT. DO NOT BE THE PRODUCT.

"This shit's intense," Jackie said. "Why do they hafta fuck
with our show?"

We were nearing the end of the episode. Neither of us had
paid any attention to the cartoons. The address showed up on
the screen.

Jackie noticed the piece of paper on the coffee table where
I'd scrawled the address last week. I grabbed it and walked over
to my computer. "Let's see if there's a number that comes up
with it."

Jackie sat just behind me, staring at the screen. I typed in the
address. The first hit that came up with a map showing Channel
53's location. It wasn't that far from here, a twenty-minute drive
at most. I wasn't familiar with the location but it seemed to be
tucked inside the warehouse district. We went through twenty
pages of the search before a number popped up.

"Bingo."

I looked at the TV. *Land of Laughs* was over and the Channel
53 logo was on screen. I dug out my cell phone.

"What are you going to say?" Jackie asked.

"I'll figure it out."

She laughed. "I feel like we're prank calling someone."

I winked at her, put the phone on speaker and dialed the
number.

Jackie said: "Let me talk. Maybe a female voice will get a
better response."

The phone rang for quite a while but no one picked up. I was
about to hang up when a male voice answered.

"Yes?"

Jackie said: "Hello, is this Channel 53?" The voice didn't respond. "I had a question for you. I was watching *The Land of Laughs* tonight and I noticed the closed captioning was—"

Neither of us could recall the last time we'd heard the sound, but hear it we did, clear as day: the crash of a landline phone slamming down.

"How rude," I said. "But I have to say, I miss that sound. Those were the days when you could really hang up on someone. Now people think the call dropped. It's just not the same."

"Young man," Jackie said. "I think you might be on to something."

"But what?" I looked at the piece of paper with the address on it. "We should go over there."

"I'm not sure that's a good idea," she said.

We sat in silence for a few minutes. Jackie's phone rang and she picked it up.

"Hello? What?" Her voice was panicky. "Is he all right? Shit. Yes. As soon as possible."

She hung up the phone.

"Everything okay?"

"That was the police," she said. Her voice was shaken. "He was in an accident. He's in the hospital in Greenville."

"How is he?"

"They don't know. He's unconscious. Pretty banged up."

"What the hell."

She stood up. "They said something happened to his car. Like he lost control of it."

I didn't know what to say or do so I hugged her. Whenever I hug Jackie, it's awkward because I have to stand on tiptoe and she has to bend over.

"Can you take me to Greenville?"

"That's two hours away."

Tears started flowing down her face. "Please, Sean? If I take a bus it'll take forever. You don't have to work tomorrow, do you?"

"No," I sighed. "Let's go."

She grabbed her backpack and we left. For the first time in a while, I was glad I hadn't smoked anything. No way I could have made a two-hour drive in one piece otherwise. We set out on the highway toward Greenville. It was hot outside and the cicadas were making a racket. I kept the AC on high and the music low. We drove in near-silence the whole way there, only stopping once for gas.

By the time we arrived, it was eleven. The cops were waiting. Jackie learned a bit more from them about the accident. Her fiancé lost control of the car and went straight into a railing. He didn't hit it head on. He'd worn his seat belt, thank god. But the airbags failed to deploy. He ended up hitting his face in the windshield but he hadn't been speeding so the impact wasn't severe enough to cause him to go through it. He smacked his face, bounced back and ended up hitting the steering wheel. The safety glass shattered, sending shards into his face and arms.

Jackie demanded to see him. The doctor said he was still unconscious and lost a lot of blood. They'd cleaned him up but he was still in traction. They were certain he hadn't injured his spine, but they didn't want to take any chances.

I stood outside the room, watching her sob over him. Part of me, I hate to admit, didn't want to be there. What if he woke up and demanded to know who I was?

I talked to the cops for a bit. They were polite and concerned about the man. One cop was big and burly. He looked angry.

"So how did you end up in this scene with her? That's what I want to know."

"Jackie and I are in the same class in grad school," I said. "She doesn't have a car. I usually pick her up and drop her off at the subway. So when she got the news, she called and asked if I could help her out."

"That's nice of you," he said. His tone didn't make it sound like a compliment.

"It's the least I could do. I mean it's her fiancé. She cares about him a lot."

The other cop shook his head. "Toxicology's negative. We had a speed trap set up about a mile and a half back from the crash. When he passed us, he wasn't speeding. No previous violations either. Doesn't make any sense."

The doctor arrived and spoke to Jackie for a few minutes. He put a hand on her shoulder as she exhaled. Without warning, the fiancé woke up screaming. The nurses sprung into action, jabbed a needle in him. His eyes relaxed. He fell silent.

Jackie came out of the room in a daze. "Doctor said he's got a couple fractured ribs and his arm is broken, but his spine is fine. He's in a lot of pain and shock. He's probably going to stay here for a day, maybe two, but he'll be okay."

"Thank god," I said.

"In the meantime, the car's in a shop down the way. They're fixing it."

"Do you want me to stay?"

"Nah," she said. "Thanks for the ride. I'll walk you to your car."

She turned around to eye the cops as we walked. "I hate cops," she whispered. "Always in your business."

When the sliding glass exit door opened we were met with the same blast of heat and incessant sound of cicadas. For the next three months, each night would be like living in a loud buzzing radiator.

Jackie gave me a big hug. "Be safe getting home."

I stopped at a gas station for some trucker coffee to keep me awake for the ride. I had a nagging thought somewhere in the back of my mind that wouldn't take shape. Maybe the caffeine would wake it.

I was somewhere outside Atlanta city limits when it hit me. Jackie's fiancé had a brand new smart car. It was only a short while after I called Channel 53 that we heard about his accident. Was there any possible way those incidents were related?

By the time I got home, it was past three. I had just put the key in the door when I noticed a brown package sticking out of my mailbox. I took it, let myself in and turned on the light.

It was a little smaller than a shoebox. No label. No address. I shook it, and heard a rumble. If I weren't so exhausted, I would have called the cops and left it unopened. People don't tend to leave you happy packages in the middle of the night. But my sense of street smarts wasn't there. I unwrapped the package and opened it without thinking,

Inside was a blue telephone. A landline. Under it was a small envelope, and inside it a note with a small map drawn on one side, and an X marking a spot. On the other side was a phone number with two sentences written in small block letters underneath:

Don't ever call again unless it's at this number, on this phone and only from these coordinates. Leave your cell phone at home when you come.

I slept until noon and woke up starving. There was a restaurant down the street from me called Here And There that had good coffee and brunch. It was usually packed on Sundays, but I managed to snag a seat at the counter, order up a western omelet and a giant mug of coffee.

I thought about calling Jackie to check in on her. Instead I sent her a text. "Just checking in on you," I didn't hear anything back.

After breakfast, I went back to my place to pick up the landline and map. It proves how much the Internet is ingrained in our lives that I wanted to get online, and enter the address so I could see what the precise location looked like. Seeing as how I was already connecting a car crash to a phone call, I thought it might be a good idea to stay off the Internet.

I stared at the map. The coordinates, as the note had called it, were located on Moffett Lane, a side street behind Grand Avenue. Grand was a bustling street with shops, bars and restaurants. I'd been to Grand dozens of times. Parking's always easy to find, either on the street or in a cheap parking garage. I didn't even know Moffett existed.

The location was far enough away that I'd have to drive there, which meant I'd have to stop for gas as the trip to Greenville left me with less than a quarter tank. I pulled up to the gas station by my house and went inside the store to pre-pay.

It was the first time I'd noticed how many cameras there were. One on every pump, one overlooking the entire lot. Inside, there were seven that I counted. I'm sure I missed one or two.

I went in with my head down, and didn't look at the cashier. I just said "twenty on pump ten," dropped the cash on the counter and went back outside.

I turned my back to the pump as I filled up. In the past twenty-four hours my best friend's fiancé had been in a car accident the cops couldn't explain the cause of. It happened after we made a phone call to a TV station with closed-captioning that was warning about evil organizations that could control your car. To top it all off, someone left a landline phone with instructions on where to use it in my mailbox. For once it seemed like my paranoia was justified.

I got back in the car and headed towards Moffett. If the gas station was causing me to try and hide from being seen, I thought the opposite would be better now. Park on Grand, so it looked like I was going shopping or eating, and walk to Moffett. Hide in plain sight.

I took the first open space I saw. I was ten short blocks away from the coordinates. I got out and started walking. I pretended to be a regular shopper, taking my time. I darted into a card store, trying to think if I knew anyone who had a birthday coming up. No one came to mind. I bought a small blue notebook and pen instead.

I window shopped the rest of the way, past a men's clothing store, hipster barbershop, and a few restaurants and bars.

At the intersection where I planned to turn right, I stopped and patted my pockets, as if I were searching for something. I looked at my watch and then took off down the street leading to Moffett Lane.

I'm not sure why I put on a pointless pantomime or what I thought it would accomplish. I assumed I was being followed. Perhaps the person who gave me the phone was spying on me from a window.

Once on Moffett, I fished the map out from my pocket to get my bearings. The designated spot was one more block, on the other side of the street. I crossed at a stop sign and made a left.

The street was tree lined, residential, and quiet. All of the houses were Craftsman style. Was I supposed to knock on a strange door and ask someone if I could plug in my phone? Not sure how I planned to do that without arousing suspicion.

When I got to the spot, it made a bit more sense. The location was a park about the size of three house lots.

I entered through the wrought iron gates and stood there, looking around. How on earth would I be able to use a phone here? The trees were neat and trim. There were rose bushes, and a wildflower garden that was doing its best in this heat to stay alive. The flowers were dropping petals like nature-made potpourri.

I spotted a brick-lined path. It was the kind where people spend money to sponsor the park and in return have their name inscribed on a brick. The names meant nothing to me; it was just some vanity project for people in the neighborhood. Who would care beyond that? I sat down on an empty bench, put the box containing the landline on the seat next to me and wondered what to do next.

Maybe it was all a practical joke. I reached into my pocket, searching for my phone before realizing I'd left it at home as instructed. Funny how much I rely on that stupid phone. When I'm waiting in line, or taking a crap, I pull it out. To think I spent years without it.

I put my chin in my hands, rested them on my knees, and stared at the ground. That's when I saw the plug. It was right between my feet. A square hole, meant for plugging in landline phones or modems. There was a plug in the box, no more than two feet in length. Just long enough to plug it in and talk while hunched over.

I dug the phone out of the box, and put it on the ground. Then I moved the box in front to kind of block the phone from view. Not that anyone was in the park. I was not at all surprised to hear a dial tone. I dialed the number on the piece of paper and let the phone ring. This time it picked up after the third ring. It was the same male voice as before.

"Hello."

"Thanks for the phone."

"What do you want." Not asked as a question, but a statement.

"I want to know about the subtitles," I said.

"Don't ask if you can't handle the consequences. You saw what happened last night."

I gripped the phone. "That was an accident. I talked to the police."

"That's rich," the voice said. "Because the police are always trustworthy, right. I heard the scanners," the voice continued. "The only accident was that she wasn't in the car. They assumed she was. They won't make that mistake again."

"You're telling me it was on purpose?"

"Everything they do is precise, or at least with precise intentions. There are no coincidences or flukes. They know that you know, and they assumed she knew, too."

"Who are they?"

"I gave you the phone to warn you."

"You were a little late. My friend's fiancé could have been killed."

"That's how it goes, I'm afraid."

I looked around the park. No one was there. "If you don't start talking I'll come down to the station."

"A threat. How nice."

"I'll report you to the police. I'll tell everyone I know about the subtitles."

"Do you really think the average person cares about privacy?"

I thought about it. "I don't know. Probably not."

"They're too busy living out loud in public twenty-four hours a day. Generation Selfie. Meanwhile the most disreputable people have infiltrated every ounce of our daily lives. From the news you see to the so-called fact checkers who fact-check the news you see. All of it is fabricated to fit the same narrative. All of it lies. What you have to realize is, everything I say is just the tip of a giant toxic iceberg."

"If they can control your car, they can control everything." I recited.

"And your watch. Your oven. Your pacemaker. They control and monitor every aspect of your life." The voice was silent.

"You wanted your message to be heard. Now two people have reached out to you. What's really going on?"

"Read much Orwell? Animal Farm? 1984?"

"Of course."

"Tell me," the voice said. "What would have happened if the book publishing industry collectively decided not to publish those books?"

I didn't respond.

"You searched last night online and found nothing recent about me, didn't you."

"How do you know?" He ignored my question. "You can't just broadcast that shit and not expect people to ask questions. You gave me this phone, didn't you?"

"I have to go to this length to establish a connection that is truly secure and even then nothing is guaranteed. Especially with someone like you."

"What's that supposed to mean?"

"You think you're taking precautions. You're not on Facebook. You have only an analog TV. You use Ad Blockers." The voice laughed. "You have no idea how deep it goes."

"Then tell me what's going on," I shouted. No one was in the park except a squirrel. It ran up a tree at the sound of my voice.

"Not now," the voice said.

"When?"

"When your friend comes back. Like it or not, she's in as much trouble as you are. And you'll have to watch out for her from now on."

"How the fuck am I supposed to do that if you won't tell me—"

He broke the connection.

I hung up the phone. Hey, look at me. Hunched over on a parking bench screaming into a landline. Not suspicious at all, I thought. I went straight back to Grand and practically ran back to my car, not one minute too soon. I forgot the parking police are total assholes in Atlanta. If you are three seconds over the allotted time, they'll write you a ticket.

The particular one was busy filling out a ticket for the car just behind mine. I threw open the car door, slammed it shut and took off. Sorry, meter maid, it's not your day.

A crazy thought occurred to me. Did the voice on the other end of the line know I was about to get a ticket? Is that why he hung up, in the hopes I'd go back to my car in time? If so, I owed that guy a thank you. It didn't seem possible. But if the past few days were any indication, anything was possible.

I hadn't heard from Jackie in a few days. Then I got a text Wednesday morning:

I'm back. Can we meet at J's at noon?

I answered "K" and turned by phone off. J's was our nickname for Johnny's Pizza. It was a small joint not far from school. It looked like it hadn't changed since the 70's. The décor was faded, they played the classic rock station on the radio and they had an old TV that only showed game shows or sports. There was no Wi-Fi. Students complained all the time, but the owners said the same thing to all of them: "If we had Wi-Fi you'd buy one slice of pizza and never leave." They had a point.

Jackie sat with her back to the door. She was drinking a Coke from a large red cup. We made eye contact but neither of us said anything. I handed her a piece of paper where I had written, "turn your phone off." She looked like she hadn't slept in a few days.

I ordered us a couple of plain cheese slices and a Diet Coke for me and then sat down.

"How you holding up?"

Jackie frowned. "We had a fight. The first thing he wanted to know was how I got to the hospital. I told him you drove me and he was pissed. He was all, 'Why you lettin' some dude drive

you that I don't know?' Then he wanted to know all about you
and who you were, that kinda shit."

"Shit," I said.

"I told him he should thank you for driving me all the way
over there in the middle of the night, but he wanted to know
why you were the first one I called. It went on and on."

"Sorry," I said. "It's like how else would you have gotten
there?"

"Right? He said I should have asked one of my girlfriends. I
finally said look, I'm here because I love you. I came as fast as I
could. If that's not enough to make you understand how much
I care then maybe we should rethink this relationship."

"That's heavy."

"I stayed a couple of days and when the car was ready, I
drove it over to the hospital and left it there. Then I told him I
had class and had to get back."

"What'd he say?"

"He was still in a shitty mood but he understood. He
apologized for snapping. I don't blame him, I mean he went
through a lot."

"But he'll be okay, right?"

"Yeah. He's driving back today. Meanwhile, I ended up
taking the damn bus back. Took three hours with two stops."
She saw me tense up. "What?"

Johnny's was empty except for the guy behind the counter
who was busy making a pizza. I leaned in and spoke with a
hushed voice, filling her in about the phone I found, talking
to the Channel 53 guy from the park, and how he said the car
crash wasn't an accident. When I was finished she just sat there
shaking her head.

"Sounds like a nut job."

"I thought so too, at first. But then I got to thinking. You were bragging about your smart car. And the subtitles were talking about if they control your car, they control everything."

"So what do you think we should do?"

"Go back to the park."

"When?"

"Right now," I said. 'We can be like The Bloodhound Gang. 'Whenever there's trouble, we're there on the double.' Let's get to the bottom of this."

She exhaled. "Sean, we need to talk."

I sat back and against the booth. "Oh, shit. Fine, let's talk."

"Sean, you're like my best friend. You mean the world to me. But we have to stop hanging out. I can't jeopardize my relationship with my fiancé. You know what I mean? I'm gonna marry this guy."

"This guy who controls your life," I said. "This guy who tells you what to do and when to come home and gets upset when you hitch a ride to see him in a fucking hospital because you didn't clear it with him first who the driver should be."

You don't have a right to judge him. You don't even know him."

"And he doesn't know me. But he's judged me all right." I shook my head. "You know what? Forget it."

"I don't want it to be like this either but you have to see where I'm coming from. If we keep hanging out, it'll only make my relationship worse because I'll have to keep lying about shit, and that's not who I am. I want us to still be cool. We just can't hang any more. I'm sorry."

I stood up and left a couple of bucks on the table for a tip like I always do. "I'm sorry, too. Just remember what that guy on the phone said. Like it or not, you're involved in this mess."

"What does that mean?"

"I had planned to find out with you. I'll find out on my own."

Jackie frowned. "Sean—"

"Just one thing. If we're not going to hang out, you'll have to find another chauffeur. Clear it with your man first, though."

I regretted what I said as soon as it left my mouth. But the damage was already done and I was stubborn. I got in my car and headed towards the park. Halfway there, I turned around. What was the point? Let it be somebody else's problem. I had enough on my plate.

At the same time, I was tired of school and the way life was turning out. While Jackie was majoring in fashion and designing these amazing dresses, I had zero inspiration.

I had a POV on my art that started with an concept I call Technological Extinction Burst. Behavioral psychologists explain extinction burst like this: If a child knows throwing a temper tantrum will get their parents to give in to its demands, the child will continue to display that behavior. If the parents stop reacting to the tantrum in the same way, not only will the child persist, the behavior will intensify, before giving up all together. That intensification followed by giving up is what is known as extinction burst.

I had this concept in which outdated technology was the same way. As we move away from cable TV, the networks try even harder to capture our attention. Landlines advertised with greater gusto during their final years of true relevancy and so on. There's a weird technological denial on the part of the technology as it's in the process of getting replaced, a strange desperation on the part of both the inanimate object and its creators.

I was painting over all these outmoded pieces of technology as a way of demonstrating their extinction burst point. Mimeograph machines. Calculators. I even took an old black and white TV and "preserved" it in a plastic cube.

During a recent presentation during class my professor didn't like the concept. She told me I was a Luddite.

I told her Technological Extinction Burst was a comment on how older technology tries to hang on in the face of rapid progression. It was calling into question our willingness to take perfectly good machines and throw them in the trash, causing a lot of physical waste just because we believe that new is always better. In that sense it was environmentalist art, too. Furthermore, as an artist, my role isn't to come up with the answers but to present questions. I ended my diatribe by saying if she thinks painting older forms of technology as part of a conceptual exploration of Technological Extinction Burst made me a Luddite, then she should probably fail anyone who is doing traditional oil on canvas. So yeah, I was a big hit with my professor.

Even though I believed in my concept, I was starting to lose interest in it. We had three more months to go and it was required that we have a minimum of six finished pieces as part of our concept. I had four. There was a month left. In my justification though, the mimeograph machine cost me three hundred bucks, not to mention the cost of paint supplies. Sometimes inspiration comes right away and other times it's like you have to work twice as hard to produce anything. I was now in the "work twice as hard," stage and I wasn't happy about it.

I was also very upset with Jackie. We'd been so tight. Now what was I going to do? I shrugged it off and went home and did something I hadn't in a while. I packed a bowl and got blitzed. Then I went to bed at some point and woke up and decided the hell with class. I didn't want to see Jackie. I stayed in and stayed high. But I didn't watch TV. I listened to music and read and did some drawing, which I hadn't done in forever.

I was drawing landscapes from images I found of remote cabins on a website devoted to them. I loved imagining myself in the scene as I drew. Here I was returning from a mountain hike to my little cabin at the base of the Swiss Alps. Or after a long day of skiing, sweating in the hot sauna that was part of my A-frame in Western Finland.

Of course I would build the cabin myself. It had plumbing and electricity and solar paneling, too. There'd be Wi-Fi, but I wouldn't rely on it. It would be so remote that no one would bother me here. I'd even grow my own food in season. The rest of the time, I'd drive to the nearest town a half-hour away to pick up staples. I got lost in this reverie and ended up drawing for a few hours. It felt great.

On Friday, I went to school because I had two classes. They passed without significance. That evening I ended up going to a bar with some guys I sometimes hang out with just to get out of the house and out of my own thoughts for a bit. We ended up watching boxing. I had no idea who was fighting and I didn't care. It was nice just to be somewhere different and think about something else for a change.

I got home at a decent hour and tucked myself in. Saturday morning, I was up bright and early for no reason at all. It occurred to me I hadn't heard from anyone in a few days. My mom always calls to check in. Weird. That's when I remembered my phone was off and I hadn't turned it back on. I hadn't missed the incessant need to check it for social media updates, or answer text messages. Quite the opposite.

When I turned it back on I had six voice mail messages and eighteen text messages. Three of the messages were from my mom. The rest were from Jackie. I called mom back first reassuring her everything was fine. She's convinced I live in a city that is the murder capital of the world and I'm only one neglected phone call away from dying in the streets. And people think pot makes *me* paranoid.

I didn't get a chance to read any of Jackie's text messages let alone listen to her voice mail messages because she called the second I hung up with my mom.

"Jesus, where the hell have you been," she said.

"You sound like my mom. It's only been a few days, Jackie, what the hell."

She spoke in frantic bursts. "We were jumped coming out of his restaurant. Oh god. Thank God he was carrying his knives—."

A shiver went up my spine. I gripped the phone and interrupted her. "Jackie. Hey. Jackie, girl. You're rambling and it isn't making any sense," I said. "I think you've been drinking."

"What? You know I don't drink," she said. "Besides it's like ten in the morning."

"Jackie," I said in a very deliberate tone. "It is clear you are not yourself. I think we should meet later, in person, when you aren't drunk. Because clearly we should talk in person."

"Of course. You are right. I'd love to meet you later. And you're right. I need to drink lots of water. So I can sober up."

"Let's meet at six."

"Okay. Where?"

I had to think. What would be code that we would get but no one else? "Hey, Super Girl, you hear what Big Willie was getting up to?"

Jackie was confused. "Uh…"

"Pushin' sushi."

"Damn. Again? Motherfucker be crazy."

"I know. I'm gonna have a word with him."

"Seven o'clock?"

"Done."

Jackie met me outside the sushi joint. It felt weird because neither of us had ever eaten there before. We just got delivery.

"Cell phone?" I said.

"Left it at home."

Before either of us could say another word, she was bending over to wrap me in a hug.

"I'm so sorry. Please tell me we're still tight." she said.

"Of course we are," I said. "Always will be."

We left and went back to my place, walking through alleys and taking side streets, looking over our shoulders.

I grabbed two cans of Coke from the fridge. I decided it might be better to stay outside, so we walked to the common yard. There was a wooden gazebo that no one in my apartment complex ever uses. I figured it would be a good spot to chat. No electronics. No cameras around.

"First off, how do you know it wasn't just regular muggers? You were downtown late at night."

She sipped her Coke. "We closed down and were leaving out the back door when a group of dudes pulled up in a fucking Lexus, like one of those modern ones, right? You following me?"

"Yeah."

"So two dudes get out and they said: "We warned you.'"

"Definitely not a mugging."

"This dude who spoke ran at us. Next thing I know my fiancé pulls out his chef's knife. The running dude got slashed. He and his friend panicked and got in their car and drove away. This is next level shit. Fuck these people."

Is your fiancé okay?"

"Yeah he's fine. I told him about everything and he's like okay, y'all need to fix this, but be safe. He said if we need help he can call somebody but he doesn't want to be part of it any more than he already is."

"Can't blame him."

"He told me to tell you thanks for driving me to the hospital. The three of us are gonna have to all meet up after this is over."

I wiped my brow. I didn't realize how hot it was until then.

Funny thing about the south. Sometimes the heat just creeps up on you.

"I don't want to shut you out. The past few days have sucked without you."

"I feel the same way," I said. "You mean the world to me, but I don't want to fuck anything up between you guys."

"I know. And I love you, too."

We held on tight to each other for a while. In that moment, we made a pact with each other. We were in this shit together. And we were going to get out of it together.

I pulled away as if snapping out of a trance. "Jackie."

"Huh?"

"It's Saturday."

Without saying a word both of us left the gazebo and ran back to my place. It was only six-thirty. I turned on Channel 53 anyway. I made sure the closed-captioning was on.

I can't recall ever watching Channel 53 before eight in the evening. I don't know what I was expecting. Still, I was surprised to see a broadcast of Alfred Hitchcock's "The Man Who Knew Too Little."

It was the scene where Doris Day was singing "Que Sera, Sera," as loud as she could, hoping someone would hear her. The closed captioning was not typing up the lyrics, though.

TECHNOLOGY ISN'T THE ENEMY. THE PEOPLE WHO RUN THE TECH COMPANIES ARE. THEY ARE IN BED WITH THE STATE. THEY CALL THE SHOTS. OUR GOVERNMENT IS A PUPPET RUN BY TOTALITARIANS WITH APPS. TURN OFF THE PHONE. UNPLUG THE COMPUTER. THEY ARE LISTENING AND WATCHING.

WE HAVE NEW INFORMATION TO SHARE. INTERESTED PARTIES SHOULD GO TO THE RENDEZVOUS SPOT IMMEDIATELY. REMEMBER, IF

THEY CAN CONTROL YOUR CAR THEY CAN CONTROL
EVERYTHING.

We looked at each other. I started searching for the phone
that was left in the mailbox, but couldn't find it anywhere.
Jackie helped me look. We turned the place upside down and
found nothing. I started to panic. Maybe they'd been in my
house. I started tearing up the place like a mad man. Then I
remembered it was still in the car.

The drive over was tense. I kept looking in the mirror, making
sure nothing was out of the ordinary. I parked on Grand, much
closer to the spot this time. We half ran to the park, found the
bench unoccupied and sat down. The park was dark with no
light illuminating the bench. I fumbled with the cord, plugging
in the phone. It picked up after the second ring.

"Yes."

"We saw the message."

"Come here in a half hour. Before it's too late."

The phone went dead. I unplugged the phone. Jackie grabbed
my arm. I looked up and saw a man was standing in front of us.
A white Lexus was just outside the park, its engine running. He
was dressed in a blue t-shirt, with a lanyard around his neck.
He had ear buds in his ears. He looked like he'd just gotten off
work at the Apple store. Except for the gun in his hand.

He smiled. "It's too late."

My foot touched one of the bricks next to where the phone
was plugged in. It was loose and moved with ease.

"Now we're going to make it simple," the man continued.
"Get in the car, and no one gets hurt. You try to scream, I
shoot."

Jackie saw my foot and patted my hand. She stood up to her
full height and moved in front to block me. I ducked behind
her, picked up the brick, and put it behind my back.

My pulse was racing. If only there'd been time to whisper

a plan. We knew each other like we knew ourselves. We took three steps towards the man. He beckoned us with his gun.

These people tried to kill Jackie's finance. No way they'd let us live. I made up my mind. Jackie would live, even if I had to die. The man held his gun in his right hand. I was left-handed. Maybe that was an advantage.

"C'mon guys. Move it."

Last year, I took fencing classes. Whenever I squared off against a right-hander, they found themselves at a disadvantage. I hoped the same applied.

We were three feet from him when I screamed, having no idea what Jackie would do.

She lowered her body and rushed him. At the same time, I turned sideways lunging in his direction.

Jackie connected with his knees. His gun hand flew out of his hand. My brick connected with the bridge of his nose, making a satisfying crack. I don't think I'd ever hit anyone as hard in my life. The man fell in a heap on his back, blood running from his nose. He was out cold.

I found the gun and put it in my pocket. I grabbed the phone, too. We ran to my car, both of us were shaking with adrenaline. We came upon the warehouse district where Channel 53 was located. We killed the lights and rolled past the buildings.

Jackie pointed. A dirty Channel 53 logo hung askew on one of the buildings. We parked and walked up to it. No sounds. No light inside that we could see. There was only a small overhead light hanging above the door with a tempest of moths circling it. I was about to bang on the door when Jackie stopped me.

Just to the left of the door was a container. The kind used for cigarette butts. And just above it, an outlet for a landline. I tiptoed back to the car, fished out the phone and plugged it in.

"This is really getting silly," I said.

"Right?"

The same voice spoke before there was even a dial tone. "Wait there." Thirty seconds later, Uncle Bob let us in.

He wasn't wearing a cape, but a green button-down shirt. He was taller and thinner in person. Uncle Bob slammed the door behind us and set an alarm.

"We don't have much time. They'll be here soon."

He led us through the dark warehouse toward a corridor illuminated by dim neon. We turned right and entered through a doorway. Jackie went in first. I heard her gasp. To the right was the "Land of Laughs" set. It was much bigger than I anticipated. In front of it were two old cameras, the kind that didn't use film but videotape.

If the set hadn't changed since 1991, what I saw on the left was futuristic. Dozens of state-of-the-art monitors showed different locations of what looked like a giant campus. On one screen, a line of people used key cards to badge into a building. On another screen, a group of men sat lunching in a large kitchen.

A man sat in front of the monitors, controlling the camera angles with joysticks.

"That's the Diddle headquarters," Uncle Bob said. "Looks like such a happy place, doesn't it? Good little worker bees. Providing their magically free services, in exchange for just a tiny bit of data, of course" His sarcastic tone changed. "They're taking over our station."

I shook my head. "That's not what we read. We heard you sold it."

"You read a load of shit. Some story their PR companies cooked up when we told them to go fuck themselves. No amount of money could sway us. Imagine my surprise when I read the news. 'Channel 53 plans to shutter this month,'"

He studied the screens. "They used their influence to get our broadcast license cancelled. Then they got to the mayor.

He's quietly using the powers of imminent domain to take our building. Claimed it was for a revitalization effort. But he's just going to hand it to them."

"What'd you do?" Jackie asked.

"Threatened to go public. That's when the car crashes started. First the bus. Then your fiancé."

Jackie opened her mouth. Nothing came out.

"That's right," Uncle Bob nodded. "His accident was deliberate. They meant to send you a message. Same way the bus crash was meant to send me a message.

He typed something on a keyboard. A monitor brought up a montage of news stories about car crashes. A somber reporter stood in front of a burned out bus. The lower third headline said TRAGIC BUS ACCIDENT KILLS 30.

"Remember this? Twenty-five people from Channel 53 rode that bus every morning. Not a private bus like they have in Silicon Valley. A regular bus. That means there were people on board who died who weren't connected to us."

"I remember that story," I said. "It was a new bus, right?"

"Part of a new fleet," Uncle Bob said. "Super efficient. Smart buses. Generously donated to the city by the wonderful CEO of Diddle.

Jackie said: "If they wanted the station that bad, why didn't you just say fuck it and take their money?"

"They aren't interested in the station. They're interested in swallowing us up. We're the one piece of information they want to suppress." He pointed to the *Land of Laughs* set. "That show is only one part of it. We change the subtitles on all of the shows and public domain movies we broadcast. A whole underground exists of people who are getting wise." He stared at us. "We're talking a proper resistance movement. Not those bullshit kids on college campuses egged on by geriatric professors who are getting one last vicarious thrill. Those idiots are trying to shut down speech they don't agree with." He waved his hand across the room. 'We want all speech out there. All of it."

He closed the news clip. "Their greed got the best of them. But they won't win. We're still here. And you've joined us."

I put my hands up in protest. "All we did was read the closed captioning."

Jackie nodded. "I didn't sign up for no resistance movement."

He pointed to the others. "These people are the last of Channel 53's employees. They believed in the cause years before any one else. Others like you may not have signed up, but you read the writing on the wall so to speak. What gets seen can't get unseen. Whether you want to be part of it is irrelevant."

"All we wanted to know was what it meant," I protested.

"Exactly," he said to me. "So you called. And the moment you dialed the number, Diddle started listening." Uncle Bob spread his arms wide, smiling at us. I half-expected him to start speaking in his TV voice. But he didn't. He was still talking like a regular person. Which made his last sentence that more unbelievable. "Thank god they did."

Jackie raised her hand. "Why is that a good thing, exactly?"

"Simple," Uncle Bob said. "You're a honey trap."

When we didn't respond, he continued. "You reached out to me, and I saw it as a perfect opportunity to get to Diddle. On the surface they are an 'internet of things,' company. In reality, they are a technocratic dictatorship. They are less than six months away from global enslavement. And the last thing they need is someone finding out."

"Oh, come on," Jackie said. "I get being anti-corporate, even being against Silicon Valley's overreach. But you're talking Illuminati shit, Uncle Bob."

He walked over to a row of lockers. "First it was email. Then it was the music and entertainment websites. Then advertising exchange sites for revenues, analytics, their own social media site. Whatever they didn't have time to make, they bought. Video game streaming companies, day trading sites. News corporations."

He spun the dial on one of the locks, wrenched the locker open. Inside was a Kevlar vest, and two guns. His *Land of Laughs* outfit was also there.

Uncle Bob removed his shirt as he spoke. "After they had the online world sewn up, then came the physical products: Smart phones, TV's, appliances. Self-driving cars. All the while, they lobbied governments around the world, to grease the skids, sometimes years in advance before they even had any locations there. Just like that miniseries of the aliens who pretended to come in peace, they are liars. They lavished the poorest countries with money for infrastructure improvements. They wanted to disrupt power generation, oil production, and more. But all their disruption comes at a price."

He buttoned up the white dress shirt, put on his black jacket and cape.

"This is totalitarianism with emojis. Soon the roving electric eye will follow you everywhere, restricting what you can say and do and eventually think. And people will be too busy updating their status messages or arguing online with strangers to realize it. The people who run that corporation see humans as playthings. I wouldn't be surprised if they tried to start a war just to see what would happen."

Jackie threw up her hands. "Okay, I was tracking with you for a while there, Uncle Bob, but this is crazy territory."

Uncle Bob looked at the monitors. "Bring up audio on conference room A."

One of the men did as instructed. A group of people sat in the meeting room at a large oval table. At the head was Michael Samson, the C.E.O of Diddle. He was wearing Diddle Specs as usual. As he spoke, videos streamed behind him: A meeting at the UN. The queen asleep in Buckingham Palace, The President and Secretary of State in a briefing. Russian officials working in the Kremlin.

"If governments are so worried about leaks, I say it's time to make everything public," Samson said. He pointed to the screens. "These are all closed circuit broadcasts for now." He smiled. "Wouldn't want anybody to know. But next month we'll start streaming, unofficially, to our beta testers." The room laughed.

Uncle Bob stared at us. His eyes were blank. "Crazy, huh?"

One of Uncle Bob's monitors was trained on the parking lot outside Channel 53. A white Lexus appeared, followed by six more.

"Look," I said.

"Ah," Uncle Bob smiled. "Perfect."

"Perfect?" Jackie said. "You're out of your damn mind."

"Quite the opposite," he said. "While they've been trying to shut me down, I've been busy infiltrating their offices. Former Channel 53 employees have been very helpful. While they're planning to broadcast the world's governments, we've been secretly recording their meetings. Sharing them with Interpol, too. For all Europe's faults, it cares more about privacy than America does."

He spoke in his *Land of Laughs* voice. "They think everyone is asleep at the wheel. But they're about to get an ACME-sized surprise."

He tapped the shoulder of the nearest employee. On one of the monitors, we could see the inside of a Lexus that had just parked outside. A driver fumbled with a door that wouldn't open. The automatic seat belt tightened around his shoulder. He struggled to remove it.

The car started again, revving its engine. The tires screamed in reverse. I shut my eyes as it raced towards another warehouse, hitting it with full force. The other cars careened out of control, smashing buildings, and running into each other.

The first car now lurched forward toward Channel 53. As it picked up speed, we saw the driver, face contorted in pain, let out an inaudible scream. Just before impact, his seatbelt relaxed. The Lexus collided with the building. His head went straight through the windshield. Then the screen cut to black.

Screams came from The Diddle conference room. They were watching the live feed outside of Channel 53. Several employees stood up, and moved toward the exit.

Uncle Bob spoke into a microphone.

"No use trying to run, kids."

The conference room broke out in complete chaos. Some tried to use their phones to no avail. Uncle Bob continued to speak in full character. "Doors locked? Devices scrambled? For a giant tech company, it's incredibly easy to hack your conference rooms. Almost as easy as the software in those white cars." His voice was mocking in its sadness. "I'm afraid the authorities won't like today's conference room broadcast. Not one bit. What would the good kids out there in television land think if they knew?"

On one of the screens, a long procession of black SUV's raced on the highway toward Diddle's mega-campus. I counted twenty of them.

Uncle Bob nodded to two employees. They got up from the table and walked to the *Land of Laughs* cameras. Uncle Bob took his place on the set.

On all but one of the monitors in Diddle's conference room, the *Land of Laughs* title appeared in its usual puke green typeface. Michael Samson took off his Diddle Specs. "You don't seem to get it," he said. "We own you now. You think you can threaten us? Shake us down?"

"On the contrary," Uncle Bob said. "It's not money I'm after."

"What, then? Your want your stupid station back? You can have a whole fucking network with us." Samson's face turned red. "What the hell do you want, you fucking prick?"

A SWAT vehicle with a battering ram broke through the gates, stopping just outside the building where Samson stood, white knuckles pressing against the conference table. Men and women in black suits headed towards the building with guns drawn.

"Language," Uncle Bob said. "This is an all ages show. Don't you know the kids are watching now?" Uncle Bob looked around. He then leaned in and put a hand to the side of his mouth. In a stage whisper he said: "You're live on the air."

Samson's face fell. There was a loud commotion outside the conference room. He walked to his chair in a daze, and fell into it.

"Good evening, groovy girls and boys of all ages. This is your friendly host, Uncle Bob." He smiled wide. "Boy do we have an excellent show for you tonight!"

CHAPTER 4

Buzzards And Dreadful Crows

It's still out there. The tree with the tangled roots. Only now it's lying on its side, covered with crude oil. Looking like a giant piece of broccoli drenched in black salad dressing.

And they are still out there, too. Out on the perimeter of the property I been working for two decades now. They got their guns on their hips. I can see 'em with my night vision goggles. They're itchin', all right. But they know not to come in. They don't want any more publicity. They don't want it to end up a bunch of statistics like in the other incidents. They're tryin' to wait me out. They'll be waitin' a long time because I been on this land a long time. I ain't goin' nowhere.

First I had a cherry orchard. Then when the disease came and wiped them cherries out, I tried potatoes. Those worked for a few years before that stopped, too. My eldest kept sayin' I needed to try and make the land fallow, but my eldest don't understand. There are only so many subsidies you can get for not growin' stuff.

When it looked like the ground wouldn't work any more and I was just collectin' subsidy after subsidy and feeling worthless, my eldest said why not try lettin' it lay fallow for the ten hundredth time, I said how 'bout another suggestion. He picked up the soil and looked at it and said "beets."

Those beets took the soil like crazy. Soon we had beets coming out our earholes. We were seein' red, peein' red, and shittin' red, too. But it put us in the black for the first time in a good long while.

We became known around here as the beet people. And then I thought, you know, maybe the tree was the problem that kept killin' the other crops so why not remove it before it killed the beets, too. Those thick roots had caused me no end of trouble and cost a crate load of money over the years.

When I said let's get rid of the tree, my eldest said for once I came up with a good idea, so then I knew it was good because he didn't say stuff like that too often.

I didn't have enough money to pay to have it removed so I said hell, it's my land, anyway. I'll do it myself. If I'd known though, I would've paid. The extra crop space would've paid it off sooner or later. The again if I'd have paid, someone else might've tried to cash in.

First I took the chainsaw to it. Took near one week in between everything else. Not like I got much help from anyone. Back when I was younger, I could've just looked at a woman and gotten 'em pregnant. I got six kids, but I only know two of 'em. My eldest and my youngest, who's a good for nothin' shit.

My eldest was busy helpin' with the beet harvest and I was cuttin' down that monster tree. And when it got down to the stump, it turned into a whole other mess. Had to rent the biggest tree stump remover I'd ever seen. But it did the job, Lord, even if it had to do it in sections and even if it took me near twelve hours.

So then there was this giant brown tree on the ground on its side, and all these leaves all over and these tangled roots like hard balls of spaghetti. I turned the machine back in, thinking

I could haul everything later and maybe sell the tree to the lumber yard and use a wood chipper for the roots because they weren't good for much of nothin' like my youngest.

But the day I planned on givin' the stump remover back, I went out there and the field was a big greasy mess. My eldest realized what we were dealin' with.

We had our ups and downs. Some years were leaner than others. Crops got switched out. We just came off a great year, my best as a man and a farmer, and now this? This'll ruin everything.

You crazy, my eldest said. We rich. I didn't understand it then. But it was only when the feds showed up and threatened me with jail if we didn't leave did I realize how rich we were.

It's been a month now. My eldest says we on the news every night, and everyone's out there protesting for us. They say it's just like the government to make sure a black farmer don't make it in this world. We a minority of minorities he tells me.

I don't understand most of it, if you want to know the truth. I left school to help my daddy when I was fourteen, which was more schoolin' than he had. I can read and write. Despite everything and the kids I don't see and the ladies who came and went sooner than most crops, I done okay. My daddy died poor. I built my house and tended the land, and kept to my own and never made any trouble. Now this. Feels like I'm winning the lottery, and losing everything else at the same time.

My eldest was on the computer, readin' me the news every day. Daddy, he say. They are settin' up for an injunction against you. If we don't vacate, they gonna jail us. I ask him what an injunction means first. Then I say, but it's our land. I got the deed. But my eldest say they consider it federal land now. They can do what they want when they want. Oil is a resource.

I watch the TV most nights after I finish. The people on the news, on one side they talk about how the government want to keep the black man down and we are a family of heroes for standing up to them. Like the new civil rights people, or some such. What they are offerin' us is a joke. We deserve more. On the other side, they say it's my duty to vacate land because we need the oil and we at war, and I should be a patriotic American and accept my fate.

I could vacate in ten minutes if they paid me enough, but if they don't pay what it's worth, no way, man. And I told them that. And I told my eldest to tell the lawyer he hired to tell them. And so I settle in. Because those people out there have guns and I never been in trouble with the law before.

Now the game has changed. My youngest good for shit, he left this morning. Done and snuck out. And the authorities out there, they nabbed him. They said they'll charge him if I don't come out, cause he was there, too. He's part of it. Why that dumb bastard left I'll never know. My eldest thinks they kidnapped him. You know how they are, Daddy, he said. They just like buzzards. They circle and wait until we get weak. Then they make their move.

The phone's been ringing for weeks, but we stopped answerin'. At first I wanted my side heard, and planned on talkin' to every journalist from here to Humboldt County. But my eldest said, keep silent. Let the lawyers do the talkin'.

We don't even have to pay them. They took the case for free.

Even though it's late, my eldest is back on the computer, readin' up on the story. I tell him why do that? You livin' the story. He just keeps on with the buzzard talk.

I wait awhile. Then I go around the house turnin' off all the lights. I wait till it's quiet, and then slip out to the barn. There's no moon tonight. But I know my land like I know myself. The sky is black as oil. Up, down, left, right. Everywhere is oil. I walk outside like a shadow. Then I head into the barn.

I got myself a little pen light I keep on my keychain for just in case. And I turn it on for a second, just to get myself straight and see what I'm lookin' for. I snap the light off and go over to the corner and pick it up. Feel the weight in my hands. It's not that far to where I'm going that I can't carry it.

My eldest is a bright boy. He's been to high school, all the way through, and is now in college. First in our family. He's bright, all right. I know it. But in this case, he is so very dumb. Those people out there, they ain't buzzards. Because buzzards only eat dead things. I may be dumb but I been workin' the land long enough to know the difference.

The guys out there with their fingers on the triggers, they more like crows. They see an opportunity and take it when they can. They crafty. You can't fool 'em with scarecrows and you can't chase 'em off.

One time when we was growin' potatoes we had crows for days. Wouldn't be more than two weeks growin' in the ground before the crows would gnaw them all down. We tried everything that year, except shootin' them. Lights. Sounds. Scarecrows. Coyote urine. None of it worked.

What ended up was, we poisoned the potatoes. All of them. And I didn't do it thinkin' the crows would eat it 'cause they got too much smarts to do that. But what did happen was, they just up and left. They realize they been fuckin' with us too long and now we fuckin' with them. They wanted them potato plants more than anything. So we made it so they couldn't have it.

I got myself this propane tank in my hands and it's all the way full up. And I got five more of them back in the barn. And what I plan to do is, set 'em all out in that black oil sludge. And then I plan on getting my gasoline tanks, and pourin' that on top, too.

And then just before dawn, I'll tell them they need to leave and go right now. And when they don't. I'm gonna light myself a firecracker from the stash my dumb for shit youngest likes to set off every Fourth of July. And then throw it out in that black pool. And I'll keep doin' it till one of 'em sparks. One way or another, I'll make them birds leave.

CHAPTER 5
Feed Me

At the intersection of Main Street and Abbot Kinney in Santa Monica is a small yellow house. Both the lower and upper rooms have fed well-heeled diners the best French cuisine this side of New York, let alone Paris. For the past ten years, Chez Pic has challenged, dazzled, wowed and astounded guests thanks to two chefs.

The first chef, Jacques Pic, opened his namesake restaurant in 1995. From the start, it was a celebrity hang out, with the biggest names (and no names who wished they were big names) making reservations months in advance to have the pleasure to enjoy whatever Chef Pic placed in front of their hungry eyes. And to be seen eating there, of course, was just as big a perk.

Pic trained in France, under traditional militant guidance. He was known for being contentious to sous-chefs, wait-staff and customers alike. For the first two years, Chez Pic was a revolving door of abused and disgruntled employees. But then Pic assembled an A-Team of beautiful but courteous denizens with one singular goal: to serve the public the best food they would eat in their entire lives.

If Pic found a server calling in sick to go audition for a commercial, they were fired the same day. He didn't care about any other art except cuisine. He'd throw scalding hot pans across the room at sous-chefs who hadn't kept their *mise en place* in order, make college students and seasoned servers sob with his explosive rage. God help anyone within screaming range should a soufflé not rise to his perfection, or the court bouillon have too much celery.

The more drama occurred, the more popular Chez Pic became. Seeing the potential in his character, a producer once offered a lucrative sum to film one of the very first reality TV shows in his restaurant. Pic didn't just refuse the producer. He banned him from ever returning to his establishment. When asked about it later, he said "I am not in the business of making gauche pornography for overweight Americans."

What he passed up in money, Pic made up for in integrity. Besides, with his menu prices and long waiting times for reservations, he did well enough to purchase the small house in cash.

Chef Pic was adored by celebrities and respected by his employees. While he considered the former to be culinary cretins with all the money but none of the palette, he paid his staff well and counted on them more than they knew.

His temper was as legendary as his drinking habits. As his fame grew beyond Santa Monica, Los Angeles and soon the rest of America, Pic's alcohol intake increased. So did his temper.

In 2002, Chez Pic was awarded two Michelin Stars, the first American restaurant outside of New York to achieve this honor. For one week, Chez Pic celebrated by creating a tasting menu reflecting the best of France. A particular favorite was his coq au vin, prepared with a real rooster, and bottles of Bordeaux from a small producer in France he championed called Chez Plume.

At the height of Pic Mania, the chef was volatile and unreliable; his kitchen staff was the true culinary geniuses. They were the ones finding and sourcing ingredients that turned Pic's drunk dreams into amazing realities every week. The brilliance was still there, but the man had all but disappeared in a bottle.

One night, Chef Pic had finished a bottle of wine and was halfway through a good bottle of cognac when a c-list celebrity couple entered the restaurant. Roman and Kelsey were the stars of a reality show called Plastic Surgeon Love, a show featuring two plastic surgeons, Roman and Kelsey, who were in love. Every week they'd give women boob jobs or tighten their faces or bleach their assholes, or make men's crows' feet disappear or tuck in their stomachs, and then fight with each other and in dramatic fashion and then make up in dramatic fashion.

One TV critic called Plastic Surgeon Love "emblematic of a deranged Hollywood who believes love isn't love unless it's out of control, abusive, and self-obsessed enough to consider mutilation in the name of staying young a form of religion." Plastic Surgeon Love was a massive hit. It had just been renewed for its third season.

Roman and Kelsey showed up late for their reservation, insisted on cocktails before dinner, and ordered specials with their specific modifications. Any other night, this was enough for immediate dismissal. But Chef Pic was in a sadistic mood. He dismissed them with his hands and told the cooks to make it "their way."

By the time dessert came out, Chef Pic had finished his bottle of cognac. He decided it was time to meet the famous couple.

When Chef Pic walked (or swerved as it were) through the dining room, the guests would stop their talking and sit silent, hoping he'd approach their tables. If you spoke in the right tone and were appreciative enough, you might get a nod, smile, or even a wink from the genius. A visit from the chef was like a blessing from the Pope. Roman and Kelsey in contrast were two blasphemers who kept chatting loud and oblivious.

Chef Pic walked past all the other diners without looking. He reached Roman and Kelsey's table interrupting their conversation. His voice was husky and loud.

"So, I trust we have pleased you tonight, no? Normally we do not make modifications to our menu but for you—" he smiled and spread his arms in a mock show of humility.

Roman and Kelsey were frozen with Botox and stuffed with silicone, as if they were made from stiff balloons.

"I've had better," Roman said.

Chef Pic laughed. "Oh really? And where have you had better *carnard aux olives*? You know this duck was flown in from my farm in France this morning, yes?

"Ah you know," Roman said. "It was good. Just not great."

Kelsey chimed in. "And the fish was too salty."

Chef Pic's smile turned tight as if he, too, had work done. "Too salty," he said. "You know I taste everything that leaves my kitchen, to make sure it is to my liking."

"Well," she said. "It may be to your liking, but not to mine."

"Perhaps you should not have modified my recipe," Chef Pic said. "As someone with twenty years now in the business and two Michelin stars, I do know what I am doing."

Kelsey swallowed the rest of her after-dinner drink. "We disagree."

"*Une minute s'il-vous-plâit,*" Chef Pic said. His voice was calm as he walked back to the kitchen. When he returned, he had the same tight smile on his face. To the untrained eye, Pic looked nonplussed. They only giveaway was the meat cleaver in his hand.

Pic strode over to Roman and Kelsey's table. Before they could react, he raised his arm above his head. When it came down, the cleaver connected with Roman's hand, chopping it off in one go. It lay in an ever-growing pool of blood, still holding his fork.

Kelsey's face turned white. She screamed, but Pic was not finished. He chopped her fork hand off as well. And then slashed with abandon until both diners lay across the table motionless. With his own pulse subsided and vision returned, Pic's first thought was that the bodies looked like two red snappers marinating in wine. Except of course, their eyes weren't as bright.

In the pandemonium that ensued, guests and staff alike ran for dear life, fearing they might be next. By now, though, Chef Pic was calm. He pulled up a chair, finished the woman's glass of wine and looked down at the carnage.

When at last he spoke, his voice was devoid of emotion. "Perhaps you will learn next time, that the chef is always right. No?"

The three-ring circus trial ended after fourteen months. Sentencing was handed down. The jury decided Chef Pic should be given the death penalty for stabbing and slashing his guests no less than thirty times each, mutilating their corpses and more. There were even health code violations, which was as much an excessive tendency on the DA as it was a comment on California's strict restaurant regulations. And while being sent to death in California was as rare as true beluga caviar, only a few years later it looked as if Pic's number was up after all.

In what many thought was a sign of the apocalypse, California elected a very hardline Republican governor. He was hard on crime, setting aside a sizeable budget to build more prisons. When it came to the death penalty, Governor Ipswich didn't create a proposal for Californians to vote on, but steamrolled it through in an overarching bill called "Crime Stop." Hidden among the details for job growth through rebuilding prisons and increased jobs for rehabilitation for non-violent offenders was a proposition called 170C: the death penalty would be expedited for the most vicious criminals. It was viewed as both a scheme to save taxpayer money and a serious way to deter further crimes of this nature from happening.

Chef Pic would be second execution of that year. The first was a notorious Mexican drug cartel leader who had also butchered people with a knife. Chef Pic was quick to point out to inmates and journalists alike that unlike the Mexican, he'd done a much better job of it. "I am no barbarian. Like my cuisines, everything I do is with the true heart of an artist."

Chef Brian Straight had taken the morning off, leaving his sous chefs in charge of procuring the day's orders. Receiving the fresh fish and meats, shopping the farmer's markets for produce, and preparing the menu. He'd hired the original staff back when he'd taken over Chez Pic. He trusted them and treated them like family.

His staff didn't know what he was doing that day. But they were used to his odd days off. Unlike a lot of workaholic chefs, it wasn't unusual for Straight to be spontaneous, announcing he was going hiking or driving up to Napa. Those days fueled his creativity and never ceased to be a source of inspiration. Once on a hike, he saw some quail, and ended up creating a tasting menu based on the dish. It was a huge success.

Early that morning, Chef Straight called his executive chef and told her he was taking the day off, giving no further explanation. He told her to serve the same menu as the night before. This in itself was not an odd request; they often kept the menu the same, sometimes for as long as a week, except for the daily specials. His executive chef hung up and thought nothing more of it.

Chef Straight hung up the phone and hopped in his Audi A6. The drive to Adelanto took longer than expected. By the time he'd cleared security, he was almost ten minutes late. When he'd passed through the last doors to the visitation room, Chef

Pic was already waiting for him, sitting between the bulletproof glass dividers, phone in hand.

"You're late," he sneered.

"Traffic" Straight said. "You might be surprised to know this but I've never had occasion to come to this part of California. It's not like there are wineries here."

Pic laughed. His voice was gravel. His eyes were bloodshot. His Gallic face looked like it aged fifteen years.

"Why'd you call me here?"

"Why didn't you change the name of the restaurant?"

"The name had equity," Straight answered. "Also, your last incident notwithstanding, I was a great admirer of everything you'd done to put Los Angeles on the map. I wanted to continue the tradition."

"And you did, too. Your restaurant with my name now has a third Michelin star," Pic said. His eyes flashed.

"This is true. I continued to uphold your tradition and perhaps I surpassed it, too."

"Oh I have read all about it," Pic said. "Your truffle tasting menu was met with outrage at first. Now others try to do the same."

"Everyone knows truffles are powerful. The difference is the amount used. A little goes a long way. Divide a little by half and you have a starter. Plus we both know what attracts people to truffles."

Pic smirked. "Smells like sex, no?"

It was Straight's turn to smile.

"And now you bested me by one star. And yet, you have kept my name on your doors."

"That's correct. The name on the door is a name on a door. It never had to be my name. I was content to become a success regardless. I would like to think if we'd worked together, you might have passed the torch when it came time."

Pic stared through the glass for several seconds, contemplating this notion.

"This is something no one will ever be sure of," he answered. "But one thing I do know for certain."

"And what's that?"

"I am scheduled to die in two weeks' time. At ten in the evening, October the seventh."

Chef Straight did remained silent, not knowing what to say. After a time he managed a "Sorry."

"I am not," Pic said. "While I feel no remorse for those pigs who had no respect for my cuisine, I have more than paid my price. To be locked up here with no way of cooking," he said, waving his hands. "They wouldn't even let me work the kitchen, do you see? It's torture."

"I can imagine."

"Well," Pic said. "If this is the rest of my life, I want no part of it. No, I will embrace my final moments. I will go out enjoying my life."

"This is a very interesting subject, but I have to ask, why did you call me out there?"

Chef Pic laughed. "*Mais, c'est facile.* Chef Straight: I want you to make my last meal."

Chef Straight felt his mouth go dry. "What do you want me to make?"

A guard tapped his shoulder. Visiting time was over. Pic smiled at Straight. "You're the head chef now. I am in your hands."

Two days later, Chef Straight was opening the restaurant in the morning when a reporter from TMZ appeared on a motorcycle.

"So what will you make?"

Chef Straight was startled. "What do you mean?

Tonight is the same menu as last night. We do have a special, Veal tournedos in crème sauce with mushrooms."

"I mean for The Butcher Chef."

Chef Straight frowned. "I don't know yet. "

"Ah, c'mon. Give us a hint."

Chef Straight turned to the man, unsure whether to look at his face or his camera. "It's clear you don't understand cooking. It takes me a month to plan out tasting menus here. The regular menu is subject to availability of ingredients. For something of this magnitude, I don't even know where to start."

"Not even a clue."

"None."

The motorcyclist turned his camera off. "That's no good. I don't think we'll be able to use any of that."

"If it makes you feel any better, I don't give a shit," Straight said.

Chef Straight unlocked his restaurant and closed the door behind him. The rest of the staff was waiting.

"Sorry," he said. "Some TMZ reporter wanted to know what I was going to make."

"Well?" Sylvia said. While it was easy to get the kitchen staff to return, Chef Straight had a hard time coaxing back the servers. Most were too traumatized. Only Sylvia returned.

"Well, what?" Straight asked. "I don't know. I have this restaurant to run, you know? I can't serve him our current tasting menu. He's too aware of it. I can't do anything modern. He's a traditionalist. I'm not going to whip out molecular gastronomy tactics on him. If I made lecithin foam he'd spit it out and say he made it better with his spit."

The staff laughed.

"I just need to think. It'll have to be something rustic. Not fussy. And filling. If it's his last meal, he should enjoy it. Besides, I have no idea what kind of kitchen set up they have."

James, the bartender, spoke up. "Why not do a whimsical take on prison food? Potatoes and spaghetti and moonshine?"

"Funny. I can guarantee you somewhere there's a chef with a prison food concept already in the works. Probably open up on Melrose. They're all douche bags up there."

It took Chef Straight another day before he decided to do a menu from Bretagne, or Brittany as his English grandmother called it. The western most area of France not only contained a wealth of amazing regional delicacies, but it was Chef Pic's birthplace. Chef Straight would start by transporting him back to where it all began.

He planned a simple tasting menu with very little in the way of alterations: One half dozen *belons* flown in from Cancale. It was just the start of oyster season but so far it was an exceptionally good year. Straight would serve them three ways: two with only a lemon slice accompaniment, two with a traditional mignonette, and two with his homemade wasabi salt.

Next would be Monkfish *à l'Aromoricaine*, a simple homey stew with the ugly and underrated monkfish as the star. Through some connections (and despite the trade embargo with Iran) Straight managed to get enough Iranian Sargol saffron to make the dish sing so loud it would make Chef Pic's eardrums bleed.

And for a charming ending, *clafoutis*, with imported French black cherries, he had soaked in cherry brandy. The secret move was that the brandy didn't come from France but from Oregon. This might be seen as blasphemy by Pic, but there could be no denying it: the cherries were better from France, but the Pacific Northwest distillers made better cherry brandy.

Chef Straight was happy with his choices. To be sure, it was simple. But perhaps this is what made it so audacious. Food can take you on a geographical journey, it's true. But it can also take you on an emotional one. Instead of bending over backwards with culinary alchemy, Straight would penetrate Chef Pic's emotional core with dishes that might cause dormant memories to come flooding back.

Straight called the prison to inquire about the kitchen setup. He was not surprised to learn the people working there couldn't answer his questions. After several minutes of conversation, Straight decided to bring his own pots and pans. Corrections Officer Jones saw no issue with this, provided they run it (and everything he brought in) through the metal detector.

Straight implored the officer to understand time was of the essence with perishable foods. "It's not like I'm going to serve him pasta and potatoes. I'll be bringing live oysters."

"As long as you comply, it'll move quick," Corrections Officer Jones said.

Straight was doubtful, but realized he had no choice against authority. If he played nice and kept the oysters on a lot of ice, everything should be fine.

"Believe me, I'll be more than happy to comply. And so will my sous-chef. "

"You're what now?" Corrections Officer Jones asked.

"Sorry. That's the name of the person I'm bringing with me to help prepare the meals."

"That's not going to happen."

"What do you mean? If I prepare these dishes by myself, it'll take hours. I need someone skilled to help."

"Oh don't worry about that," Corrections Officer Jones said. "We have a work rehabilitation program here. Randy'll work with you."

"Randy."

"Yeah, he's been working the kitchen for four years now. Guy can make anything and can make a lot out of nothing. Why, just last week he made this mac and cheese that had jalapeños in it. You don't usually hear the inmates giving compliments but they ate that up like nobody's business."

"The problem is I'm not making jalapeño mac and cheese, although I admit that is a good idea. I'm serving raw oysters with wasabi salt and making monkfish stew."

"The only words I understood you say were oysters and salt," Corrections Officer Jones said.

"What I mean is these aren't easy dishes to make, and it is Chef Pic's last meal."

"Let me explain something to you in plain English. A producer who was tight with the governor pulled the string to make this thing happen for Pic in exchange for the movie rights to his life-in-prison story. On top of that, the governor is trying not to look like too much of a hard ass because his poll numbers are in the toilet."

"What does that mean?"

"It means no one cares about Pic's last meal. You are there to make the governor look good and give good PR."

"Oh," Straight said.

"Oh is right," Corrections Officer Jones said. "It was already a headache getting you clearance. It's way too late to get clearance for one of your crew."

"So Randy's my sous-chef," Straight said.

"Bingo."

Corrections Officer Jones was working the afternoon Chef Straight arrived at the prison. Whether out of sympathy or negligence, he didn't know, but Straight wasn't held up more than three minutes clearing security, and that was only because the officers mocked him for taking live oysters to a prison.

Once in the kitchen, Corrections Officer Jones introduced him to Randy who offered his hand. His handshake was warm and friendly.

"Hi, I killed some people a while back but all that's behind me, praise Jesus. I'm a new man now. I'm set free."

"You have ten more years to go before you're even up for parole," Corrections Officer Jones reminded him.

"That's ten more years to be a blessing and witness to those who need it most, Praise Jesus."

Corrections Officer Jones shook his head. "Hey Straight, I have two officers here that will be standing by. They won't get in your way unless Saint Randy here decides to do something stupid like he did last month, didn't you?"

"We have all sinned and fallen short of the glory of God," Randy said.

"Your sins added two more years to your sentence, Randy."

Corrections Officer Jones left without waiting for Randy to respond. Randy turned and said "What should I do first, Chef?"

Straight looked at Randy. His eyes were beady and he had a dirty brown mustache. "Let's wash our hands first. Really good, with soap and hot water. And then I'll decide what you should help with."

After washing up, Straight announced they'd make the dessert first because it would take the most time.

"I love me dessert," Randy said. "Is it pudding? Like Jell-O?"

"Not exactly. Tonight I'm only making French dishes for Chef Pic."

"Oh that's right," Randy said. "That French guy's mostly kept to himself. We heard what he did to those customers. We leave him alone. So no Jell-O?"

"No," Straight said. We're making something called *clafoutis*."

"Clown Footee?" Randy laughed. "Doesn't sound like something I'd eat. What is it?"

"It's kind of like a cherry cake."

"Gotcha. So how do I help you make this Clown Footee?"

Straight turned the oven to 325F, and got out a large bowl. "I want you to whisk everything I put in this bowl."

Randy saluted. "Roger that."

Straight added the milk, eggs, sugar, vanilla, flour, melted butter and a small four-ounce vial of the cherry brandy to the bowl.

"Get that nice and incorporated."

Randy attacked the bowl with his whisk like he was trying to make concrete.

"You can go a little easier."

Randy nodded, easing up on the whisk. Once finished, Straight placed a large cast iron pan in front. Randy poured the batter into the mixture.

Straight removed the lid from a container of pitted cherries and started putting them on top. Randy also helped.

"This looks real nice," Randy said. "Smells nice, too."

Straight took the juice from the container and also poured that on top.

"Oh man, " Randy said. "That's like extra good, right?"

Straight placed the pan in the oven and set the timer on his phone for 30 minutes, which was ten minutes beneath final cooking time. He never trusted an unfamiliar oven and wanted to make sure the *clafoutis* didn't burn.

"While that bakes, we'll start on the other courses."

Straight decided Randy should be in charge of chopping by placing vegetables in the processor. The inmates who worked the kitchen weren't allowed knives. Straight could always blame the texture of the ingredients based on circumstances; despite his legendary reputation he was sure Pic would understand after spending this long in jail. But all the excuses in the world wouldn't get him off the hook if the dishes weren't up to standard in terms of taste.

After five seconds, Straight stopped the processor.

"Why'd you do that?" Randy asked.

"We are making a mignonette, not shallot soup."

"What's a mignonette?"

Straight sighed. "It's a traditional accompaniment for oysters. Minced shallots, red wine vinegar, salt and pepper."

"What's a shallot?"

Straight was about to berate him, the way so many chefs had berated Straight when he started. From his first rung position as dishwasher it was years of yelling, pots being thrown, verbal threats, and intimidation to make him the chef he was.

Then he remembered Randy wasn't training to be a chef. Randy had, as he said, murdered some people. Straight wasn't sure if "some" meant two, or twenty; he didn't want to be the next. Straight took a deep breath and said "Shallots are the things you just chopped up. Think of them as little onions."

"Shallots. Roger that." Randy nodded. "What now?"

Straight grabbed a spatula and scooped the shallots out into a metal bowl. "Nothing at the moment. I'll just finish this." Straight added vinegar, salt and pepper to the shallots. He put the sauce on a bag of ice in his cooler to keep it chilled. Next he took out the ingredients for the second dish. He removed the monkfish from the cooler. Randy gasped.

"What the hell is that, an ugly motherfucking alien?"

Straight smiled. "It's called monkfish. And you're right. It is ugly. But it tastes great."

He picked up a knife and started removing the seven layers of skin, dorsal and fins.

"Please give me something to do so I don't have to watch that," Randy said. "I'm gonna hurl."

Without stopping, Straight instructed Randy to chop the onion, shallots, and garlic, whirring the processor for about ten seconds only. "And when you're done with that, open the can of tomato paste and tomato puree.

Once the Monkfish was cleaned and skinned, Straight placed another cast iron pan on high heat. While that was heating up, he dredged the monkfish medallions in flour.

"How's the onion mixture?"

Randy held up the bowl. It could have been minced a bit more but he would make it work. Straight went over to his cooler and fished out a bottle of wine and a small bottle of cognac.

Randy rubbed his hands together, licking his lips. "Now that's what I'm talking about," Before he could move, one of the guards stepped between them.

"Sorry," Randy said. "Forgive me, Lord. Old habits die hard."

"Hey Randy," Straight said. "Can you put a pot on with some water? We're going to make some rice, too."

Without taking his eyes off the bottle, Randy nodded.

"Now I'll need you to back away from the oven," Straight said.

Randy looked hurt. "But why? I thought I was doin' okay."

"It's for safety." Working fast, Straight added a mixture of olive oil and butter to the pan, swirling it around. The butter bubbled and sizzled. He took the monkfish medallions and put them in the pan, seasoning with salt and white pepper. He flipped the medallions and seasoned them again. Straight then grabbed the bottle of cognac and added a few splashes.

"Stand back," he cautioned.

Randy took two steps back and watched as Straight lit the cognac with a match. It caught fire, sending an orange and purple flame toward the ceiling. Straight took the pan off the heat and put it on a trivet.

"That's crazy, What'd you do that for?" As the flames died down, Randy sniffed. "Oh. I see. Man, it smells fantastic. Also that's a great color. Nice even browning."

Straight set the monkfish aside, and looked at Randy.

Randy smiled. "When it's TV time, I like to watch food shows. You know last week I made mac n cheese and I added jalapeños? The guys loved that."

"So I heard. Can you add the rice to the water? Stir it for a minute, add a pinch of salt, then turn the heat down and cover it."

Randy did as he was told. Straight was impressed. Despite the circumstances, he'd employed people who were so lacking in talent they couldn't follow even the simplest directions without screwing up somewhere.

Straight placed the pan back over the heat, turning it on medium this time. He added another glug of olive oil and started sautéing the onions, shallot and garlic, being careful not to brown them. He then added the fish stock, tomatoes, wine, dried thyme, bay leaves, and saffron. He turned the heat up to let it boil.

"That's not all I did to the mac and cheese, though," Randy continued. "I found this stuff the Mexicans in here love called ancho powder. It's like some kind of chili pepper. I added that as well as some other stuff. I call it Mexican Mac. I wish I had some left for you to try."

Straight let the pan boil so the sauce would reduce. "Let's check on the *clafoutis*."

He opened the oven and they both peered in. Randy inhaled and closed his eyes.

"It's too bad you aren't the cook here. When I get out, maybe I can apply for a job with you? I'm a good learner."

From behind them Corrections Officer Jones said "Randy, you'd have to stop getting into trouble to ever get out."

Straight saw the cake needed another ten minutes after all.

"You almost ready, there, chef?"

Straight added the Monkfish back to the pan, spooning the sauce over it. "Ten more minutes."

"Pic is waiting. And we don't have all night," Corrections Officer Jones said.

Even in jail there was a hurry to make everything come out at once. There was never a moment to coax the flavors into coming together. No spontaneity allowed. One had to whip them together as fast as possible. It was hard to believe the circumstances that led to this moment. Most chefs would have jumped at the opportunity to cook for someone of Pic's stature. But they also would have been nervous. There was no denying today would either be Straight's finest moment or his biggest disappointment. It all came down to the ingredients, and Pic's disposition.

Straight grabbed his oyster knife. "Randy, can you add a bed of that ice on that pan, please?"

"Sure, no problem, Chef."

Straight placed half a dozen of the shucked *belons* on the ice. He added the mignonette to two, added the two lemons on the lip of two other shells, and sprinkled the tops of the final two oysters with wasabi salt.

He then removed the *clafoutis* from the oven and stuck a knife in the center. It came out clean. The crust was perfect. Golden in some parts, a little darker in others. The cherry brandy brought a new layer to the smell. Straight couldn't help but smile. Pic was going to love this.

"Leave this where it is, okay? It needs to cool before we cut it."

"Randy smiled. "You can count on me."

Chef Pic sat at a table in a small room by himself. He had requested candlelight and a proper place setting for ambiance, but this was met with laughter. He had also requested a good bottle of wine. This too, was met with firm denial. The room was adjacent to the lethal injection room.

On the other side of the lethal injection room was another

room for reporters, lawyers and the victims' families. It was packed. There were three reporters. One from TMZ, one from the L.A. Times and one from CNN who worked the L.A. beat. The rest of the group belonged to the family who were all too happy to tell their story in the hopes of turning it into a new reality show.

Chef Straight knocked once and then entered. Pic's face was ashen. His hair seemed to have greyed more. His eyes were resigned.

"Bonjour," Chef Straight said.

"Ah," Chef Pic said, his face coming back to life. "I have been looking forward to this. It is the last thing I will ever look forward to."

"I hope this will suffice. The kitchen is meager as you know, but I have tried to do my best. I had sous-chef Randy helping me."

Pic laughed. "I have worked with worse." His face turned grave. "I want you to know, my friend, you will not be judged by me tonight. I cannot bear to judge a man when I myself am meeting my final judgment. I am French. We are all Catholics in the end."

Chef Straight nodded. "Perhaps we can think of better things for a few moments more." He presented the first dish.

Chef Pic's eyes widened in disbelief. He stared at the plate. When he looked up, his eyes were shiny. "*Belons.*"

"*Bien sur,*" Chef Straight answered. "I thought hard about what to serve you. What I finally decided it was only appropriate to take you back to where you began before you—"

"Go where I am going," Pic answered. "*En effet.*" He took the prison napkin and unfolded it, placing it on his lap.

Chef Pic started with the lemon version, squirting just a drop on each one. "You know, I have not had these in so long. And truth be told, for most of my life I wasn't a fan. But now,

I wish I could live to be a hundred and eat nothing but." He finished the second one.

Chef Pic then scooped up the mignonette versions and ate them one after the next.

"I apologize for the texture. Chef Randy didn't know what a shallot was."

Pic laughed. "This does not surprise me. But it is still excellent. So simple, just like this. Unadorned." His eyes rested on the third pair. "But now these. I am curious."

Chef Pic picked one up with delicate fingers and inhaled. "Ah-ha!" He slurped one oyster and let it linger on his tongue before swallowing. "Wasabi salt?"

"Correct," Chef Straight nodded.

"This, again. Simple. Yet unexpected. East meets West. The grassy notes of the wasabi mix with the oyster liquor." Chef Pic bowed. "Bravo, Chef Straight."

Back in the kitchen, Randy busied himself by washing the processor, mixing bowl and containers. If he proved himself now, perhaps when he got out, Chef Straight would remember. He mused on this for a moment. And then he saw the oyster knife.

Chef Straight came back in to the kitchen. "Randy, chef Pic sends his compliments."

Randy spun around. "Wow, I don't even. It's an honor. Sir. Chef. Sir."

"Now on to the next course. Can you plate the rice for me? Here's some dried parsley. Sprinkle it on top. It'll be perfect by the time I present it.

Randy scooped out a small mount of rice and added the parsley, while Straight added the fish and monkfish à l'Armoricaine to the plate.

"Perfect," Straight said. "I have to say, you work well under pressure. I'm impressed."

"Thank you," Randy said. "Really."

Straight picked up the plate. Noticing a stray dot of sauce, he wiped it with a towel. He walked through the corridor and into the room where Pic was leaning forward in his chair, excited to see the next dish.

"Such heavenly smells. Can it really be?"

"*Lotte à l'Armoricaine.*" He placed the dish in front of Pic who placed his nose an inch away. He inhaled. When he opened his eyes, they were moist. "I am ten years old again."

Chef Straight smiled. The plan had worked so far.

Chef Pic took his fork and broke into the monkfish. He mixed the sauce with the rice and savored each bite.

"*L'impossible,*" he said. "Persian Saffron?" His eyes met Straight. Who did *you* kill to get this?"

They both laughed. But Pic's laughter stopped when he noticed the time. He began to eat with more determination. He held his knife and fork in true continental style, flipping the fork so it was upside down.

"Do you know what is the biggest tragedy of this perfect meal?"

"No wine?"

"Well yes, of course. But besides that. The tragedy is not having you to eat with me."

Chef Straight was taken aback. Pic waved him away with his fork. "Oh, I know my reputation precedes me. But I was only like that to people who deserved it. These little shit actors and these so-called Hollywood moguls. They are slugs, all of them. But you," he said, still chewing. "You are an artiste."

"That means a lot."

Chef Pic looked up at the clock, his eyes far away. "My time ends tonight. But to know that you stepped into Chez Pic and not only kept my name alive, but kept the passion—" He broke off, his eyes welling with tears. Chef Straight walked over to put his arm around him. "I wish this were a different evening."

Chef Pic pulled himself together and patted Straight's arm. "Thankfully, there is a dessert course, no? At least we will have a sweet ending."

Chef Straight returned to the kitchen. The *clafoutis* was now cool enough to handle. He flipped the pan and placed it on a large plate. He picked up a shaker full of powdered sugar and handed it to Randy.

"Randy, this is the final dish of the night. I would like you to do the honors. Can you dust the top of that with powdered sugar?"

"Oh yes, Chef. I would be honored, indeed."

Straight heard an edge in Randy's voice. Nevertheless, Randy did as he was told and did it well. Not too much sugar, but just enough to put the finishing touches on a mouth-watering dessert.

"Just beautiful. Really. I mean it, Randy. You did a great job tonight."

Randy remained silent, but gave Straight a tight-lipped smile. Behind him, the guards shifted on their feet. They weren't interested in food talk. Only discipline.

Straight decided to bring out the entire *clafoutis* for slicing tableside. It was dense, and the smell of cherry was intoxicating. He only had to enter the room before Pic erupted into applause.

"There is part of me that knows that cake will be so perfect I don't even have to taste it. But the other part—*le professionnel*—simply must."

"I understand completely," Chef Straight said. "What's more, I would be upset if you didn't, for there is a subtle surprise in store for you." He carved a generous slice with a plastic knife and placed it before him.

As before, Chef Pic learned in and inhaled. "Cherry essence

is pronounced. The cake texture correct." Chef Pic took his fork to the cake and took a bite, with slow deliberate chews.

"But what is this? It is not *Kirschwasser*."

"You are right," Chef Straight said. "This is a cherry brandy from the Pacific Northwest."

"But how can this be? It is brighter somehow. It tastes more of cherry," Chef Pic said.

"I know. And I came to the conclusion that this cherry brandy is better than the ones that come from France and Germany. And I wanted to see what your opinion was, too."

Chef Pic kept eating the cake, chewing with a thoughtful look.

"So? What did you think? Of the entire meal? Please tell me. Don't hold back. I must know." Chef Straight said.

Pic started to answer but his voice was cut short by the sound of gunfire. His eyes turned to pin points. Then the light went out of them. Chef Straight watched as the bullet entered Chef Pic, who fell face down into the *clafoutis*, his blood mixing with the dark black crusts of the baked cherries on his plate.

Chef Straight turned around to see Randy holding a gun in one hand and the oyster knife in the other. The knife he held in front of Corrections Officer Jones' throat. The knife was bloody.

"Food time's over, guys. Sorry but I have to run. Lord forgive me for what I have done and what I am about to do."

Chef Straight held his hands up. "Randy, please don't."

"Oh, I won't," he said, his voice gentle. "Not to you. You were nice to me." He held the oyster knife tighter. "But this guy? I'm going to do to him what I did to his friends."

Before Straight could react. Randy took the oyster knife and slit Corrections Officer Jones' throat. He lay gagging on the floor. It must have been a full five minutes before he died.

"Chef, I need you to do something."

"What's that?"

"I need you to give me your chef's jacket and your chef's pants. I wish you had a hat. Why don't you have a fucking chef's hat?"

"Randy, real chefs almost never wear those."

"Well give me your fucking chef's shirt. And those fucking checkered pants, too."

Straight disrobed as fast as he could, throwing the clothes on the ground. Randy disrobed as well, keeping the gun on Straight.

"Now you are going to shut the fuck up and sit here. I am going to lock you in. Believe me when I tell you it is for your own safety. There's about to be a riot. I am not lying to you," Randy said. "I am trying to be a better Christian. I am still working on it and I have a long way to go."

Straight was at a loss for words. He felt cold. Randy fished in his new pockets and found Straight's wallet. He opened it and took out all the cash: five hundred dollars. Straight had meant to go to the farmer's market that night.

Randy threw him the wallet as well as his prisoner's chef jacket. "Wear that. I'm not taking your cards because they'd find me immediately. Sorry about the money. But look, someone will find you. Show them your ID. They'll know who you are, don't worry."

"Randy."

"You don't understand, man. This place does things to you." An alarm sounded. Randy headed to the door, yanking it open. He turned back at the last minute. "I also add Mexican crema to the jalapeño mac n cheese. I'm telling you. It'll change your life."

With that, he closed the door and locked it.

Straight stood next to the two bodies. Pic's face lay on his plate. The rest of the *clafoutis* was unscathed. He missed the other two dishes. Straight had tasted the sauces in the kitchen for quality control, but that wasn't the same as sampling the dish. Such a shame.

He could hear shots being fired and screams outside. There were dozens of footsteps running down the hallway. The noise was deafening. He couldn't tell where it was coming from. Or going to.

Straight snagged a chunk of cake and ate it. Just as he expected, it was as good as he thought. The cherry brandy really brought the whole dessert together. He looked at Pic's dead body and chewed.

The worst part to Straight was that he would never know what Pic thought of the overall three-course menu. The separate components he seemed to approve of, but what of the whole meal?

Straight longed to hear his thoughts. Was he taken back to his childhood days? Was he filled with nostalgia? And when the emotion wore off, how did Chef Straight, stack up from an objective culinary standpoint? And what wines would Pic have served? Straight thought perhaps a champagne for the *belons*, and a heavy Chardonnay for the monkfish. A port with the dessert almost seemed too obvious. Perhaps Pic would have chosen something else?

None of these questions would be answered now. Straight sighed, and took another chunk of *clafoutis*. He bit into the cherries, the juice spilled down his chin. At that very moment, a group of prison guards burst through the door. Straight turned around, with blood red cherry juice dribbling down his face, hands in the air and screamed: "Don't shoot! I'm a chef."

The following week was a blur. The governor called to personally apologize for the ordeal he put Straight through. "We know how much you mean to Los Angeles, and really to this state," he said. "We're sorry for the unfortunate events."

The Governor had promised to dine at Chez Pic at a later date. As if that would make everything all right.

That same day, the Governor held a conference where he stated any plans to accelerate the death penalty would not be halted. In fact, it was imperative, he said, to stay the course. As a result, his approval rating soared.

Chef Straight would not have been surprised if Randy had turned up at the restaurant, looking for a job. And he half-considered harboring and employing a fugitive if that moment occurred because it wasn't every day you found an employee worth their salt. Sure he killed people, but he could take orders. That counted for something.

As it turned out, Randy had other plans. Two weeks after the ordeal, the news reported Randy had crossed the border into Mexico and was shot and killed just outside of Tijuana. The news story was a little hazy on the details, or how he got shot, but Chef Straight was certain it wasn't over Mexican mac and cheese.

A few weeks later, Chef Straight introduced his kitchen staff to a new menu, which included *belons,* the monkfish and the *clafoutis.* The staff thought they were his best additions ever. They always said that, though. That was the problem. It was so hard to find good honest criticism any more.

CHAPTER 6
Superfreaky Memories

The room was packed with account executives, strategic planners, producers, interns, digital strategists, public relations execs, media buyers, UX designers, and clients. The art directors, copywriters and creative directors were not in attendance. They were watching a lecture with a celebrity who'd recently starred in an action film that bombed and had nothing whatsoever to do with advertising. Either way, there were plenty of rubes in the room. I wasn't worried. My presentation would go viral soon enough. I treated the Cannes Festival of Creativity as the necessary evil that it was.

I touched my computer. A slide appeared on the screen behind me. It showed a cheesy stock photo of a businessman with a toothy grin, throwing money into the air.

"What I'm about to say is controversial. Are you ready?" Not one person answered. "Here goes: Digital and social are bullshit. You are wasting hundreds of millions every year. And if you stop lying to yourself and put your bullshit metrics down—if you do something rare in this industry and are one hundred percent honest—you'll know that needle hasn't moved at all. Not one inch or mile or kilometer for you metric types."

I clicked to the next slide. It showed an infographic from a study commissioned by an advertising trade association. Over the past five years, the amount of money ad agencies spent on digital and social media increased twenty-five percent on a year-over-year basis. And yet the actual return on investment (calculated in terms of response, click-through, and actual sales conversion) was a flat line.

I paused a moment, letting the words sink in. I gave them the shot. Now it was time for chaser. "Clients: you are wasting money. Ad agencies: you are hoping no one notices because you never got over the first dot com bubble burst and you desperately want that kind of money again. And you're jealous of media because they're making money hand over fist by selling a pipe dream."

I clicked through the slides depicting banner ads, a featured storiy, on a social media site and mobile advertising, too. "Programmatic advertising? Bullshit. Multi-paneled carousel units? Bullshit. Mobile units? Bull. Shit. Am I clear?"

Two people got up and made their way to the exit.

"You fell for your own lies. And you've been walking around with your eyes closed, hoping no one would notice." I clicked to a slide that showed someone behind the wheel of a car, eyes closed.

"You are asleep at the wheel. But luckily, while you were sleeping, I figured out a way to not only save the industry, but earn potentially untold billions, with minimal effort."

I clicked to another slide. It was black. There was one word written on it in a unique typeface, created by a Brazilian designer. It cost me fifty thousand dollars and it was worth every last cent. The word in question was Dreamverts™.

"Since advertising began, we've tried to get the consumer's attention where they spend the most time. All we've done is condition them to ignore us."

I clicked to the next slide, showcasing three social posts that went viral. After a beat each one of them disappeared. "Even the few social media successes haven't translated to anything beyond a momentary increase in chatter, or a temporary increase in traffic to the website. Objectively speaking, this has not translated into increased sales. People are spending time with the brands. What they aren't doing is spending money."

I looked around the room. All eyes were on me. Good. It doesn't matter if they have questions. I could have cared less if they were skeptical. I was going to sell them the same way I sold a global campaign for that swimwear brand that turned it from a laughing stock in America into a juggernaut. With the same patience, humor, bravado and showmanship. They were going to buy what I was selling. They had no choice in the matter.

Todd sat in Doctor Emily's office, lanky legs crossed, hands folded, composed. The doctor always chatted with her patients after their exams, making them feel welcome. It was one of the reasons The Sunrise Retirement Community won top honors year after year. Personal attention. Loving care. And of course, the best medical staff around.

As its name implied, Sunrise was cheery. Guests (as they were known) were vibrant, possessed all faculties, and were wealthy. Todd was no exception, having turned a small clothing store into a worldwide chain before selling it to a larger company for close to two hundred million dollars. Sunrise was less a retirement home and more an exclusive resort for people who refused to give in to old age.

"Your tests all look good, cholesterol's low, blood pressure is great. Your weight's held steady. Your full MRI shows nothing out of the ordinary." Doctor Emily said. "Still taking those long walks?"

"Of course," Todd said. "Only now that it's summer, I take them at dawn rather than at midday. I can't stand the heat."

Doctor Emily nodded. "Just as well. Don't want to worry about skin cancer. If there's nothing else, I guess we'll see you in a year." Todd help up a hand when she stood.

"There is one thing," he began.

"Oh?"

"Doctor Emily. I'm not one for flights of fancy. Nor am I a hypochondriac. I'm smart enough to know you can't believe what you read online, especially when it comes to medical websites. I've always said the CDC should be more involved in regulating them. They prey on the vulnerable and uninformed alike."

"Very true," Doctor Emily said. "So what is eating you?"

"This is going to sound strange. But for the past two months I've been obsessed with two words. I'm fixating on them. Day and night. Is that a sign of anything bad?"

"Which words?"

He paused. "Oak pussy."

Doctor Emily stifled a laugh.

"I don't know if those words are supposed to go together or if they are unrelated. But the words 'oak,' and 'pussy,' are always in my head."

Doctor Emily made a show of thinking hard. "Todd, everything checked out, including your brain. And I've never known a fixation of words to be a sign of anything except perhaps obsessive-compulsive disorder, which you certainly do not have. You could be tired, or stressed, but it could just as easily be nothing."

"Nothing?"

She nodded. "In the same way that getting a song stuck in your head is essentially nothing. Annoying, perhaps, but insignificant."

"I do hope you are right. I think you are. But I have to say it is annoying."

Doctor Emily showed him to her door. "I can refer you to a therapist if it keeps up."

"I'm not that far gone," he joked.

I'd earned a reputation over the years of being a great creative director. Sure as hell had the boatload of awards to prove it. But ever since I started my own shop two years ago, people talked shit about me. What has he done since he went out on his own? Does he even have clients? It's like they wanted me to fail. They had no idea how wrong they were.

A hand rose from the audience. I recognized the woman. She was an account director. I'm sure we'd worked together at one of the dozen agencies I'd been to before I started my own shop.

"Dreamverts™? Is that some kind of VR experience?"

"All in good time." I was going to savor this moment. Why rush the mind fuck? "First I need to explain how I ended up here."

The next slide featured the name of my agency. "I started Sidewinder two years ago with the humble idea of changing the ad industry as we know it. Throwing out all the traditional stuff, really giving it a rethink, starting with the people. I brought in folks who had all kinds of different backgrounds to be part of a think tank. They weren't tasked with solving client problems, but the ad industries' problems."

I clicked through some slides showing various charts and graphs. "I've already covered a lot of this. But it's worth noting a lot of clients have gotten wise. A major cereal company just yanked a hundred million dollar ad spend from digital, because they came to the same realization I did. That digital ad spends are bullshit."

"You keep saying that," someone in the audience said.

"And I'll keep saying it, too. Everyone seems to love the word 'disruption,' don't they? Well I'm going to give you disruption that will make your brains melt." I heard my own voice rising to zealot level. I coughed to clear it away.

"The idea of Dreamverts™ came to me about three years ago. It took this long to get it right."

The next slide showed a beautiful woman in bed, eyes closed, looking peaceful. "I kept thinking that spending money on digital and social was so pointless it was like trying to advertise to someone in their sleep. Then it hit me. Why not do it?"

"Do what?" someone asked. I looked for source of the voice. It came from a producer I worked with when I lived in Toronto.

"Advertise to people while they slept. In-dream advertising."

The room erupted in laughter.

"So funny," I said. "Almost as funny as convincing your clients to spend an extra two hundred grand to film behind-the-scenes of your spot for salad dressing. Not sure about you but I've never seen BTS with more than five thousand hits on YouTube unless you paid for the views. But I digress."

The next slide featured two different gifs that looped an animation of brain activity. "The brain on the right depicts normal activity of someone browsing online. The brain on the left is when people are asleep. Note the most frenzied activity is when they are online, like Twitter or Amazon or CNN or Facebook or whatever. It's complete overstimulation. Who can pay attention to anything in that mental state? By contrast, the brain on the left is calmer. Not completely still, far from it. It's just a different kind of frenetic energy."

I clicked to the next slide. This one had a different gif. A cartoon sponge absorbing a lake-sized amount of water, over and over again.

"When they are browsing online, they suffer from information overload. It doesn't matter how clever, simple, or creative you make your ads. Banner ads, social posts, featured stories—they all might as well be white noise. But when people are asleep—particularly when dreaming—their brains are very receptive to information. The question I dared to ask was, what if we could figure out a way to reach the consumer when they were the most receptive to our messaging at a time where there is little to no competition for their attention? How much more exponentially effective would our ads be?"

Todd left the doctor's office and headed home. At the last moment, he changed his mind, left the Sunrise grounds, and caught a bus towards town. He didn't have a particular need to go there. It just seemed like a good idea. He had no reason to stay home. It was two in the afternoon. The sun was shining. It was a gorgeous day.

He could stop at Wentworth's bookstore, chat with the owner, pet Trixie the trusted bookstore's mouser and buy a new paperback. Or take in a movie if anything was worth seeing. His next-door neighbor Carla had mentioned something about a French restaurant that had just opened. He could have an early dinner. If it was good, then perhaps he and Carla could make it a date, albeit a platonic one. Neither had interest in the other beyond friendship. He hadn't had interest in anyone in a while.

Oak. Pussy. Dammit all, he thought. What do those words mean? Why do they appear? Why him? He'd never been much of a drinker, never took drugs at all. Hadn't had a stressful day since he sold the company. His brain wasn't on the fritz. What was this strange development and why now?

He thought back. Two months ago. It was a Wednesday. Did something different happen then? No. It was a day like any other. He was sure of it. He got up, had his breakfast, took his morning walk. Answered some correspondence. Checked in with his stockbroker. Had lunch. Thought about napping but didn't. Listened to music. Had dinner. Emailed his daughter.

Watched the news. Met up with friends at the Sunrise bar, and then made it an early night. In short, it was a regular day. If anything, Todd felt he'd been in a bit of a rut the past year or so. It all felt too familiar.

Then the words came while he was in the shower. He grabbed the soap, lathered up and thought Oak Pussy. Except it wasn't really a thought, was it? No. Just words. Oak Pussy. Or Oak and Pussy. Or Oak. Pussy. His mind churned. Oak was easy enough. But was Pussy a cat or a vulgar slang? If so, did that make Oak a phallic symbol too, or just wood? It was confounding.

Doctor Emily mentioned the phenomenon of songs that stay with you. Earworms. In this case the words stayed with him, but with no melody to accompany them. No meaning that he could see. But disturbing in their persistence somehow, like an ominous sign he couldn't read.

Todd stared out the window, still lost in thought. No school buses in summer, still too early for rush hour. Traffic was light. What was the name of that French restaurant? Chagall? Chantal? Something like that. The thought of food made his mouth water. For the past year he'd watched his weight with the discipline of a prizefighter. With the good news from Doctor Emily, it was time to indulge for a change.

He glanced out the window once again, realizing too late, he'd missed his stop. He stood in a panic, touched the bell to alert the driver and walked to the front of the bus. The next stop was four or five blocks away. It wasn't the hassle of walking back that irked him. It was more that his wandering mind had been the cause of it.

Todd reached out a hand to grab a railing as he made his way to the front of the bus. He was surprised how crowded it was. Every seat was taken except three. Nurses, construction workers, college students, businessmen, and the occasional tramp—everyone was represented.

If only he could drown out the two words that haunted him like nonsensical ghosts. Think about the bookstore, or Trixie the cat, or the restaurant. He wondered what kind of French restaurant it was. Something regional, or old standards? Either was okay with him provided the name wasn't Oak Pussy.

"I see I have your attention now. Good." I changed the slide again. On this one was a photo of a geek wearing a VR headset arms outstretched. He looked like a zombie.

"Many of you think VR has vast potential. Like five years from now, a budget for a VR experience will be as everyday as print. Perhaps some of you have already produced some concepts involving VR. I wouldn't know since I don't watch case study videos, which is the only way most people would even hear about it. Regardless, I'm here to tell you that what's up here in our head is truly untapped territory. At least, it was until now."

I changed the slide once again. Now I would grab their attention with a two-minute animated film that went into just enough detail to make them understand without giving away anything that would threaten my patents. I talked over the film to give a brief explanation of how it worked.

It opens on a woman getting ready for bed. She closes her eyes. An old-fashioned alarm clock with two hands starts spinning. The film then goes inside her head, revealing a smaller version of herself. She sets up an old projector. On the screen is a Dreamverts™ logo followed by a message that reads: Your Brand Here.

When the film stopped I said, "Obviously, this is an oversimplification, but you can get the gist of it."

A voice interrupted. I couldn't see where it came from. "Are you really proposing to advertise to someone against their will?"

"You mean beyond what we already do?"

When the laughter died down, the voice continued. "But this is different. They're asleep, for God's sake. What you are talking about is subliminal advertising."

As a kid, I'd heard about subliminal advertising. The story went that a soda brand added in a single frame of their drink during a movie. The frame would go by so fast it would be imperceptible to the viewer. But their brains would recognize it all the same, propelling them from their seat to the concession stand. I was kind of sad when I learned it was an urban legend.

"There's a difference between subliminal and subconscious. Besides, you're not seeing the bigger picture here."

A client spoke up. I recognized her as the CMO of a financial planning brand I pitched once. I didn't win the account. "What I'm seeing is probably unethical and farfetched at best."

"Sounds like you're the one spewing the bullshit," another person said.

"Instead of rolling my eyes, I'll prove it to you. Would you like that?" I stepped away from the podium and walked into the audience. I looked around the room until I spotted the first victim, a junior account executive.

I pointed. "You had a dream last night, right?"

"I don't know. Maybe." Her face turned crimson. "Yes, okay? I had a dream last night."

"Tell us about it." I smiled in encouragement.

"It was unusual because it was, well, kind of erotic. I dreamed I was having sex with my boyfriend in a Spanish villa."

"*Muy caliente*," I said. "Go on. Without the graphic details, of course."

"I remember after we were done. I went into the kitchen. I asked him if he was hungry. And I opened the refrigerator."

"You opened the refrigerator," I prompted. "And?"

"And I saw a jar of Jif peanut butter. It was so striking I wrote it down in my dream journal this morning." The expression on her face went from realization to horror, before ending on unbridled anger. "You bastard. You violated me. You fucking bastard." She tried to charge me, but was stopped by an art buyer friend of mine I hadn't noticed earlier.

"Show of hands. Anyone else have a vivid dream involving Jif?" Sixteen hands went up. "Congratulations! You experienced Dreamverts™."

Todd reached the front of the bus just as it slowed. He glanced at one of the passengers. What he saw made him stop in his tracks. A man in his late thirties clutched a messenger bag. He wore a newsboy cap and brown t-shirt. Two words were written on the shirt in white blocky letters.

"Oak Pussy," Todd shouted. The man looked up, startled. He got up and ran off the bus. Todd chased after him.

"Wait!"

The man headed north at a brisk pace. He kept glancing over his shoulder. Todd followed after. Five blocks later, he watched the man enter Wentworth's bookstore.

Todd waited, letting his breathing go back to normal. He pushed open the door and went inside. Trixie was in her usual spot in the window, fast asleep. Mr. Wentworth stood behind the counter, flipping through a magazine. He looked up when he heard the bell on the door ring.

"Nice to see you, Todd. Been a few months."

"Indeed it has," Todd said. "Time for some new books."

"Or old ones, eh?"

Todd looked around the store. The man in the brown t-shirt was nowhere to be seen. He walked through each aisle, picking up books and putting them back without even looking at their covers.

"Help you find something?"

"You see a man with a brown t-shirt come in here?"

"When?"

"Few minutes before me."

Mr. Wentworth took his time answering. His voice was cautious. "What do you want with him?"

"To talk to him. That's all."

"About anything in particular?"

Todd pointed to his chest. "He had the words 'oak pussy' written on his shirt."

Mr. Wentworth's face was blank. "Those words mean something to you?"

Todd told him what little there was to tell.

"So I just figured that if he had it on a shirt, he'd know what it was. Is it a fashion brand? Or is it a band name? A movie?"

Mr. Wentworth switched the "Yes, We're Open," sign so it read "Sorry, We're Closed." He then locked the front door.

"Figured there had to be more. Come on."

Mr. Wentworth led him to a door at the back of the store. He'd assumed it was an office or storage room. When Todd pushed open the door, he was surprised to see the room was not only larger than the bookstore itself, but filled with a few hundred people.

Waves of anger threatened to turn the audience into a mob. I went back to the podium for safety as much as to regain control. "Calm down, everyone. I'll explain." Their anger subsided. I took a deep breath, exhaled, and plunged in.

"Sixteen of you dreamt about Jif because you kept your mobile phones on your bed stand at night. Proximity is key. As long as your phones are within six feet of your bed at night,

Dreamverts™ will work. The majority of the population sleeps next to their phones. Young, old, black white, doesn't matter. All demographics are represented. By the way, this is true on a global scale."

A client I used to work with when he was on a different brand raised his hand. "What do dreams have to do with our phones?"

"Sorry, that's a trade secret."

The junior account executive sat with her arms crossed. "The number doesn't seen very high. Sixteen."

"I'm sure there were more. But for this particular focus group I only chose twenty-five of you. That's a 64% response and retention rate for product placement. How many of your digital ads ever received that kind of response?" I held up my hands. "Don't bother answering."

The same client raised his hand again. "Can you guarantee those numbers??"

"With almost near certainty," I said. "The average person sleeps seven hours a night and has anywhere from four to six dreams per night, maybe more. The odds are always in our favor."

I clicked onto the slide showing a booze bottle and a marijuana leaf. "Our studies show the difference in retention of people who were drunk or in any other way impaired was negligible." The next slide showed a pill with an RX on it. "Same with sleeping pills, anti-depressants. In other words, Dreamverts™ doesn't just cut through clutter. Dreamverts™ negates clutter entirely."

The client raised his hand again. I ignored him.

"I need to stress that our research didn't only come from those of you who were, shall we say, organic participants in this focus group last night. Far from it. We've conducted multiple studies over the past year and three months. We've done our homework. We've got the numbers. And I stand by those numbers."

An executive creative director cleared his throat. I'd only seen him at award shows. I avoided him like the plague. He was the type who would bully people into drinking shots with him. By the end of the night he was so loaded he couldn't stand. He was known behind his back as Peter Pan.

"This sounds like a great shortcut. But at what price?"

"Morally?"

"Financially." he smirked.

"We can talk one-on-one if you are serious. There are a lot of variables, but for argument's sake, I can tell you the starting price is equal to if not more than what you'd pay to produce and run a thirty-second Super Bowl spot. But while the Super Bowl can reach hundreds of millions, it's a grapeshot approach. This can target everyone in your demographic by country, city, neighborhood, even by a street. This technology doesn't come cheap, but it's a small investment considering we can beat your KPI's without even trying."

It was time to end the presentation. I smiled and turned to the last slide in the deck that once again featured the Sidewinder logo.

"I realize this is a lot to process. But I'm open all tomorrow. Come seek me out, ask questions and try to poke holes in it. You won't be able to. but by all means, try. Thanks for listening."

I went back to my hotel room. Cannes was hot as shit as usual. I could have mingled with people I'd worked with in the past, drinking rosé at scandalous prices. Instead, I sat on my room's balcony, sipping Amaro Nonino with ice, and waited for the texts and emails to come. It didn't take long. First, a client texted asking if they could set up a one-on-one meeting at my earliest convenience. Then the CCO of an agency that had lost its luster at the turn of the century wanted to have breakfast. Another client sent a smarmy email suggesting lunch. And a Scandinavian art director sent a flirty DM to my Twitter account wanting to meet for drinks in my room. I answered her first.

Twenty minutes before the Scandinavian art director arrived, I received a frantic text from Jake, the head of Sidewinder's IT department:

Know you are in Cannes but this is really important. Have an issue. When can you talk?

I frowned at the message, and then picked up the phone.

"Hi, room service? A bottle of rosé please. Dry, not too fruity. I'd also like the escargot, the squab and John Dory, and for dessert, let's go with the *assiette à fromage*. Oh, and a bottle of Pastis. Perfect. *Merci.*

I undressed, hopped in the shower and got ready for my date. I was used to Jake's panic attacks. They happened with regularity. He could wait.

He lost count around the two hundred mark. There were three times as many. Men, women, young, old, all sitting in rows. Almost all wore the same brown t-shirts.

"Todd is a long time customer," Mister Wentworth said, by way of introduction. "He came in here not five minutes ago wondering what Oak Pussy meant."

"Hello Todd," the group said in unison.

Instead of responding, he turned to Mr. Wentworth. "Do you know what's going on?"

Mr. Wentworth gestured to a chair. "Please."

Todd sat, eyes wary. Mr. Wentworth moved to the front of the audience.

"I will recount everything for Todd's benefit as much as ours. Starting approximately two months ago, possibly as much as three, all of us came to the realization that the words Oak

Pussy held a large but inexplicable significance in our lives. As many of you are frequenters of my store, we naturally met up. Slowly the word got round, and the rest of you appeared and now here we are, trying to understand this phenomenon."

Silence. The room was cool. Todd stared at the collection of people. None of them shared any common trait. It was, he noted, a perfect portrait of diversity. He saw representatives of every race. Men. Women. He wasn't sure, but he thought there were a few transgender as well. The religious were represented, too. Sikhs, a rabbi, and imam, and two nuns. No doubt many members of other religions as well as atheists were gathered. Not to mention everyone on the color spectrum.

Mr. Wentworth smiled. "Todd, I don't know how I became the organizer of this group. But I've had this large back room for quite a while. I used to keep my collection of rare antique books here, but that still left more than half the room unoccupied. Once I sold off my collection, I planned on leasing it out to another business. Before I could though, this thing started happening. The room's where we have our weekly meetings."

Todd looked around the room. "What do you meet about, exactly?"

"We meet to try and figure out why we are all so fixated on these words. What does it all mean?"

"I still think it's something perverted," a man with a heavy accent I couldn't place said. "Pussy. Disgusting."

A woman in a grey shapeless dress shook her head. "But it must mean more than this. It's not like this is a sex cult."

"If it was, I'd have gotten some by now," an old lady said.

When the laughter subsided, the rabbi said: "Be that as it may, the significance must mean something. I have searched the Torah, the Talmud and even the Zohar and have come up blank as it were."

The nuns and imam voiced their agreement.

A young man with a pierced cheek, wearing a t-shirt with Darwin's face on it nodded as well. "From a pure scientific and atheist standpoint at least, none of it makes sense. I keep thinking we're under some sort of collective hypnosis. The collective cognitive imperative, if you would."

A girl, in her late teens laughed. "You make it sound like the ghost of Jim Jones is pulling our strings. You seem to forget there is no leader here. If we've all jumped on some bandwagon, it has no driver."

The two argued back and forth. Mr. Wentworth clapped his hands. "Please, this is getting us nowhere. Last week we agreed to come up with suggestions as to what Oak and Pussy might mean. Now then, has anyone had any success?"

The room fell silent. Mr. Wentworth looked at Todd. "How about you? Anything you can contribute?"

Todd looked around the room. "Unfortunately, no. Except, I went to my doctor today for a check up and mentioned it."

"Yes?" Mister Wentworth said. "And?"

"And nothing. She said it was one of those things. Mind playing tricks on you. Like when a song gets stuck in your head. Nothing to worry about."

"Your doctor is an idiot," the man in the Darwin t-shirt said.

"Now, now," Mister Wentworth cautioned. "Todd, how did you come to uh—"?

"All I know is two months ago I was in the shower and the words came to me."

"Me too," the woman in the shapeless grey dress said. "I told you it was connected to water." She smiled at Todd. "Are you an Aquarius like me?"

Others did not share the same experience, however. The words came to some while driving, or eating breakfast, or sitting in a meeting, or drinking coffee or reading a newspaper.

One person even admitted the words appeared while they were having sex with their partner.

"This is getting us nowhere," the rabbi said. "And yet the words are there as strong as ever."

A chubby man in a short-sleeved dress shirt stood up. He held a piece of paper in his hands. "Look, we're all bringing our own cognitive bias to this. And maybe that's helpful because each point of view is like looking through a lens. And if the lens is blurry, we look though another lens."

The imam asked: "And what is your lens?"

"I work for the state parks and recreation department. I started thinking. Let's assume for a moment that the words have to do with nature." He held up the paper for the room to see. It showed a satellite map. "Now this is a map of the largest park in the state about an hour from here."

"Go on," Mr. Wentworth said.

The man pointed to a demarcation line. "Well, it just so happens that there is a large pussy willow arbor here. It's kind of a landmark along this hiking trail. Some couples even get married there." He looked at the photo and then looked around the room. "This arbor is in a clearing. But surrounding it is an oak forest. Might be a long shot, but maybe this spot has something to do with it?"

I woke up early next morning and telephoned room service for *deux café completes*. The Scandinavian art director and I had enough time for one more romp before the breakfast arrived. Good day so far. I chugged my coffee, squeezed her ass as she went out the door, jumped in the shower and went downstairs for the first of many breakfasts, lunches, drinks and dinners with prospective clients. Word had gotten around fast. My phone was blowing up.

"Hey it's Jake, we really need to talk. I know you're in Cannes but shit is hitting the fan here and it's not going to—"

"You know I don't go in for that technical shit. Whatever it is, I'm sure you'll fix it. I trust you."

"This is important," he protested.

"So is this," I yelled. "I've got at least eight potential client meetings today. Possibly more. I'll be coming home fifteen pounds heavier from all the food and drink. But if I even sell this to like two people, we are set for life, do you understand? I just walked in the elevator, so I might lose you."

His voice was desperate. "Listen to me. We have a huge problem on our hands. Like, Hindenburg huge."

"What? How?"

No answer. The elevator opened. I hurried out to call him back. Before I could hit redial, I was stopped by one of the clients who attended my presentation.

"There you are. Ready for breakfast? You must tell me more about this. I trust you have not only metrics but hard costs?"

I put my phone in my pocket and smiled. "Of course."

Over my second breakfast that morning, I laid out specifics in a granular way that was different from my general presentation. More detailed, and with more numbers.

The client whistled. "You know, that's a lot of money."

"You saw it work with your very own eyes. I didn't know any of those people."

"Oh, I know," the client said. "It worked on me as well. And we'd never met before." He shook his head. "It's just really a lot of money."

I flagged a waiter for the check. "You're the head of yet another company who recently pulled fifty million of your digital spend. I understand you feel a bit jaded by the people who sold you a bill of goods. But I'm telling you this is real innovation that brings real results. For half your digital ad spend, I can guarantee at least a sixty percent response rate and increase in sales. Within six weeks."

I signed the bill, letting him see my black American Express card in the process. Sure, it was a cheap trick. But people fall for cheap tricks in Cannes. Besides, stupid things always impress people.

"Think it over. Sorry to rush. I have seven more meetings today."

He stopped me. "I am on board. Believe me. I just need to meet with our leadership team and head of finance. They're going to want to unpack this first. Really understand the process. Is there a PDF of the presentation you could send me?"

I shook my head. "Not even if it were password protected and your entire company including the cleaning crew signed an NDA. There are people within my own company who haven't seen this project."

"I can respect that. You just need to understand, even though I'm CMO I don't pull the purse strings regardless of what people say."

"Tell you what. Let's meet up in the next couple of weeks when we're stateside. Bring the people you need to convince to L.A., or I'll come there and do a closed-door presentation. But only to the real decision makers."

"I appreciate it."

"I'm in no rush. Business is booming."

That last part was a stretch. But he needed to believe that I didn't need him. He needed me.

We shook hands, and I went to the bathroom to take a shit. I'd stick with coffee until dinner.

Mr. Wentworth decided they should break off into small groups to get to know each other and discuss further before calling it a day. Todd sat with the imam, rabbi and three other people whose names he forgot as soon as he was introduced to them. They spent the rest of the afternoon on into early evening getting nowhere before giving up.

"Okay," Mr. Wentworth said. "Are we at least all in agreement that we should go to the pussy willow arbor?"

The group murmured in approval.

"I think Friday would be best. Try to get off work. If you can't, we'll just have to report our findings at the next meeting," Mr. Wentworth said. "Make your own travel arrangements." Todd agreed to carpool with his group. One of the women had an SUV that sat seven, more than enough room.

Bringing the room to order once more, Mr. Wentworth said, "I almost forgot. For any newcomers, please grab a t-shirt on your way out." He pointed to three large cardboard boxes lined up by the exit. "We've only got smalls and mediums left. But I'd encourage you to wear it in public. We might find some more people before Friday."

As they were leaving the building, the rabbi grabbed Todd by the arm. "Excuse me if I'm being forward but I couldn't help but notice you didn't say much."

"I guess I was taking it all in. It's a lot to process."

The rabbi laughed. "There's a Yiddish saying *Klieg, Klieg, Klieg-Du bist a Nar*. It means 'You are smart, smart, smart—but you are not so smart.' Some of those theories I heard today were far from smart. I can say this for certain. Perhaps you were wisest of all for staying silent."

"Not so sure about that," Todd said. "More like I just didn't have anything to contribute."

"But these words must have meant something to you, otherwise you wouldn't have sought out their meaning."

They both stopped at the bus shelter. "You know, my life was going along fine until this incident. Sometimes I wish it wasn't routine, But it wasn't terrible. Then all of a sudden these two words that might have no connection to each other got me thinking about mortality and worried about my sanity. Meeting everyone else today has given me a sense of peace."

The rabbi nodded. "That you aren't alone. Connected to humanity, yes?"

"Exactly," Todd said. "I've been living a nice life. I used to live large." He held up his thumb and index finger. "Lately it's been life with a small 'l,' if you get my meaning. But this experience has shown me that I'm still connected to a larger world."

The rabbi patted Todd on the back. "And to think you just said you had nothing to contribute."

The bus came and the rabbi bid him goodbye. Todd was halfway home before he realized he'd forgotten about the French restaurant. He was too far away from town to stop and walk back and as good as it was, he didn't feel like eating at the retirement community restaurant.

He got off at his stop, crossed the street and continued down the boulevard, looking for a suitable restaurant. He bypassed Star of Siam, a Thai restaurant he found lackluster. Same with Athena's Greek Palace. Three blocks later, a stained-glass window piqued his interest. The blackboard sign on the sidewalk indicated a new restaurant was open for business. It was an upscale tavern serving elevated traditional pub fare. While this in itself was inviting, the name of the pub made him laugh. It was called The Cat And Fiddle.

He was shown to a large green booth and was handed a thick menu. The server was wearing a plaid dress that he guessed was supposed to resemble traditional pub attire.

"If you like scotch, we carry dozens."

"Brown liquor and I are not friends," he said, and ordered shepherd's pie and an English lager.

By the time my meetings ended, it was past nine. I was at

that stage in Cannes where I needed a new liver, gastric bypass surgery and new vocal cords. I was tired of clients, tired of advertising, tired of snooty French people and the world in general. All I wanted was a bath, and a good night's rest.

There were four messages from Jake on my hotel phone, three emails, not to mention a bunch of text messages, too. I emailed him a one liner, saying I was not available to discuss but he would have my full attention on Friday when I was back at home. With that, I closed my laptop and got in the tub.

I'd ended up talking to nine people that day. If one client or one agency got on board with Dreamverts™ it would be game over for the ad industry as we knew it. Not to mention a shit ton of money for Sidewinder.

We were a small operation. Six full-time. Six freelancers. I kept it lean with as few layers as possible. The full-timers had equity and were going to make out like bandits. That pleased me to no end. All were good people and great coworkers, both traits a rarity in this industry. They deserved every dollar coming to them.

Through the open balcony, the never-ending douche bag brigade raged on the streets below. I pictured sloppy grinding to Eurotrash music, expense account assholes trying to figure out how to open champagne magnums, and lusty heads of accounts that go by some code like "It's not cheating if you're out of the country." I hated them all and couldn't wait to suck as much money out of them as possible.

I slept with that delicious thought in mind and woke up to a midmorning sun blazing through the window. I checked out of the hotel and made my way to Menton, a little town just across the way from Italy. It is a beautiful place very few in the ad world ever frequent, thank God.

A few mornings on the beach and solitary nights of eating dinner on my balcony overlooking the sea set me right. My eyes saw no static banners, billboards, or TV spots. Not even a print ad in the local newspaper. I ignored all social media and kept my phone turned off. In the two days I spent there, the only real conversation I had was with a realtor. I entertained the notion of buying property. I looked at an exquisite seven-room villa with a pool that cost just over two million Euros. I was assured the seller would accept a lower offer. Tempting though it was, in the end I decided against it. How often would I really go to Menton, anyway? I'd rather get something closer to home.

By the time I got to Nice international airport and was seated in first class, champagne in hand, I was ready to go back to work. I'd arrive in L.A. early Thursday evening, get a good night's rest and then take Friday to deal with whatever was making Jake spaz out every hour on the hour.

Like most people who work with computers, Jake could be a little awkward, a little too technical for his own good. But he knew his stuff. He and his team of freelance programmers and testers took made the back end run like a ship. But there were some days were Jake could be so uptight he'd drive everyone in the office crazy. I kept telling him to lighten up, all would be fine, but he never listened. Just as well. It was one of the reasons I trusted him so much. He was there to find the exploits and patch them, look for bugs and remove them. And above all, make Dreamverts™ the best fucking thing to happen to advertising since Bill Bernbach.

I just wish sometimes the guy would give it a rest for a bit. We'd gone into beta and would get results soon. I could understand having some measure of anxiety, but you had to draw the line somewhere.

I popped an Ambien and folded my seat down to turn it into a bed. We'd chosen a cross section of five hundred people in a small town in northern Virginia as the first beta test. All seemed well. What was all the fuss about now?

Ah well, I thought. Can't solve it from thirty-five thousand feet in the air. It would wait. Just need to keep our eye on the ball, I thought. And with that I fell into a blissful, dreamless sleep.

Once the SUV was filled, the woman drove her group to the park. It was just after eleven. With so many cars arriving at the same time, parking was difficult. They ended up having to drive on the other side of the park to a different lot.

Mr. Wentworth had emailed instructions the previous night. Wear your brown t-shirt. Print out the map to the arbor. And call him if anyone got lost.

Todd got out of the car clutching his map and feeling foolish.

"We look like cult members," the rabbi said.

"Or worse," the imam said. "Like we're on a cheap vacation tour."

Although Mr. Wentworth had said the group of people numbered close to six hundred, only a third were able to show up. Todd saw them descend upon the arbor from all corners of the park. He took his time, smelling the earth and subtle sweetness from the yellow blooms of golden Rain trees. He noticed everyone else getting caught up in the beauty of the park.

He felt someone walking close by. It was the woman who drove the carpool. "Such a beautiful day isn't it?"

Todd agreed that it was. She looked like she was in her late fifties, and well taken care of. Her pale skin was smooth. Her eyes were blue. Her hair was the color of straw.

"It's funny," she said. "I'd been keeping this SUV for ten years now. But my husband died a while back and my three kids are all grown. It's the first time in a while so many people have been in it."

"And what an excursion to make," Todd said.

Her laugh startled a pair of resting sparrows. "I don't know what to make of it, to be honest. One afternoon I was sitting on my porch watching the world go by and oak pussy showed up like an alley cat I couldn't shake. Up until then, I'd been lost in my own head. Wondering if I should sell the big house, the SUV, but never doing anything about it. Stuck in a rut."

"I know that feeling well. If it weren't for oak pussy, I'd still be going about my daily routine. Sleep walking, really."

They walked together in silence, veering from the concrete path to walk on the grass.

"It's almost like we're on a picnic," she giggled. "By the way, my name's Emma."

"I'm Todd. That's a nice name," he said.

"You think?" She wrinkled her nose. "I always thought it sounded old-fashioned. Most people call me Em."

"Well, Em, it's a pleasure to meet you. I think we share the same kind of life in a way. Only I went one step further and downsized and moved into a retirement community. I feel like I could have waited another decade to do so. Kind of silly, right?"

"You had your reasons," she said.

"I lost my wife, too. Our kids are also grown. One lives out of state, the other lives out of the country."

"So the nest got too empty."

"Something like that."

"Look," she pointed. A long willow arbor bridge stood a hundred yards before them. On the other side, they could see the rows of oak trees, just like the parks and recreations man described. The rest of the group had already assembled.

"Guess we got distracted."

She took his arm. "Come on. Let's see what this is all about."

They reached the arbor, taking their places among the group. Mr. Wentworth took a head count. Todd saw him mouthing each number.

"That's one hundred fifty of you." He turned to the parks and recreations man. "So? This it?"

"This is it," he said.

"Do we wait for something to happen, or what? I'm confused," a man said.

"No idea," the parks and recreation man answered.

Em spoke up. "I have an idea. I don't know if it'll lead anywhere, but it's something, at least."

Me Wentworth nodded. "Let's hear it."

Em bit her lip. "This might sound crazy, but what if we all walk though the arbor to the oak trees? See what happens?"

Mr. Wentworth thought about it.

"Couldn't hurt."

They lined up at the entrance of the arbor. Mr. Wentworth gave the signal, and walked through it. A person followed. Then another. And another. When it was their turn, Em and Todd walked together. She took his arm again.

Everyone walked in silence through the arbor as if part of an ancient ritual. They reached the other side, and continued toward the line of oak trees. When the last person joined, they stood motionless, waiting for something to happen.

"So that's that," Em said. "Sorry."

"Nothing to be sorry for," a woman said. "It was a stupid idea to begin with, coming here."

"If you had a better one you could have mentioned it," the parks and recreation man said.

Mr. Wentworth held up his hands. "Please, please. Let's not start fighting. We all agreed to come here thinking it might lead us somewhere but keeping an open mind in case it didn't. I don't know about the rest of you, Oak Pussy is still stuck in my head. But it's looking likely that we're not going to understand why that is. This experience has been a strange one to say the least. I'm grateful to have met you all. But I don't think I'm going to pursue this matter any more."

His words hung in the trees.

"So you're giving up," the rabbi said. "Just like that?"

"By all means, feel free to pursue on your own time. But I've got a bookstore to run and a life to live. If you believe this is a sign from God, well, either God's not being clear enough, or he hasn't finished saying what he's got to say. So I'll check back later."

It was hard to argue the point. And yet no one was in a hurry to leave, either. They shared a special bond. No need to break it up just yet.

The imam and the rabbi joined Todd and Em.

"I must say I'm disappointed," the imam said.

"Me too," the rabbi said. "Why would anyone halt their pursuit of the unknown?"

"Isn't that what makes us different from all other animals? The quest for knowledge?" The imam shook his head.

Em shrugged. "Maybe he just prefers to get his knowledge from books."

They walked back to the SUV without speaking. Em drove them back to town.

"Regardless of today's outcome, I don't think this was wasted time. It's been great getting to know you all. Even if our link makes no sense, we're still linked," she said.

She dropped them off one by one, saving Todd for last. She pulled up outside the retirement community. Neither was in a hurry to part.

"Thanks for the ride."

"Thanks for the walk," she said.

"Glad you enjoyed it. I love walks," Todd said. "I take long walks every morning. Sometimes five or six miles."

"Do you? That sounds lovely. I should try that some time."

"Hey, Em? This might be out of the blue, but I found a great new restaurant down the street. It's sort of a British pub, with a more interesting menu. You wouldn't by chance want to have dinner there tonight?"

Em smiled. "I would love that, Todd. Is eight too late?"

Todd reassured her it was not. He loved eating late. They exchanged numbers. After a moment's hesitation, she leaned over and kissed him on the cheek.

"See you tonight."

No one ever came to work at Sidewinder before ten. L.A. advertising agencies tended to get started later. The only people who came early to work were those who had meetings, juniors or interns trying to impress, or losers who had no life and were married to advertising.

I got up early, still a little groggy from the Ambien. I went for a quick run, then showered, ate breakfast and caught up on the news. It was ten-thirty by the time I entered Sidewinder.

I greeted the receptionist, picked up some mail and walked through the main workspace.

"Okay Jake, let's talk."

We went into my office, and I closed the door. I paused to look at a print ad for our sole client so far: Glenmorangie scotch. The ad was just a pack shot of the bottle with the logo on it. I thought it was shit but had it framed so when the clients came for meetings they would think I cared. For the record, I did care about their business. That's why I was going to grow the fuck out of it using Dreamverts™.

"What's all the fuss?"

Jake ran his fingers through his hair. "Our beta testing got fucked up."

"Fucked up, how?"

"It's like this—"

Before he could continue, I held up a hand. "Spare me the nerd talk and act like I'm four."

"With Dreamverts™ there are two methods of delivery. First, you've got preprogrammed dreams with ads baked in. It's a self-contained unit, right? And second, you've got ads that find their way into organic dreams."

"Yes, I know. We prefer to keep it organic because it's less invasive than a pre-programmed dream unit. Listen to me. I sound like an account guy. What's your point, Jake?"

"In each version you have front facing messaging that people see in their dreams, and stuff for the developers on the back end. Are you tracking?"

"So far."

"Well I kept wondering why we weren't getting much of a read out from any of the five hundred beta testers. It's been two months. Nothing. Sales of Glenmorangie haven't budged. Not in bars or liquor stores. It took six and a half weeks but I finally found the bug."

I sat up. "Okay, so you found a bug. Did you fix it?"

"Finally, yes."

"So what's the problem?"

Jake exhaled. "The problem is all the previous research is corrupted."

"Corrupted? You mean everything is fucked?"

"Yes."

"How fucked?"

"This is where I'll have to get a bit technical. You see, the bug I found had to do with the meta tags."

I stood up, opened my desk drawer and brought out a bottle of the scotch. I poured myself a generous measure. "English, Jake."

"Okay, sorry," he said. "Meta tags are like key words. They're content descriptors that help us research the effectiveness of the ad. Just like on a website. If I'm a user on a website I don't see them. Same with Dreamverts™. The dreamer who experiences a Dreamvert doesn't see it. This is all back end stuff."

I swallowed the scotch in one go. "Fine. Meta tags. What's the big deal?"

"The big deal is, the bug I found caused the meta tags to show instead of the actual Dreamvert."

I choked on the scotch.

"Wait. Hang on. Are you telling me for the past few months that five hundred people have seen your meta tags instead of our fucking ad? Is that what I am hearing?"

Jake nodded. "That's why we haven't seen any movement in sales at all."

"I know I don't know much about what you do, but wouldn't these meta tags be at least related to the product?"

"They can be. But they don't ever include the brand name."

I pinched the bridge of my nose. "But you used the word 'scotch,' didn't you?

Jake didn't answer.

"Jake."

"The thing is, in a million years I never would have thought that anyone would see them."

"What words did you use?"

"'Oak,'" he said. "And, um, 'pussy.'"

I gripped the glass like I was about to throw a fastball.

"Oak because Glenmorangie is aged in oak."

He nodded.

"And pussy." I said. "Why pussy, exactly?"

Jake babbled. Developers. Programmers. Computer geeks. They are a special breed. Because they're not only perverts, but also pranksters. They like hiding things for other computer geeks to discover. He went on to give a detailed history of all the instances in which such Easter eggs were planted and discovered by other geeks. He explained that his particular Easter egg was meant as an inside joke for some developer friends of his who are the type to go looking for stuff like that and that he was waiting for them to discover it.

The ramifications of the focus group seeing the meta tags and having a dream about the words oak pussy for the past one and a half months were unknown at this point. But in a way, he said, it was good to know because all developers like to be the first to discover bugs and fix them.

He reassured me that the bug was fixed but suggested we should start another beta test with another group if we wanted to get accurate results.

At this point I'd finished half the bottle of Glenmorangie. I chased him out of the office, threatening to take away his life, and his equity in that order if it wasn't sorted and a new beta test launched by that week. Then I went back in my office, slammed the door a few times and sat down.

My inbox was full of emails from the clients and heads of agencies I'd met. The phone rang. I put my head in my hands and let it keep ringing.

"Oak pussy. What a bunch of meaningless horseshit."

CHAPTER 7
Eye of Fatima

Six months before my mom died, I flew back to the east coast over Christmas to visit. She'd been on chemo for a year and a half and had planned on having the week of Christmas off from her treatments, but her state was so advanced, her doctor advised against it.

"Best I can do is get you in on Monday. That way, when Christmas rolls around on Sunday you'll feel better by then like you usually do."

That Monday, up early from being on L.A. time, I took her to the chemo center. My brother had given up his job to take care of her. The least I could do was let him sleep in and have some nights free for the week I was home.

With her frail state, weight sliding off her bones, and the cancer spreading from her bowels to her liver, it was hard not to assume it might very well be our last Christmas together. We approached that inevitableness on tiptoe. More often than not, we tried to ignore it. We took life a day at a time the way we are given them. And if on some days she felt sicker or was depressed, who could blame her?

The chemo treatment center was fantastic, as were most hospitals in the area. We were lucky her insurance covered the majority of it. No one would have described the place as looking cheerful, but the nurses were. They tried their best with a Christmas tree and faded window decorations that looked like they'd been hauled out from a poorly kept paper box once a year since nineteen eighty-eight.

My mom shuffled in wearing her usual blue Doc Martens, black jeans, spiked bracelet, Sex Pistols sweatshirt and leather jacket. She was seventy-two.

"The kids have it the worst here," she said to me, while we sat waiting her turn. "I mean the ones with parents who need to come here. They have nothing to do while they wait."

"That's awful," I said. There were dentist's waiting rooms that had more character.

"Hey, do you have any extra money? I was thinking, there's a toy store across the street. Could you go over and buy some stuff for them? I want to do something. I'll pay you back."

"Don't you want me to wait with you?"

"No, no. We have to get something for the kids. Get a bunch of coloring books and crayons, and books they can read, up to age twelve or so. And some blocks. Toys. Stuffed animals. I don't know. Just get a bunch of shit. But I'll pay you back."

I went out into the freezing cold and walked across the giant parking lot from the treatment center to the Toys R Us and tried to figure out what to get. I even talked to the salespeople who had no idea what kids waiting for their cancer-stricken parents and relatives would want as amusements. Most of them had smart phones, anyway. Once I wandered the aisles, however, I got caught up in it. I've seen kids in family restaurants lose their shit over free crayons. No smart phone game would compare to something tactile. I ended up spending a half hour and two hundred sixty five dollars in there.

When I came back I had eight large plastic bags of stuff. Some of it was educational. Some of it was silly. Stuff for girls, boys and neutral toys, too. I got a few things that just looked cool and might inspire some kids who liked to use their imaginations. That's what I would have wanted.

When I got back, my mom was busy entertaining the nurses and other patients who had become friends over the past year.

She winked at me. "What happened, kid? You get lost in the toy store?" And then with a perfect a comedic pause. "How old are you, again?"

Once the laughter subsided, she was quick to brag. "He's a good kid. He works in advertising like me. He may write all those commercials you see on TV, but I feed him the best headlines, though."

"She's not lying," I said. "You should see the scripts I've passed off as my own."

Ten minutes went by before I realized she'd been done for a while now. She was in no hurry. She's there to keep them company, make them laugh and have some laughs. Besides, the chemo hadn't hit her yet. The next day would be a mess, and she'd send me out to get extra toilet paper, "just in case."

She never wanted me to see her suffer. It's the reason I suspect she decided to die the day I was supposed to fly home in May, six months later. The day after the same doctor who wanted her to have a good Christmas had to tell her she had at most, six weeks to live. Her nurse kept her company that night. She asked if it hurt to die, and the nurse said no she didn't think so, she'd seen people die before and it was the exact opposite in fact.

Her nurse sent me a Christmas card a year later, with a short handwritten note. All those toys I got from the Toys R Us were still being put to good use. Not only that, but the little area had inspired others to donate. What started as eight bags was now quite the set up.

Tucked inside the card was a photo of the waiting room with

the nurses standing by the children's section smiling and giving the camera the thumbs up sign. They had also chipped in to get an engraved sign and hung it in that area just above the toys. It read: Helen's Corner. What was once a drab area in a waiting room was transformed into a safe space for kids to ward off sadness, sickness and boredom.

Instead of crying, I laughed out loud. In light of that touching tribute, my first thought at seeing the photo was that I wish I had also done something about the Christmas decorations, too.

We both shared the same desire to change the things we hate the most. At the top of that list is seeing people suffer who don't deserve it. Tacky decorations were a close second.

Three years and one day after that Christmas, I sat in the hallways of an emergency room with my wife. She'd been throwing up on and off for a week. She also suffered from crippling body aches, chills, fever, and had coughing spasms so violent they were causing migraines. When the thermometer read 102, I insisted she go to the ER.

I bundled her up and dragged her to the car. The weather was heavy with humidity and fog. For an L.A winter it was downright chilly. But even though I've lived here for five years, I never realize it's Christmas until the actual week.

I'll see Christmas lights winking on apartment balconies and wonder why they're there. "Here comes Santa Claus," will play in the mall and I won't understand why. When a nativity scene appears in front of a church it'll give me pause. Something about baby Jesus and barefoot surfers in black wet suits eating tuna poke or tacos just doesn't go together.

This Christmas we took it easy. We stayed in, opened our presents, and then went to bed. By the next evening, we were on our way to UCLA Medical Center in Santa Monica. There was no traffic to speak of. I found a parking spot right outside the entrance at a meter that didn't require payment after six. When I checked the time it was 5:50. I figured I'd chance ten minutes.

We got signed in and sat for a while. Then they called her name and took her to a small room to learn her symptoms and check vital signs.

They led her back to the waiting room where this time we sat for a half hour. We were both wearing masks. Me, because I didn't want to get anything from anyone and her, so she wouldn't give anything to anyone. The waiting room wasn't all that crowded. There was a couple with a kid, a man with his pregnant wife, a Mexican family of four, and four teenagers who did nothing but take selfies the entire time.

The teenagers didn't want to sit in the actual waiting room but instead blocked the entrance to it. They took endless photos of themselves, posing in different positions. They had to have been waiting for someone, but their "rich kids with no class" stench was so strong it was almost like they were taunting us with their health.

I was considering removing my wife's mask and having her cough on them, when a guard came over and told them they could either go in and sit down or wait outside but they couldn't block the entrance. They scowled, but obeyed. Their photo shoot was over, anyway. They slunk in and joined the rest of the sickies.

On the TV was an informative video in Spanish demonstrating the proper way to cough and blow your nose and wear masks. I watched it all the way through fifteen times.

The couple with the young baby were called first. UCLA Medical Center is primarily a pediatric one, and the baby was having an allergic reaction so they were in the right place. The poor kid's cheeks were pomegranate-colored and swollen. He was howling when they walked away with the nurse.

After that, it was the pregnant wife's turn. She was

complaining of severe dehydration. Her husband looked like it was the fifth time he'd taken her there that week. He'd moved beyond concern and now had the look of a husband who believed his wife was doing this to him on purpose.

Ten minutes later, they called my wife's name. She got up and walked a few steps before turning back. "You are coming, right?"

It was the first time I'd been in a hospital since my mom's death. They walked us down the hallway, past rooms filled with other patients. All the rooms were taken. They led us to a gurney just outside two rooms. The first room was large enough for three patients, who could enjoy privacy curtains. The next room was only large enough for one person. A nurse was standing outside of the smaller room, looking anxious.

My wife flopped on the gurney.

Our nurse asked how she was feeling. Her voice was so weak, the nurse turned to me to interpret.

"She's been throwing up a lot, she had a fever of 102 before we got here, and she's headachy and coughing and her coughs cause her headaches. I had stomach flu but I've been fine for three days. This is much worse."

The nurse nodded. "We'll take some blood and see what's going on. And some urine. Can you pee?"

My wife nodded and managed to get back up. A post-Christmas miracle: We were right next to the bathroom. The nurse handed her a gown. "Put this on while you're in there."

My wife poked her head out from the bathroom, motioning me to come help. I took her bottle filled with pee and unhooked her bra so she could put on the gown, all while trying to be a gentleman and block the open bathroom door. I went back out and sat on a chair next to the gurney.

To my left, I saw the large area where the nurses took phone calls, and looked up records. In the middle of the table was a four-foot Christmas tree with little doctor-themed ornaments: skulls, bones, giant pills. I didn't see a syringe or an IV drip ornament, but that would have been a nice touch.

On the flat screen TV, a Yule log in a fireplace burned. It was a much more festive atmosphere than I had expected. The nurses were a tight unit, alternating between "can you hand me a blanket for patient X," seriousness to making in-jokes with each other. Even with sick people around, it looked like a fun place to work.

I stood up to have a look around the room. On one gurney, a large Hispanic woman lay on her side, playing with her phone. A doctor explained to her she had severe acid reflux disease and she really needed to think about losing weight or it would only get worse. His voice was impatient, as if treating acid reflux was beneath him and he had better patients with more interesting maladies to tend to.

A different couple came in carrying a toddler who was screaming its head off. An older Japanese man in pajamas was also on a gurney outside a room. His wife accompanied him. He was explaining to the nurse how he had diarrhea and self-diagnosed himself as having flu.

All the while the nurses milled about like desensitized bees.

I was thirsty but the hypochondriac in me got squeamish at the thought of the water fountain. I watched the Yule log burn, listened to the frenetic sounds. My wife came back from the bathroom and flopped down on the gurney again. "I'm cold." She shivered.

I flagged a nurse, asked for a blanket. She rushed over to us and placed it on it her. She asked if she needed anything and then left when the answer was no. Just as fast, our original nurse showed up with a contraption built to take various kinds of blood samples. As he searched for my wife's veins, the anxious looking nurse who'd been outside the small room all this time came over.

""He still won't leave. He knows the drill."

Our nurse rolled his eyes. "So get him some juice and crackers and if he doesn't leave with them, call Bob."

She hurried away, got the juice and crackers, and went back in the room.

"Now," he said to my wife. "Sorry about that. And I'm sorry it's taking so long to get a good vein. I think it's because you're dehydrated. There we go."

The needle found the vein and he filled three vials, one after the other. Then he slapped a bandage on her arm. He told her the analysis wouldn't take too long. They'd have an answer in an hour or so.

As soon as he left, my wife ran to the bathroom to vomit, came back defeated and covered herself with a blanket. Once again, I flagged a nurse to explain what happened. They got her a nausea pill, which worked quicker than any pill I've ever taken in my life, and gave her an IV drip to deal with the dehydration.

The anxious nurse went ahead and called Bob, who turned out to be a very large security guard. It took him a few minutes to appear, but once he did I knew why he was a security guard. He took up the entire hallway. He poked his head into the room and said "Time to go, Jack. Now."

Out staggered a homeless man who couldn't have been older than thirty-five. He didn't seem sick. I figured he may have just wanted a warm place for a few hours. The guard escorted him out the door. The man tried to take the blanket with him, but the guard prevented that. "I was once in medical school," he said out loud to no one in particular.

The next hour I took in the chaos. My wife was feeling more stable. I was getting more anxious. At one point I looked up to find a man in handcuffs and shackles standing next to me.

A cop was guarding him. Great, I thought. Just what we need: A prisoner-patient. I saw a film like that once. It didn't end well.

To keep from thinking about that, I looked in the large room next to me. The pregnant wife from the waiting room was asking for another IV drip. They were in the middle, with the curtain half closed.

"Another one?" her husband said. "Are you sure? Yes. I know. Okay." He left the room to find a nurse.

To the right was a quiet African American family who couldn't decide whether or not to wear facemasks. The older woman was waiting to be discharged. From their conversation, it sounded like she was having hip trouble.

On the left of the large room was another older woman. Her two grown daughters were doing their best to ignore her. One was texting. The other left every twenty minutes for a cigarette. She reeked of smoke. The older woman sighed a lot. Every so often she'd say something to her kids in a heavy accent I couldn't make out. She seemed antsy and annoyed with her children who weren't listening to her.

"I think I'm still running a fever."

It took a minute before I realized it was my wife talking. I got up and walked to the nurse's station and explained the situation. A nurse said she'd be over with a Tylenol. I also asked if she knew how long it would be before the doctor came to see her. She looked surprised.

"You're still waiting? Let me get him. I'll get her the Tylenol first, but then I'm going to get him." The nurse shook her head.

Five minutes later, a doctor appeared with a young man carrying a clipboard.

"Hi, I'm Dr. Austin. This is my stenographer. Don't mind him."

The stenographer looked like he just started shaving last

week. Dr. Austin inspected my wife while I filled him in on the symptoms. First he took out a penlight and checked her pupils.

"Have you been traveling lately?"

"Oslo," my wife answered.

"Why there?"

"I'm from there."

He felt her stomach, listened to her lungs. "Mm-hmm. You go anywhere else?"

"My plane had a connection in Paris. A bunch of people was on a connecting flight somewhere in Africa.

"Do you know where?"

"Somewhere with a French sounding name."

"Can you sit up?" She got up and he continued listening to her lungs, placing the stethoscope on her back. "How long ago were you traveling?"

"Three weeks ago."

"I was going to say this is flu, and it probably is. But we're seeing a lot of things coming back from overseas travel this winter. To rule anything else out, I want to have a look at your blood work."

The doctor walked through the nurse's station and plopped himself in front of a computer. I could see images on his screen. I had no idea what they were.

"It's just flu," I said.

"It's just flu," my wife said. "My body is really hurting now."

My wife came from Nordic stock; it was not like her to complain. Once again, I stood up and asked the nurse for help. She rushed over.

"On a scale of 1-10, how bad is the pain?"

"Six, maybe seven," my wife answered.

"I'm going to get you some morphine," she said. "I'll be right back."

I looked at my wife. Her face was pale and her light blonde

hair was so damp with sweat it looked black. We'd been there three hours and so far they'd given her a Tylenol, a blanket, and an IV drip.

"You still thirsty?" I asked.

"Very. This stuff doesn't quench your thirst. It drips out so slowly. How much is left?"

I looked at the bag.

"More than half full. Or half empty, depending on your mood."

"It's so cold when it goes in. I wish they would heat it, but I guess they can't."

The nurse came back, and added the morphine to the drip. My wife slumped down on the gurney and her eyes fluttered.

"It's just flu," she mumbled.

I didn't know how long viruses or bacteria took to gestate, but it seemed to me if they suspected Ebola they would have put us both in quarantine. Then again if it was Ebola we would have known a lot sooner because you die from that quickly, don't you? What are the chances of picking up anything that severe from a plane? Then I remembered the kid with TB whose father worked for the CDC and had flown a few times despite being on a no-fly list, and then I stopped thinking about it.

"Oh, God." I looked at the floor and hung my head and without thinking about it I started to pray. "Please help my wife. I don't know what's wrong but please let it just be flu. This is bad enough. Please heal her."

Doctor Austin didn't come back until another hour later to tell us my wife had a severe case of flu that had developed into pneumonia. He wrote her prescriptions for nausea medication, antibiotics, an inhaler, and some codeine cough syrup to take at night.

"You'll have to take it easy for about two weeks, but you'll be fine. I'll write up your prescriptions and discharge papers and a nurse will be along to help you."

I stood up and thanked him, relieved. It was now after ten.

"Okay so it wasn't just flu but at least it's treatable." I put my hand on my wife's knee. "How you feeling?"

"The morphine is so great. I want to go home while it lasts."

Once again I stood up but a nurse was on her way. "We're just waiting on your discharge papers but I'll be able to help in a few minutes. Just let me get some things."

I realized with some degree of dark humor that my wife's urine was still sitting in a cup on the gurney. I pointed to it.

"Oh we won't need that," the nurse said. She took it and threw it in the biohazard bin.

I saw one of the daughters in the room leave for what had to have been her tenth cigarette of the night. The other doctor was nowhere in sight.

The older woman got up from her bed. She was wearing a maroon tracksuit. Her steps were slow and labored as if each one were an effort to get to the exit.

Our nurse reappeared with discharge papers for my wife to sign. I was just about to ask if I needed to sign anything when I realized the older woman was standing right in front of me.

Her skin was olive. Her hair was cut short and was dark brown with flecks of blonde and grey. She was sucking on a mint and smiling at me.

Her track jacket was open at the neck. She wore a necklace. It was an upside down hand made out of gold in an intricate interlocking pattern. The hand looked like three regular fingers and two thumbs on either end. In the center was an eye made from cobalt.

Under the hospital lights the gold pattern flashed and flickered. The eye looked as if it were alive and was staring at me, or through me. The woman's presence was jarring, not the least of which because she invaded our personal space so much. Another few inches and she would have been in my lap. Despite this, her presence was not unwelcome, at least not to me. There was something familial about her.

She bent over until her face was in line with mine. When she spoke her voice was strong, but quiet. I still couldn't place her accent.

"I saw you."

I had no idea how to respond to that. The nurse was struggling to remove the IV. My wife's eyes first went to the woman, and then me. She looked stoned and perplexed. The woman touched my cheek as much to get my attention as to caress it.

"You were praying, yes?"

"I was."

She smiled at me. "I knew. Because I could see from in there," she said, pointing to her room. "I saw you."

She winced and pointed to her leg.

"Do you want me to pray for your leg?"

"The swelling is so bad and has gone from here to here." She pointed from her ankle to above her knee. "They are doing tests." She winced again, and her eyes met mine. "Please pray."

From the corner of my eye, I could see my wife sitting up now. The nurse was also watching us. Her mouth was open.

"What is your name?"

She smiled. "Valentine. I was married to my husband fifty years. I was from Persia. Long time ago."

"Do you speak Farsi, Valentine?"

"Yes, but thank God I don't have to. I live here. In Santa Monica. Where are you?"

"We live in Venice."

"Oh," Valentine said, dismissing Venice with her hands as if I had mentioned a Podunk town in another state. "I am six blocks from here. I can walk. When I can walk," she winced again. "I hurt so much. They can't give me anything. I don't want to be here any more. I want to not hurt. It has been months now, that I come."

She stood up. I did the same. "Do you want my seat?"

"No, no," she said, shrugging off the pain. "I want you to pray like you did for your wife." She leaned in to whisper something to me. When she did, her necklace jingled. "My daughters, they don't care about me."

I couldn't remember the last time I'd prayed, and now I was praying twice. But when someone you don't know asks for that kind of help you don't refuse.

I had no idea if Valentine was Muslim, Christian, Jewish, or none of the above. To be on the safe side I just used the word God, figuring that was as good a name as any.

"Dear God, I pray these doctors find the cause of Valentine's pain and that you give them science and wisdom to heal her. Amen."

When I finished, I looked over at my wife. Even though her IV drip was removed, and papers signed, the nurse was still there. Both had witnessed this scene. And both of them were crying.

"Amen," Valentine said smiling. "You see? I knew." Valentine touched the amulet. "You know this?"

I shook my head.

"Hamsa, The eye of Fatima. We wear for protection. My daughters, they don't care. My eldest, she smokes all the time she's waiting here. She just wants my discharge papers so she can get me home. But I won't leave until I know. I won't die until I know."

"You won't die," I said.

"I am seventy-eight," she said. "God takes me, I don't mind.

I want to see my husband again. I have had a good life. I would just want to live the rest without pain."

She held out her hand. I took it. We stayed like that for a long moment. She smiled with her entire face, her eyes, as much as her mouth. There was far too much meaning behind that smile for me to interpret. When Valentine at last let me go, she flashed me the amulet one more time. Satisfied, she turned to go back to her room.

"Thank you young man. You said Venice, yes?"

I nodded.

"It is late. Take your wife home now. You have much longer to go. Lucky for me, I am not that far."

CHAPTER 8
Electric Lash

The bus driver shook her head at both of us. Her hand jerked the lever, opening the door with such force the bus rattled. "I don't care what you read online." She emphasized the last word. "If you want to go downtown, you need to take the 30. Not the 105." A few passengers up front voiced their agreement in the same tone of voice.

Bryce put his gold iPhone 7 back in the pocket of his burgundy jeans. "Your metro app clearly needs an overhaul. Come on, Jay."

I followed after. The bus driver snapped the doors shut, missing the heel of my shoe by an inch. We were on Sunset Boulevard, right across the street from the Whisky A Go-Go. It was eight forty-five on New Year's Eve.

"We should have taken an Uber," Bryce said. "What is it with you? You know public transportation here isn't like New York. We were on that stupid bus for almost two hours."

"But the price surge," I protested. The sky was black with a light grey layer of rain clouds. Even though it was much colder in New York, I buttoned my coat collar.

Jay pulled out his iPhone, opened the Uber app and scowled. The surge rate was ten times the normal amount. "At least we would have been there by now. Instead, we're in Touristville. Hollywood, U.S.A. She might as well have dropped us at The Grove."

The rain started falling in large drops, staining my light green bomber jacket. Winter in Los Angeles wasn't all that inviting. That's why I liked it so much. Something about it not being warm and sunny made everyone display real emotions instead of fake ones. They were quieter, more ill at ease. In winter here, the ocean turns dark grey instead of blue. Only the surfers brave the beach. Everyone else gets pensive and stays indoors.

"Might as well grab a drink. There's lots of places over there." I pushed the crosswalk button. We waited for ages.

"That's on the west side of the street, though," Bryce said. "We have to go east."

"It's just one drink," I pleaded. "Nothing is on this side for blocks."

We looked around our side of the street. There was a half-empty Jack in the Box, and a high-rise condo under construction. The only sign of life was outside the convenience store. A homeless man stood moving his arms back and forth like he was conducting an imaginary symphony. Bryce mumbled something I didn't catch. He pulled out his iPhone again out of habit. We continued waiting for the walk sign.

Ten years ago, Bryce developed his first app, called Yes. Its sole function was to say, "yes," every time you tapped it. Everyone including Bryce was shocked when it became the fourth most downloaded app that year, netting him close to three million dollars. Bryce was now worth fifty times that amount. He was CEO and founder of YesYes: a content studio that specializes in comedy. YesYes also acts as a management company for a robust list of bourgeoning social media stars. Bryce had a knack for turning these up-and-comers into megastars. People with video views that were now in the millions.

I'm the sole creative director and one of three writers whose job it was to write comedy sketches and help the social media stars plus up their ideas until they learned how to do it themselves.

Bryce planned to put one more role on his plate in January. He planned to act as liaison for advertising agencies, making the rounds to convince the ones whose clients have deep pockets to spend a lot of money on branded content. In bigger markets, he'd trot out his A-list social media stars to stoke the fire, and get everyone excited about the possibilities. "Like putting the prettiest hookers in the window," he said.

Word choice aside, when Bryce told me his plan, I was enthusiastic. He was a great salesman. I knew he'd have no trouble getting ad agencies excited about the YesYes media channel. As an added benefit, he wouldn't have time to pop in the writers' room to help brainstorm. Bryce was one of the least funny people I've ever known.

"Some way to spend the holidays," he said. "Fucking L.A." His phone vibrated. He looked at the screen. "Know where Tristan is?" He showed me the phone. "At a secret show with Blood Orange. Look at all the people there."

Tristan was one of the other writers at YesYes. Except for sharing the same sense of humor, we had little in common. First thing in the morning, I read the international news. Tristan checked the fashion blogs to see if there are any new sneaker collaborations of interest. Although he was born on some small island in the Pacific, his diplomat parents raised him in Holland. He was known to play up one side of his ethnicity over the other depending on what he thought would impress the most. I loved working with him. Beneath the narcissism and shallowness was a pretty decent guy.

In the photo, Tristan was throwing a sideways peace sign,

smiling from ear to ear. He was surrounded by a bunch of people I didn't recognize.

"Kamasi Washington's there. That tall guy next to him is Jeff Millner, head of Ace records. That guy on his left is GiantPea, the Swedish YouTuber I've been trying to sign for a year. He does all those dumb reaction videos and Let's Play videos. Game reviews, too. He gets paid butt loads to give everything a thumbs up," he said, posing with two thumbs in the air. "GiantPea's signature move. He swears up and down the gaming companies don't pay him for his reviews. Total piece of shit."

Bryce took his iPhone back and stared at the screen. "Oh and look. There's Gigi Hadid." He sent a few smiling and thumbs up emojis to Tristan. Then he shoved his phone back in his pocket. "Remind me again why we left Bushwick to spend New Year's here?"

Back in October, Bryce held a meeting to announce YesYes was going to open an L.A. office. We thought at first it was just another fleeting brain fart. Every few months, Bryce would make an announcement about his intentions. More often than not, they went nowhere. Some former gems were closing the office so we could all work from home. Shifting our focus into app development. Creating an in-house ad agency. Turning the downstairs floor into a club/maker space/artisanal general store/prototyping atelier.

None of these ideas advanced beyond the first meeting. So it came as somewhat of a shock a month later, when Bryce called me into his office offering me the job of launching YesYes L.A. He planned to promote Tristan to Executive Creative Director New York content. If I accepted the offer I'd be promoted to Executive Creative Director of Content, L.A. The promotion came with a very generous pay bump, and a great deal more autonomy.

"You guys have this content shit on lock," he said. "This will free me up to focus on hooking the ad agencies."

Bryce worked out a deal with a Santa Monica production company where I could lease out an office until we found a suitable space of our own. We'd spent the majority of the week getting the lay of the land, having drinks with the owners of the production company and scoping out locations. There was much deliberation. Should we be situated next to the other production houses? Should we move somewhere else? I was leaning towards Santa Monica or Playa Del Rey for proximity to vendors as well as the airport. Bryce thought Silver Lake was a better choice. As soon as he saw how long it would take to get to the airport, he relented.

New offices aside, it wasn't the only one reason we'd gone to L.A.

"If I'm not mistaken, we're in L.A. because you said, quote, I want to leave New York so I can get over Julia. Remember?"

Bryce went silent for a brief second. "Fuck her, too."

We walked by the Whisky, heading west against the rain. Bryce kept up a running commentary on every place we passed.

"Too douche. Too boring. Rooftop bar? I'm sure it's fantastic with a rainy view of LA. Oh look, an Asian Fusion restaurant. How original."

I stopped in front of a bar. Bryce was so distracted by his snarkathon that he bumped in to me.

"What's this?"

The bar had no sign on its glass door. Boxy TV screens showing music videos hung in corners all around the bar. Posters dotted the dark green walls. The floor was black and white checkered tile. Bryce cupped his hands around his eyes, and peered in the window.

"Please tell me they didn't just discover the speakeasy revival concept. I know L.A. is backwards, but—"

"One drink, just to get out of the rain."

Bryce relented. "Fine. At least I can mock it."

I pushed open the door and stood in the entranceway. The place looked half-empty. A server came towards us. She was dressed in black combat boots, with black socks over her knees. Her grey jean shorts were cuffed. Her shirt was black and white checkered, matching the floor. It was open at the neck with a black t-shirt underneath. She also wore a silver cross. Black suspenders hung at her sides.

"Sit anywhere you like, guys."

Bryce made a show of looking around trying to decide. I ignored him and took a seat by the window.

"Doesn't look busy now, but you wait. This place will be jumping in an hour," she said. "My name's Meredith, I'll be taking care of you." She plunked down two menus and left. She went back to the bar to pick up some drink orders from the bartender. He had shoulder length hair. He was wearing a long-sleeved plaid shirt, and a black knit hat.

Meredith deposited the drinks at another table. She returned with eyebrows raised. "So?"

"I'll have a double vodka tonic," I said.

Bryce held the menu at arm's length. "Have any craft beers?"

"Full Sail Amber, Lucknow IPA. Oh and we've got Magic Hat from Vermont."

Bryce shook his head. "I'll just have a Heineken."

Meredith nodded. "Lime with the vodka tonic?"

"Yes, please."

"Be right back," she smiled.

"She's cute."

Bryce pulled out his iPhone and put it on the table. "Her outfit, though. It reminds me of that girl's catalog, what was it called? It was spelled with studly caps. Donna's?

"Delia's."

'That's it," Bryce said. "I almost Googled it. She looks like she got her outfit from Delia's."

"What'd you expect, Bryce? This isn't some hipster joint. It's a regular bar."

"That reminds me," he said. "The Standard isn't our only option. I saw an article on Complex about everything going on here on New Year's. He tapped his phone. "Weird. I can't get online."

Outside, the streets were slick with rain. A black limousine rolled by, wipers on high. "Looks like we missed the storm just in time."

"Go on, Mister Good Vibes. Lay on the positive energy."

"Come on, man. We're in L.A. instead of freezing New York. YesYes is going to have a killer 2017. You could try to be a little happier."

His eyes never left the phone. "I only have twenty percent battery. Fuck."

Meredith returned with our drink. Our eyes met and she smiled once again. Something about her smile was comforting. Genuine. When was the last time I'd seen an honest display of emotion between two people in real life? We had all the apps in the world to help make our lives easier. Apps for dating, getting rides, recognizing an unfamiliar song or star in the sky. Life was supposed to be so easy now. How come more of us weren't enjoying life?

"One double vodka tonic with lime, and one Heineken. You want to start a tab?"

"Nope," Bryce said.

"Okay, no worries." Did she sound hurt? She walked back to the bar.

Bryce called after her. "What's the password for your Wi-Fi?"

Meredith cupped her hand to her ear. "What's my what?"

"Your Wi-Fi password. Does the bar have Wi-Fi?"

She looked at me for help. I shrugged.

"Sorry," she said shaking her head.

That set Bryce off. I sipped my drink while he ran through a litany of what was wrong with L.A. in particular and the world in general. Music played from the speakers. I recognized the slide guitar, but it took a minute before I could place the song. "Scar Tissue," by The Chili Peppers. I started thinking about how a song can frame a time and place so well. Not that this particular song had a lot of meaning for me. But I remember the video. It showed the band driving in a convertible somewhere in the desert. Beaten. Bruised. But still standing.

"Jay? Hello?" Bryce snapped his fingers in front of my face.

"Sorry. I was just waiting for you to finish your rant."

"Funny. Can you check your phone and see if you get service?"

I sipped my drink and reached in my inside jacket pocket fished it out and turned it on. "No Wi-Fi. No 4G. Nothing."

"Is this a black hole? I can't believe there's no service here."

Meredith's voice broke in. "It took exactly one minute for me to get your drinks and you're complaining about service? You've got some nerve."

Bryce may have hated humanity but he was smart enough not to let most people know it. Besides—today's waitress might be tomorrow's biggest social media star.

"I didn't mean service from you," he said. "You're great." He looked around, trying to show enthusiasm. "This place is great." He picked up his iPhone. "I meant phone service. There's no reception here."

She turned to me.

Thinking it would help, I reached into my pocket and showed her my iPhone. "There's no cell phone service."

Meredith's face turned red. She tried to laugh it off, but

it only made her face redder. "Oh. Duh. Sorry. Some of the customers have complained about spotty reception."

"You see?" Bryce said. "It is this place, after all."

"Yeah I guess," she said. She pointed to my phone. "Also, I've never seen one like that until now. Anyway, should I get the check?"

"Let's do another round," I smiled. She walked away and my eyes made their way down her back to those black suspenders flapping by her jean shorts.

"Dude," Bryce whispered. "She's never seen an iPhone 7 before. Can you believe that?"

"They haven't been out all that long," I said.

"But everyone from CNET to the Times has reviewed it. She was totally surprised." He finished his beer.

"It just might be that she's not a first adapter like us. Believe it or not, Bushwick doesn't represent the rest of the country."

Meredith returned with our drinks.

"No shit. Just look at Trump."

Meredith said: "The Miss Universe guy? Yuck."

"Exactly," Bryce said. "You'd think that would have sunk him." He shuddered. "This whole year we've been on edge, right?"

"Tell me about it, " she said. "I've been like, what the hell's going to happen? Is the world going to end?"

Bryce nodded. "Oh my God, me too. See, Jay? She gets it." He pointed at me. "But Good Vibes here keeps telling me to stay positive. Things might look bad now, but they aren't as bad as they seem. "

"Yadda, yadda," Meredith said.

"Laugh all you want," I said. "But right now none of us knows what's going to happen. Is it really worth getting all worked up about it now?" I looked at Meredith. "I don't think so."

Meredith smiled. "You've got a point," she said. "It's New
year's Eve, after all. Can I get you anything else?"

"We're good for now," Bryce answered.

I watched Meredith walk back to the bar. She turned back
and caught me looking. Now it was my turn to blush.

"Jay, stop looking at her ass and look at the TVs."

The volume was down on all of them. One showed a music
video of a band riding scooters past palm trees. I had a vague
memory of it but couldn't place the song. On another TV, the
Beastie Boys' were mugging for the camera in high hats and
safety glasses.

"It's all nineties shit."

"The nineties are back," I answered. "Didn't Complex just
have an article about it?" He ignored my sarcasm.

We watched two guys walk up to the bar. Both had small
soul patch beards on their chins. They also wore black knit
hats just like the bartender, as well as Baja ponchos. Then a
larger group of guys and girls approached the bar. I hadn't seen
anyone come in. Maybe there was a covered patio in the back.

Bryce downed the rest of his beer, tapped his iPhone again.
"Okay, Jay. It's now ten. Here's what I'm going to do: Go
outside. Get reception. Order an Uber. And get the fuck out of
this place. If I get lucky I might make it to a real party before
midnight."

I nodded. The rain was still coming down in sheets. Two
women wearing gaudy sequined dresses teetered by in high
heels, clutching smart phones as big as their heels. They were
drunk, wet and crying. Bryce went outside, oblivious to them.
He stopped every few steps, looking for reception.

This second vodka hit my empty stomach hard. I hadn't
eaten since breakfast. Bryce was notorious for his eating habits.
He never ate regular meals at regular times. For the past month
he'd been living on Soylent, the tech-startup meal of choice.

The powder contained all the nutrients you needed to live. Just add water, stir, drink, and you are free to go back to working a hundred hours a week.

I like going to the farmer's market. Shopping at my local organic butcher. Chatting with the fishmonger to see what's just come in that day. Sharing a meal, having conversation, taking time to slow down and relax while the hectic world races by is a profound experience. Why would I want to give that up to sit in front of the computer longer than I already do?

Bryce stormed through the door, blinking the rain away from his eyes. He stood standing over me. He grabbed a napkin to wipe off his dripping phone. "Man, am I glad they finally made the iPhone waterproof." Without looking up he continued. "So, Jay. Sorry."

"No need to apologize, man. I know it's been hard since you and Julia split. It's all good."

'The fuck are you talking about? I meant sorry, but I'm leaving before you." Bryce pointed outside to five people, huddling under two umbrellas. "Those guys ordered an XL. Should be here any second. I'm the sixth person and there's no extra room."

I learned back in my chair. "I see. Now."

"They had no trouble getting one," he said. "Apparently because people can't deal with rain here, the wait time's only fifteen to thirty minutes. So you'll be right behind."

"Where are you going?"

"Those guys are going to the Ace so I think I'll start there. It was on my list. I'll get the driver to charge my phone. By the time we get there I'll be at fifty percent. Just text me when you're there. I'll come find you. Cool?"

Meredith came over at the exact same moment a black SUV pulled up in front of the bar.

"Shit. I'll get the next round. See you there."

He rushed out into the rain, and into the waiting SUV.

"His Uber has arrived."

Meredith shook her head. "He's an uber-douche, if you ask me. Sorry. I shouldn't have said that."

I laughed. "You're absolutely right. He is an uber douche."

"What about you?" Meredith asked. "Do you need the check?

"I need a food menu. I haven't eaten since breakfast."

She went over to the podium and plunked one down on my table. "We've got the best wings on the Strip. The Gardenburger's pretty good if you're a vegetarian. My favorite is the blackened chicken sandwich. It comes with fries."

"I'll go with your favorite. And can you bring a Diet Coke, too?"

"You got it," she said. She hesitated. "Listen. I don't mean to be whatever, but all of us servers get dinner breaks and I need to take mine before ten-thirty. Mind some company?"

"Love some. My name's Jay, by the way."

"Nice to meet you, Jay, by the way."

In a few minutes she came back with blackened chicken sandwiches and Diet Cokes for both of us. As far as bar food went, the blackened chicken sandwich was pretty good.

"You live around here?"

Kind of. I'm moving out here next month from New York."

"You like it there?"

"Nah. It's incredibly overrated."

She gasped. "Come on. So many of my friends have moved there. I've lost touch with them all. It has to have something."

"Well I've been there four years. That's long enough. Everything you heard is true."

"Like what?" she said. "Great art, music and culture?"

"Expensive. Rats. Cockroaches. And that's just the people."

"Ha," she said. "I'm born and raised here. Wouldn't trade it for anything." She sipped her drink. "It's not just surfing and fake plastic people. L.A.'s got a lot of hidden gems if you know where to look."

"I'll bet."

She pointed outside. "And by the way, just so you know, this much rain is not normal."

"Rain doesn't bother me."

"Me neither," she said. "I'm only happy when it rains," she sang in her best Shirley Manson voice.

"I haven't heard Garbage in forever," I said.

"Really? I love that song. Come on."

I followed her to the jukebox at the back of the bar. She plunked in four quarters in the jukebox and found the Garbage song. Then she made me turn around so I wouldn't see what else she chose.

"It's a secret," she said with a playful voice. "Now there are two songs left. Let's see what you pick so I can judge you accordingly."

The selection leaned heavy in the rock, punk and alternative territory: The Clash, Alice in Chains, The Cure, and some older stuff like Led Zeppelin. I chose Liz Phair's "Supernova," and Jane's Addiction's "Jane Says."

We went back to our food. The rain was not letting up.

"There was a big playlist before us, so it'll take a while," she said. "Don't worry, we'll hear our songs before midnight." Her smile disappeared. "Oh, but I guess you gotta go meet your friend soon."

The bar had filled up just as Meredith had said. It must have happened when we were at the jukebox.

"I don't think so." I said. "I know he was lying about the Uber wait time. And to be honest, I'm having fun just hanging out here. With you."

Meredith looked away. "I'm glad," she said. "But I have a question. What is Uber?"

"You're kidding, right?" I pointed out the window. The two women I saw earlier were busy attempting to maneuver their way into one. "You see that logo on the back of the car?"

"Uh-huh."

"That's Uber. It's a ride service. Like a taxi except it's not owned by the city. It's private."

"And you order it from your phone?"

"For sure." I shook my head. "You really haven't heard of it? It's been in L.A. for like four years now."

She looked at the table. "I guess I just don't get out all that much."

We ate without speaking. I waited for her to break the silence.

"Sometimes I look outside and I think the world is passing me by," she said. "When the bus stops I see all these ads for shows I never watch. Most of them I've never even heard of, you know?"

"I do. Maybe it's work," I said, trying to sound helpful. "Sometimes my job is crazy. Eighty to a hundred hours a week in front of the computer."

"Are you a computer nerd?" she teased.

"I'm a writer."

"Close enough."

Our laughter was the kind two people share when they are becoming more familiar with each other.

"Here you are in front of a computer all day and using your phone to order taxis. And I'm still using this." She fished out her cell phone. It was a Nokia 5110.

"Holy shit," I said. "Where did you get that, eBay?"

"Meredith! Hey Meredith. Break's over."

We looked up to see the bartender's glare. "I gotta get back to work," she said. "Want another double vodka tonic?"

"Please."

I picked up a napkin and wiped my face. On one of the TV screens, Daria was eating pizza. The bartender was changing the other TV with a remote. I tapped my iPhone. It was five minutes after eleven.

"Your drink, sir," Meredith said.

"Cheers."

"By the way, I comped your dinner. Happy New Year." I started to protest. "Don't worry about it." She winked. "Besides, in an hour the cash registers might not be working, anyway."

Before I could say anything, Meredith put a finger to her lips. Then she pointed to the speakers. Through the din of the crowd I could just make the opening guitar riff to "Possum Kingdom," by the Toadies. "Song one," she said.

She cleared away my plate and silverware. I got up and was about to ask where the bathroom was when she pointed. "Through that door and hang a right. First door on your left. I'll make sure no one steals your seat or puts anything in your drink."

The adjacent room was just as packed. I made my way past the throngs of people lined up three rows deep at the bar, found the first door on the left and pushed my way in. The bathroom was clean. It had three urinals and one stall. All were occupied.

I stood by the sink, waiting my turn. I pulled out my iPhone. It started vibrating as soon as I touched it. So there was reception after all.

"Hey dude, you want to put your pager away and move from the sink?"

I looked up and saw a large college kid wearing a backwards hat and red USC t-shirt. His pissing buddy was dressed the same way. Both looked like they spent more hours in the gym than was necessary.

"Sorry," I said.

"If you're a dealer," he said with a threat in his voice. "Then hook us up!"

He and his pissing buddy laughed and high-fived each other. I skirted around and stood in front of the open urinal. The text messages were an hour old, all from Bryce. From the way the spelling deteriorated, it seemed like he was getting super drunk:

We're at Ace. It's banging.
The fuck you at a-hole?
Pick up.
OMG Regee Waots is her.
Dude yr messing out. The girls are slamin
HNY dick

I put my phone in my back pocket. I'm sure Bryce would have a glorious time on his own making fun of everyone until he found the right girl for the night. I didn't want to hang out with him or his new rich friends. Those types of places made me uneasy. Like I wasn't cool enough to be there. I have never been one to try so hard to impress anyone or fit in.

As I peed, my eyes looked at the front page of the L.A. Times that hung on the wall. "U.S. turns over Panama Canal to Panama." "RIAA Napster Suit heats up." "Boris Yeltsin resigns, appoints Putin President."

The date on the newspaper was December 31st, 1999. It wasn't preserved behind glass like some memorabilia. It was just tacked up.

I returned to my seat and sipped my drink. Meredith came over carrying two shots, her face in a mock pout. "You missed my song number two."

"Aw man," I said. "What song was it?"

"Song Number Two. Blur.

"Proud of yourself?"

"Very. It's now eleven thirty. Let's do a shot."

I tried to sound like a cop. "Are you allowed to drink on the job, young lady?"

"Only if it's the right circumstance. It's vodka. I figured I should try to catch up."

We clinked glasses and knocked them back. I'd been drinking well vodka in my tonics. This was top shelf.

"Listen," I said. "My first song,"

Meredith stood listening to "Supernova," for a moment. Then she walked backwards to the bar, holding our shot glasses, her hips moving to the beat of the song. "Liz Phair. Not a bad choice, Mister Jay. Not bad at all."

Unlike a lot of bars on nights like tonight, no one was angry. No fights were threatening to break out. As if everyone had agreed to a ceasefire. I turned my back to the window, taking in the scene. The two backwards hat bros from the bathroom were sitting with two girls who laughed at everything they said. The soul patch baja guys stood hunched in front of the bar, one shouting in the other's ear to be heard.

For the first time since coming out here I was content. Bryce was busy being Bryce somewhere downtown. I imagined the scene in rapid progression. Bryce looking serious, slurring to a girl. Bryce trying not to spill his drink. Bryce pulling out his iPhone for the thousandth time of the night while everyone else was posing for a photo.

I heaved a heavy sigh, shook my head and pulled out my phone. I went to the back toward the bathroom.

Uber never came.
Still in H'Wood. All Good.
HNY.
Talk tmw.

I had no idea if the text would send. Nor did I care. I'd had my share of New York's bullshit to last a lifetime including the jaded neurotics, professional hustlers and relationships that would collapse before they were built.

Despite my admiration for what he built from scratch, Bryce was a difficult person to like. I planned to give YesYes L.A. one hundred percent and make him proud. But beyond that I didn't owe him anything.

When I got back to my table, Meredith was standing by it, with two shots in her hand.

"You broke the seal, didn't you?"

"Ha-ha," I said. "I have been here for a few hours you know." And then "my second song started playing while I was in there. I pointed to the speaker. Meredith listened for a moment, and then nodded.

"You passed the test," she said. " She handed me another shot. "Look." She pointed to the TV. An aerial shot of Times Square overflowed with people. The night was clear but cold. The camera cut to inside the crowd. A group of drunken shirtless dudes screamed at the camera. Their breath billowed out in the cold like horizontal smokestacks

"Do you miss it?"

"I could break out in hives just looking at it. Not in the slightest."

She linked arms with me, swaying on unsteady feet. "Good to know."

When I first moved to New York I went to celebrate the New Year there, just to say I did. Something about this night looked different from the way I remembered it. Were the cops wearing different uniforms? Was the ball smaller? I couldn't tell. And where was Anderson Cooper and Kathy Griffin's awkward drunken banter?

"Maybe they changed it up," I said out loud.

"Huh?"

"Nothing."

"For as long as I can remember, New Year's Eve has been the same. Like that movie, 'Groundhog Day,'" she said. "I've been here. Working. And when it turns midnight, every jerk in the world wants to kiss."

In Times Square the ball made its slow descent. In New York, and in the bar, came the chants: ten…nine…eight…

I turned to face Meredith. We found ourselves holding hands.

"What do you think this jerk's chances are?"

As the countdown reached two, she smiled, closed her eyes and leaned her head towards mine.

Her lips were warm. She let go of my hands and put her arms around my neck. Seemed like we were in for a good make out session. If everyone in the bar hadn't started screaming, I have no doubt it would have happened.

We opened our eyes and saw blackness.

"What the fuck," someone shouted.

Meredith's loving embrace was now filled with tight panic.

"It's okay," I said. "It's okay."

With chaos all around us, we stood like statues, holding on for dear life. Then the lights came on all at once, as if parents had descended from the basement to stop horny teenage shenanigans from going any further.

The bartender was the coolest head in the room. "Pipe down, everyone. It was just a power outage. Blame it on the rain."

The chaotic fear now turned back to revelry. From the other room, a spontaneous group sang Milli Vanilli's "Blame it on the rain." While close by, a group of people blamed it on the governor and his gray-outs. I wasn't sure what that meant; I didn't keep up with local politics in New York, let alone California.

Meredith smiled at me. "Here's where I make a joke about if you're that great at first kisses I'll need to find out how the rest of you is, oh boy, wow, I'm a bit more tipsy than I thought."

"It's okay. It was still a pretty good joke."

"She straightened up and looked me in the eyes. I'll have you know I pride myself on a being a very good girl."

"I don't doubt it," I said.

She nodded in satisfaction.

The bartender's voice rang out. "Meredith. Break time's over. Tell your boyfriend you need to work."

"Jay. If I give you my number will you promise to call me on that fancy phone of yours?"

"Absolutely. One hundred percent. Yes," I said.

Meredith picked up her tray and walked back to the bar. Without looking back she asked "When?"

"Tomorrow."

CHAPTER 9

If You Don't Like The Effects, Don't Produce The Cause

Rigby's Pianos? Mark Smith here. From Bubbly Lounge in LAX. Fine, thanks. Well, Mr. Rigby, I have a bit of a problem with your self-playing piano, the TR-300. The one with the two hundred mp3's, yes.

It is indeed a great model. Just set it and forget it, as they say. Except...No, it isn't broken. That is to say, not exactly. Let me start from the beginning. Hopefully it'll make sense. I've had the TR-300 for a year now. And it's been fantastic. The travelers come in, order wine and cocktails, and have a moment of relaxation until their flight. Bubbly Lounge tends to stay open longer, you see, ever since I noticed more and more flights were running late.

I remember when I used to fly. I used to be in marketing, you know. Traveled all the time. Racked up frequent flyer miles back when they really meant something. I was always getting upgraded first class. Now it's all but impossible. They keep raising the amount you need, you see. I was always upset that I'd arrive at an airport around ten in the evening for a red eye, and nothing would be open. So when I took over the Bubbly Lounge, I decided to keep it open till two, just like a regular bar. Oh yes, Mr. Rigby, you'd be amazed how much extra I make.

Anyway, the TR-300 was working well enough. Providing background music, unobtrusive, but nice nonetheless. If the patrons weren't doing cartwheels over the selection, no one ever told me to turn it down. Plus it helps pass the time. Better than silence.

Yes, I agree. Two hundred songs is quite generous, Mr. Rigby. But about two months ago, it started acting up. No, it wasn't skipping. It was worse than that.

Well, Mr. Rigby, the fact of the matter is, the piano started playing songs that it wasn't programmed to play.

Mr. Rigby, I have been renting this piano for a full year now. I darn well know what it plays and what it doesn't. I was being charitable when I said two hundred songs was a lot. When you operate a bar that stays open sixteen hours a day, you run through them very quickly, let me tell you.

Well, just listen, and I'll explain. It happened first about two months ago. There was this gentleman. His flight to Ottawa had been delayed for three hours, and he was none too pleased. So I did what I always do and try to make light of it. It's okay, I said. More time for you to relax, don't worry; we have a new Chardonnay, try it. I pick all my wines myself, Mr. Rigby, sometimes even going to visit the wineries. I take pride in my establishment, and you won't find one like this in any other airport.

So this gentleman settles in. He's still fuming, reluctant to let the anger go. But after a glass, he's a bit less uptight. He starts telling me his life story, as they do. And since no one else was there that night—it was around eleven—I didn't mind. He used to be the manager of this band called Pure Prairie League.

No, Mr. Rigby, I hadn't heard of them either. Once upon

a time they had a top ten hit. Back in the seventies, I guess. Anyway, he's telling me how he had managed them during their prime and then ended up in accounting. You know how life goes. You start out in one direction and go off in the next. He's telling me these stories about life on the road with the band. He's on his third glass of Chardonnay mind you, a very good one. And all of a sudden, he jerks up in his seat like a madman. The piano was playing a song by that band, the Pure Prairie League. The man burst in tears right there and then. Couldn't stop. Said he felt like the universe was trying to tell him something. All I could do was stand there, hoping someone else would come in, but also hoping no one else would come in. My establishment is respectable.

What do you mean, why? Mr. Rigby, I own a respectable establishment. No one ever gets visibly drunk in my place. I'm not about to let anyone have too much. If they get on the plane like that, they're most certainly going to end up escorted off or put on a watch list. I don't need the hassle and I don't want to be shut down. Do you have any idea how much the airport liquor license costs?

Mr. Rigby! You know darn well you don't have that song in your repertoire! And yet, here was the piano playing that song, "Hey Aimee," it was called.

No! I wish it were the only instance so I could chalk it up to a fluke. Maybe an mp3 snuck in there by mistake. It could be possible. I don't know how these things work. But Mr. Rigby, this has been going on for two months now. Every day since that night, that gosh darned piano fucks with my patron's emotions, pardon my French. Here's another example: this twenty-year old flight attendant came in and the piano played a Lady Gaga song that reminded him of his ex-girlfriend. Now, I know for a fact that piano did not come with any Lady Gaga songs, especially that particular one. He told me the song only came out this year! And this piano was playing the live version of it, which differed greatly. The poor boy almost missed his flight, he was so upset, and you know that missing a flight is different if you're supposed to be working the flight. Then there was the Indian fella from Bombay, or Mumbai, as they call it now. But he still called it Bombay. He was sitting there quietly, enjoying a Spanish red, and the thing started playing a raga. Mr. Rigby, do you know what a raga is? No? Well, I don't rightly know either, except to say that it's a type of Indian classical music. I ask you, sir, do you have anything by Ravi Shankar in your collection? What? Oh. Of course, I'll hold.

What's that? Yes, I thought so. Why would I make it up? What good would come of that? I have an airport bar to run. I don't have the time for prank calls, Mr. Rigby. Word is spreading through the airport. People are starting to avoid my place because of this darned piano.

This is what I've been trying to tell you, sir! I've had more than thirty incidents of this nature. The latest one is what prompted my call. Well, stop shouting! If you won't calm down, we won't get anywhere. Okay. You see there is a gentleman named Nick Diamonds. No, that's not his real name. His real name is Nick Thorburn; I know because I saw his credit card when he started a tab. He's a musician. What? I don't know. Hell, I don't even like music all that much, to be honest. He was flying to San Francisco to do a show. He was homesick. I don't know where he was coming from, sir. Wine makes more effusive storytelling, but doesn't always provide for explicit details.

Yes, you're right, it's probably wise to refrain from it all together, but some people enjoy it. Mr. Thorburn was telling me how homesick he was and all of a sudden that damned piano changed mid-song, from Total Eclipse of the Heart to something I'd never heard before. And that's when Mr. Thorburn lost it, sir. I mean he lost it completely.

I'll tell you why! Because that piano was playing a demo of a song he had just written that week. He hadn't even recorded it yet! He threatened to sue me, Mr. Rigby. Me! This piano is doing more than acting funny. This piano is deliberately messing with people's emotions. And that is something I can't have, sir. I'm a respectable bar owner and I want to stay that way.

Don't think I haven't thought of that. It's an insult to my intelligence. The fact is I unplugged it three weeks ago. It's still playing. You heard me right. No, I don't know how.

I just want you to come out and remove it and fix it or get it replaced. No, I'm sorry, but a week from now is much too late. My lease for your piano is well up, and I am sure I'm due for a replacement.

I don't care about your schedule, sir! This is an emergency. I will not stand for this kind of problem on my watch any longer. Every time someone comes in I'm afraid they'll leave in tears or anger. No one ever leaves happy, Mr. Rigby, I can tell you that much. The player piano has gone from playing background music to playing songs that are reaching people in places they do not want to be reached. This piano is picking at scabs, do you understand? Old, young, English speaking or foreign, it doesn't matter. Why, one time, that piano played an obscure Cuban folk song. This poor retired couple wanted to turn me in. They were ready to report me to the TSA.

Why? They accused me of implying they were members of the Communist party who were trying to infiltrate us. That's why! You should have seen how upset they were, swearing in Spanish. Not only do I not care about Cuba, I don't speak a lick of Spanish! I could keep going all night with these stories. If this keeps up, my business and my reputation will be ruined.

Wait? What? I'm sorry...hang on a minute. The piano...do you hear it? It's playing something. I can't put my finger on it, but I know that song, somehow. It reminds me of, well, it reminds me of my youth. I grew up in a small town, in the rust belt. I always hated it, but lately I've been wishing I could move back. I don't know why. Maybe it's just how you get when you get older. You realize things weren't so bad back then. In fact, they were pretty good.

You really don't hear it, Mr. Rigby? That's strange. It's louder than ever over here. I can't quite place the melody, but I know I've heard it. Years ago. You know how you know a song but can't place it? Your mind starts searching for the words? When a song gets in your head like this, it becomes an obsession. What is this song? I have to remember. As I said before, music's not my thing, but everyone has a favorite tune, right?

I'm sorry. I have to go. What I mean is, I'll call you back tomorrow. I think. I mean, yes, I will. Of course I will. But wait, what am I talking about? We need to fix this problem, Mr. Rigby, sooner rather than later.

No. No, don't do that. That's crazy. I'm fine. I'll just call you tomorrow.

I'm not sure when. Sometime in the afternoon. Really. Okay. Goodbye, Mr. Rigby. I have to go.

CHAPTER 10
You And Oblivion

When I was twelve, I took a summer course in biology. The teacher gave each of us a worm to dissect. The stinging smell of formaldehyde was so strong the entire class had to leave the room to go outside and get air. One poor girl threw up. The next week, we stuck to the woods, looking for the living instead of opening up the dead. Our teacher walked into a creek, turning over a few stones with care until a marbled salamander slithered out looking like a rock with legs.

The teacher held its wriggling body for all of us to see. "They need to be near moisture and water or they can't live. So when it gets too dry, they go underground to find water and live there."

The salamander's tail separated from its body. "They all have different defense mechanisms. Some have teeth so they can bite predators, while others excrete toxic slime. This little guy dropped his tail so he could run away. He'll grow it back later." She put the salamander on the ground. It scrambled away until it found refuge underneath a brown and green leaf.

Animal life would have made a better theme for this year's course instead of rain. Each semester, I chose a different theme as part of the lesson plan for a high school literature class. The themes made it more exciting for me than choosing from the same roster of books over and over again. The short stories and poems I selected were contemporary. They might as well have been ancient texts. None of them had felt rain.

"Who can tell me how long it's been completely dry?"

They kept their eyes on their devices, ignoring me.

The bell rang. Their heads jerked up and their chips took over. Rows of eyes twitched in hideous spasms, like bugs had burrowed in their sockets and struggled to break free.

Johnny spat out the answer. "The planet's been completely dry for eighteen years now. According to most sources."

The chips forced them to study, learn and respond. The entire class had to look up the answer. It was rare that more than one student answered out loud. The ones who raised their hands got an A+ from me. The rest got B's—the lowest grade allowed by law.

Three years ago, a rising politician came up with an answer to the education crisis. A simple, harmless chip embed would control violence, promote healthy feelings and ensure we would once again lead the world in education. Government-funded research claimed the high crime statistics and student drop out rates would fall by eighty percent or more. Scores of parents protested. The measure was nothing more than population control. Their voices got drowned out by teacher's unions, lobbyists, state-run media and government-led PR campaigns. The bill was passed without opposition.

It's true the success rate of this program was staggering from the start. We led the world in education. The violence rate dropped as well, although nowhere near as much as projected. There were myriad explanations for this, none I believed.

If you asked a teacher instead of a bureaucrat, their point of view was very different. Forced excellence didn't make kids smarter, happier or less self-indulgent. If anything, the students became more fragile. Insufferable. Any criticism, no matter how constructive, was met with hysterics.

I didn't share the news of my retirement with anyone but Mister Scott. He had twenty years in. Each day we'd meet in the break room lamenting our fate. We weren't teachers but babysitters. The new teachers with less than three years on the job had no idea what we were talking about. They were just glad to be employed, glad they weren't held accountable for anyone's success, least of all their own.

"This week a paper was published in the Global Scientific Journal of Ecology. After a four-year study, they believe our climate could be on the cusp of coming back. Just like the ozone layer and the arctic did all those years ago."

"Like we don't already know this," Harold said.

Harold represented all the reasons I wouldn't miss teaching. When he opened his smug mouth I wanted to punch him. Petulant little shit.

"I'm sure you were the first to see it the moment it was posted in whatever forum you read, Harold. But I'm asking if you know the significance."

Harold stared at his device. The chip embed didn't register my inflection as a question.

"If the scientists are right it means storms could come again. It might break up the yellow cloud. Would life as we know it come back?"

Another student spoke up, panic in her voice. "I didn't see anything about the cloud breaking up. Where are you getting this from?"

"I'm speculating."

She sat back in her chair. "You really scared me," she said. "I thought my feed wasn't updating."

"If the scientists are right, someday we'll be able to go outside without our masks. We'll be able to breathe fresh unfiltered air. And see the stars that some of you have never seen in real life."

I stood in front of twenty-six teenaged satellites, all in their own silent orbit. I couldn't remember the last time I saw kids socializing offline.

The final bell rang. I watched the kids file out one last time. I went to processing, filled out a form accepting my final paycheck and a second form acknowledging my correct bank account number for direct deposit. My pension would start the following month. It equaled 80% of my salary. I'd built up a large nest egg from investments; with my frugal nature there was no reason to worry.

The last few stragglers walked stoop-shouldered past playgrounds long since rusted by pollution and neglect, eyes glued to their screens. I gathered my things, slipped on my mask and left the school for the last time.

Mister Scott waited for me outside. He wore a black mask, and had a black motorcycle helmet tucked under his arm.

"What am I going to do now, Stef? Some of these new teachers are only a few years older than the students."

"You're the last of the oldies."

He wrapped me in a bear hug. "I'll miss our talks." Before he left, Mister Scott pointed toward the telephone pole in front of the school. "Even after all this time I still look for crows. Silly, right?"

Big Bomb vaporized a billion people. The mysterious viruses and deadly asthma that came from the yellow cloud killed millions more. Asthma was still the number one cause of death in the western hemisphere, with lung cancer a close second. Masks were now mandatory. We were told they helped, but we were told a lot of things.

One of the strangest side effects that came in the aftermath was a near complete loss of taste. Despite this, eating out still held a great appeal. Gourmet restaurants still charged exorbitant prices. Cooking shows were as popular as ever.

That night, I decided to splurge on dinner at the most expensive restaurant in the city. I couldn't remember the last time I'd gone out to eat, let alone called to make reservations. I picked up my device, looked up the number for Julia's, pressed a button and waited.

"Julia's, may I help you?"

"I know it's last minute but is there any chance you have an opening for one person this evening?"

"Well," the man said, stretching out the word. "I sincerely doubt it, but let me check. We do fill up months in advance, as you know. I'm not seeing anything," he said.

"Oh. Well, that's okay—"

"Hang on," he said with excitement. "We just had a cancellation. It's your lucky night. The thing is I can seat you in The Rain Bar at 8. Is that okay?"

"That's just fine," I said.

"Excellent," the man said. "I'll put you in the Rain Bar at 8. Please arrive a few minutes early so we can check your mask."

Julia's was a throwback to a more glamorous time. The dining area was large and inviting. On most nights, jazz musicians took up the bandstand. Several smaller dining areas made for more intimate surroundings. There was a private dining area made to look like an English gentlemen's club that could be rented for private parties. It featured a roaring fireplace, a fussy chandelier and mahogany overstuffed chairs.

Rumors swirled that there was a special dining area reserved for heads of state. No one knew what the decor looked like. A former teacher who'd inherited a fortune from his parents and was a regular at Julia's once told us it was an elegant room where diplomats, presidents and ambassadors could be whisked in and out at a moment's notice through a hidden exit.

Some of the more sensational newspapers described the door to the dining room as being impact proof. The interior supposedly outfitted with signal scramblers, an arsenal of weapons, even an escape hatch leading to either a modern fallout shelter or spaceship.

I was more interested in the Rain Room, one of three unique bars at Julia's. The Quick One was just inside the foyer. It didn't have a full menu but served the country's best cocktails from an award-winning mixologist who was also a chemist and doctor. In other words, if you were suffering from yellow cloud sickness, and needed a tetanus shot, he'd give you a booster, serve you an iodine chaser and follow it with the best Manhattan ever made.

The main bar was much larger and horseshoe shaped. One side had an unobstructed view of the dining area and bandstand. Those who sat on the other side could still see the show from the flat screen monitors, or be just as content to enjoy the full menu and the sight of a vast number of bottles legally imported or smuggled in from all corners of the globe.

As its name implied, the Rain Bar's crowning achievement was its entryway: A long corridor affixed with sprinklers to approximate the feeling of light rain. They spent a full year developing the fragrance.

The Rain Bar was by far the most popular room at Julia's. Reservations were all but impossible. Some of the richest men and women in the world were known to tip the head server thousands of dollars just to walk through the corridor and experience rain.

I'd read all the glowing reviews about the menu. If everything I put in my mouth didn't taste metallic I'm sure I would have anticipated it more. But at least everything would look amazing.

I walked the six blocks to Julia's. It was still sweltering. I took my time so as not to break into a sweat. The streets were dirty and crowded. Security guards, both human and robotic, stood on every corner. The robotic guards scanned retinas in nanoseconds while the human guards checked for body language.

Across the street, a robot guard held a vagrant in a vice grip around the neck, instructing him to drop his weapon in a variety of different languages. The vagrant held a large knife. He screamed something incomprehensible. The words that came from his mouth weren't the byproduct of Z4 or Domo or Salspark or any of the other designer drugs that had taken the place of pot and heroin when the poppies and marijuana plants died out. He was saying something in a foreign tongue, one I didn't recognize. The more he screamed, the harder the robot clamped his neck. I hurried past, forcing myself to look away. I didn't know the story and didn't want to jump to conclusions. The robots had a higher success rate in stopping crime than the human police, with fewer errors. Watching them work did nothing to reassure me. I hoped the robot would find the right language in time.

The sky turned chartreuse as somewhere behind the yellow cloud the sun disappeared under the horizon. I arrived at Julia's ten minutes early. A bouncer blocked the door. When I stopped and turned to go in, he didn't move. His weathered face had seen more than its share of fights. He was built like a ton of bricks. His facemask looked metallic.

"I have a reservation for eight," I asked.

"I.D." he demanded. I took it out of my purse. He scanned it with a device about the size of a credit card.

"You must be naturally photogenic," he smiled.

He opened the door, stepping to one side to let me in. "Wait till the door seals behind you before pressing the gold button. Have a great evening."

The door closed behind me, shutting out the noise. The

bouncer returned to his position blocking my view. I pressed the gold button and waited.

The door opened and a man wearing a white dinner jacket beckoned me in. He had a thin old-fashioned mustache, curled up on either side. His fingernails were immaculate half moons. He smelled of lime-scented aftershave. While he wasn't what I would have called attractive, his demeanor was pleasing. He couldn't have been more than twenty-three but had the air of sophistication reserved for middle-aged men.

"So good to see you Mrs.—"

"Miss."

"Of course," he nodded. "My apologies. Welcome to Julia's. Let me show you to our coat check."

"Who'd wear a coat in this heat?"

"The coat check is where we take your mask. We still refer to it as a coat check because it sounds, well—"

"Less sterile?"

"More glamorous," he offered. "If you'll just step this way. Julia's is the most hygienic restaurant in the nation. We take as much care in our environment as we do our cuisine."

I followed him down a narrow candlelit corridor. He turned to face me and gestured to his left. A woman in a see-through HAZMAT suit stood behind a glass window with doors on either side, the kind where one could pass objects safely.

"Good evening," she said. "If I could just have your mask," she said.

I hesitated.

The man in the white dinner jacket nodded. "It's okay," he said. "You will not need it upstairs."

"Will I get it back?"

"Why would you want it back?" The woman in the clear HAZMAT suit shook her head and laughed. The man cleared his throat, cutting her short.

"Please forgive Suzy. We're still training her. This is your first time with us?"

My cheeks felt hot.

"Suzy, instead of being flippant, why don't you explain to this beautiful woman Julia's policy," he said.

Suzy did her best to seem more formal. "All of our guests are issued with brand new A3s as a thank you for their patronage." She opened her side of the window, shoved a piece of paper and pen inside and shut it. "If you could please sign and initial where indicated and place it back in the door along with your mask, we'll be happy to issue you an A3."

Masks ranged in styles and effectiveness. There were bargain basement ones that protected against some elements of the yellow cloud and very little else. Others came with designer labels that increased the spectrum of protection. At the top of the list were A3 coverlets. These shielded the wearer against everything recognized by the CDC as being harmful. They came with a three-year, no questions asked warranty. They cost the equivalent of three month's teacher's salary.

I signed and initialed, removed my mask and placed it in the bin. Suzy took the mask and disposed of it. She presented me with a flat container. Inside were rows of A3s. "What color would you like?"

They had every color imaginable. I'd always worn a white mask.

The man spoke up. "Most of our first time guests choose white or black. Those colors tend to go with everything."

I looked at the spectrum. I was tired of white and didn't want black. Hot pink or neon green weren't my style at all.

"I'd like that one, please."

"Grey with a hint of purple. How regal. Are you quite sure you've never dined with us before?"

Suzy slipped the unwrapped mask through the door. I took

it from her, put it in my purse and followed the man in the white dinner jacket to the elevator.

"Not too much farther," he smiled.

The elevator slid open with a ding. He held it for me, waved a plastic card over the reader, and pressed the top button.

"Maybe someday the clouds will clear and we'll have a view to go along with the décor," he sighed.

The door elevator slid open and a woman in a smart black dress greeted us.

"Hello, it's so nice to see you," she said. I couldn't place her accent. East European, I guessed. "Your seat in the Rain Bar is ready."

There was a small aquarium next to the elevator with fish of all colors floating lazy in the crystal clear water. The hallway led to the very large dining room where seats were packed with diners. Servers glided past, silent and efficient. The decor was white with the exception of the carpet, which was light grey with white and purple patterns.

The woman stood back as if taking in the scene with me. After a beat she set off with determination. I stumbled, trying to keep up with her pace. It had been a while since I'd worn heels.

We passed the horseshoe bar where two-dozen people sat drinking and eating. The smell of garlic, steak, salmon and butter hung rich in the air. Ice cubes clinked in glasses filled with brown liquor. I looked at the diners without making eye contact. Not like I would have recognized any of them. They could have been the cast of whatever new blockbuster movie was out and it wouldn't have made any impression on me.

On the bandstand, a four piece played quiet jazz. A voluptuous blonde singer wore a silver-sequined dress and elbow-length satin gloves. She sang a song through an antique microphone I suspected was there for decoration. I didn't recognize the tune but let the song wash over me.

During my last year of teaching, I tried connecting with the kids on their level. I'd watch a few hours of Music Today or some teenaged show like "Girl's Strange Worlds" or "Dana's World" to understand them better. I'd try to equate a poem or short story with the latest hip-hop song or plot of some inane show. Far from impressed, the kids were annoyed I was trying to keep up with "their" culture.

Just as well. Their music videos were over-sexualized, the plots to their shows insipid. After two weeks, I gave up.

"Great music." I hadn't felt this grown up in years.

She shouted over her shoulder. "Julia's has an in-house songwriter." We turned left. Then right. "I'll meet you on the other side. Take your time."

She walked around the entrance to the Rain Room.

I was facing a black narrow corridor lit in a dim glow. The smell of rain was intoxicating. When the first drop hit my skin, I recoiled. The last substance to rain down from the sky came from nuclear fallout. I pushed the feeling away.

I was no longer in a narrow corridor, but surrounded by a grey mist, a low-hanging cloud of tangible sadness. Tears flowed as waves of memory came over me. I held out an unsteady hand to grab the railing. Fifteen feet above, the ceiling was painted in grey, looking like three-dimensional clouds. Was it a hologram or were they real?

I touched the walls on either side of me and felt the chill. Underneath the sound of rain I could hear the faintest hum. Drops hit a puddle on the floor, causing a ripple effect. The rain caused shivers on my skin, soaking into my dress.

Without warning, a new memory appeared. I was sixteen. I had just lost my virginity to Eric, the first boy I ever loved. We had fumbling nervous sex in the renovated attic of my house while my parents were out playing golf.

I wasn't sure what was supposed to happen or how it would

feel. He came. I didn't. Neither of us knew what to expect or what to do when it was over. After he finished, he took the condom off, unsure of where to throw it away. I pointed to the small powder room and told him to wrap it in toilet paper first so my parents wouldn't find it in the wastebasket.

When Eric returned, he apologized, and then apologized for apologizing. I was numb and wondered if that was normal. Were rites of passage supposed to be this bewildering?

It was summer. The windows were open. A sudden breeze blew away the stifling attic heat, bringing with it the sound of thunder. We hurried to get dressed before my parents got back. We were sitting on the porch just as the first giant drops fell and the breeze picked up and lightning flashed and thunder shuddered closer. The rain fell harder, raging its way into the sewer. I put my head on his lap.

After a few minutes he asked "What now?" I didn't answer.

We stayed together for three more months. We had sex a half dozen more times. It never got any better. Whatever we started with wasn't there any more. One day we both blurted out the same thing—it's not working. And then we laughed, relieved. Being a teenager was hard enough without having adult conversations.

It had been years, decades really, since I thought of Eric. The memories were so distant; they felt like someone else's. The uneasy feeling passed, and with it came a sense of peace. I listened to the rain, inhaled once more, and then hurried to the other side of the corridor, where the woman was waiting, wine menu clutched in her hands.

She raised her eyebrows. "So?"

"How long was I in there?"

"We once had a guest spend three hours in there. Had to send someone in to talk him into going to his table. After that, we implemented a half hour rule. Any longer and we start charging a fee." She smiled. "You didn't even come close. Ten minutes or so."

"It felt like—"

"Hours. Everything here does."

"Must be great when you go on break."

The woman laughed. "This is precisely why we're not allowed to go in the Rain Room on breaks."

She showed me to my seat at the bar. The space was smaller than the horseshoe bar and half-empty. She showed me a hook where I hung my purse, snatched the napkin from the bar and draped it over my lap.

"Bon appétit."

I scanned the drink menu. The prices weren't as outrageous as I expected. After some back and forth, the bartender suggested a cocktail: Lillet Vive. Made with Lillet, tonic and cucumber with a strawberry garnish.

The menu proclaimed all vegetables, flowers, fruit and herbs were grown in-house and meats and fish were responsibly farmed or grown in non-toxic pastures and labs. My mouth watered.

The bartender presented the drink with a flourish. I smelled herbs, earth and sweetness.

"Perfect pick-me-up after a sudden rain." A man about my age sat at the end of the bar, sipping the same drink. He raised his glass. I did the same.

"May I join you? I hate to drink and dine alone. Do you mind?"

"Why not?"

He asked the bartender the same question. The bartender tapped a screen to see if any large parties would be sitting there.

"It's all single diners for the next three hours. Be my guest."

The man sat next to me. His hair was dark black and straight. His eyes were grey.

"So what brings you here besides the rain and spectacular drinks?"

"I'm celebrating."

"Exciting. What are you celebrating?"

I sipped my drink again. "It's the end of a long ten-year career as a high school teacher. I realize it's not as exciting as a promotion or big stock market win."

"When one door closes, and another one opens, it's always a big deal. Congratulations. Teaching is a noble profession."

"Not with kids today."

"Kids today," he said, in an old man's voice. "Get off my lawn."

When my laughter died down, our eyes met. I looked at my menu.

"If I may make a few suggestions—"

I put myself in the stranger's hands. He said to start with the day boat scallops with pea tendrils, followed by the steamed trout with tomato aspic, and follow with lemon sorbet.

"All of those are in season," he said. "Remember when we called it farm-to-table? Now it's lab-to-table. Or aquarium-to-table."

"Don't remind me," I groaned. "So, we've established I'm a teacher. What do you do?"

"Remember the three r's? Reading, writing, 'rithmetic? Mine's more the three C's."

I snapped my fingers. "Cosmetology, comedy and carpentry."

"Close."

The day boat scallops arrived. Despite being unable to taste them, they smelled sweet, and were a nice match to what I remembered peas tasted like. Earthy and grassy. They were finished with butter and white pepper. I did my best to enjoy them, but once I put them in my mouth it was all I could do not to gag.

The man didn't seem to notice and ate with the air of a professional hedonist.

"How is everything?" the bartender asked.

"As good as ever, Richard." He pointed to our glasses. "Can we get another round?"

"Not for me," I said.

"Oh but you must. You're celebrating," he said. "Don't worry. It's on me."

I sat up straight. "Listen, it's very kind but—"

He waved me away. "Please. I imposed on you. It's the least I can do."

I nodded. "Thank you. It's good to meet new people."

"Especially ones who are of drinking age, and not students. My name's Jack."

"Stephanie. Call me Stef. Everyone does."

We shook hands.

The drinks came, and he sipped. He nodded to the Rain Room. "What'd you think? How many emotions did you go through?"

"Too many," I answered. "Sadness. Warmth. Mourning. Nostalgia. Love. Some memories were vivid. Others weren't even full memories, but flashes of them. It was intense. And after a time, I was ready to leave it. Like it had provided enough. I felt like some of the darker things I'd been hiding in my head had been washed away and replaced with, well...." I searched for the words. "New information."

"Sounds like you're describing a baptism."

"You don't believe me?"

"Oh yes I do," he said. "Transference and recalling memory. You might say it was built for that."

"And that rain. I don't know if it's a hologram thing, or just the mist, but the temperature seemed to change with the feelings."

"Oh it's real, all right. The rain and mist play a important role."

"Sounds like you know a lot about it."

Jack started to say something but I couldn't hear his voice. His words were swallowed by an ever-growing noise, like someone was turning up the knob the wrong way on an amplifier. The noise was deafening. His eyes left mine and looked behind me. Before I could turn to look, he was shouting. I shook my head, not understanding. He grabbed my wrist hard.

"We've got to get out of here," he screamed in my ear.

I looked behind me. The rain room was crackling with electrical sparks. My lungs filled with heavy metallic smoke.

I grabbed my purse with one hand while he dragged me along by the other. We headed towards an unmarked door I hadn't noticed before. The ceiling fell in large chunks all around us. Our bartender was lying face down over the bar, blood spilling from his head. The entire building shook like we were in an earthquake.

We went through the door. It stopped closing midway.

"The hatch won't work unless it's sealed," he yelled. "Help me."

We pushed on the door. With a great effort it closed, blocking out the worst of the noise.

"What the hell."

Jack touched a sensor, revealing a control panel. He entered a six-digit code and punched a blue button. Elevator doors closed. He pulled me to his body, arms wrapped tight. I didn't have time to protest. We were free falling now. Heart in throat, pulse racing, I buried my face in Jack's chest. My first night of freedom in ten years and I was going to die. What a waste.

The elevator ground to a halt, stopping before any impact. Momentum threw us against the ceiling. Then we landed on the floor with a crash. I lay in a startled heap, groaning.

Jack sprang to his feet. "Can you get up?"

"I don't know," I said. "My shoulder hurts."

He bent over, examining me. "It's dislocated. This is going to hurt. Sorry."

He put his foot on my shoulder, tugged at my arm with great force. My shoulder popped back in place, sucking the air out of me. He pulled me up, pried open the doors. My eyes couldn't adjust to the darkness. We were in an underground garage. He ran ahead, dragging me by the arm that wasn't throbbing. I coughed. My lungs were still burning from the metallic smoke.

At the sound of an explosion I hurled myself on the ground, covering my head, a reflex built on a decade's worth of high school fire and bomb drills. Jack yanked me back up to keep running.

"Come on," he shouted.

The explosion happened at street level far above us. It still echoed overhead.

We came upon a large black vehicle. He opened the passenger door and shoved me in. A second later he was behind the wheel.

Jack touched a button and entered another six-digit code. We went screaming through the garage in the darkness. Light from the vehicle's dashboard cast an orange and blue glow on his face. I lay on the seat, wiping sweat from my forehead.

"Where are we going?"

Jack punched a few buttons on the dashboard. A map of the city appeared. He zoomed out to show the surrounding states. The entire region was covered in red. The dashboard blinked. He touched a button and a man's voice answered.

"Go ahead, Jack."

"How bad?"

The voice on the speaker exhaled. "We don't know yet. There were multiple cities hit in the Northeast. We know it wasn't nuclear.

"Same group as before?"

"Yes," the voice replied. "Arrived too late to stop it but this time we got them all," the voice paused. "We're absolutely sure of it."

I was pinned against the plush leather seat, unable to sit up. I didn't think it was possible for a land vehicle to go this fast. As a kid I'd been to the amusement park many times, but no ride ever matched the speed of this car. I shut my eyes, pretending we weren't moving. Everything was still pitch black outside the windows.

"What the hell is going on," I asked.

Jack shushed me, hands gripping the steering wheel.

"Are you absolutely sure we got them all?" Jack demanded.

"Positive. They launched the code on an open line. If we'd known what to look for at the outset we could have prevented it."

Jack stared at the map in red, saying nothing.

"We traced them. They were celebrating when we got there. Just like you thought, there were less than two hundred left."

"What about their chips?"

"All but one. A guard shot himself in the head before we could stop him. We might still be able to recover it. We've already scanned the others. Some very interesting information is coming back."

"What's the civilian toll?"

The voice paused. "We won't have a true number for days. It looks like a hundred thousand. But it could be more."

"Jack," I said. "I feel weak."

"Julia's?"

"Closed," the voice said.

"What about the delivery?"

The other voice paused. "Can't say. If it did, we might know as soon as tomorrow.

"Okay."

"Jack," the voice said. "They were hiding in plain sight, too. Like you said."

The voice broke off. Jack punched a button, took his hands from the wheel. With a deep sigh he leaned back in his seat. He opened the glove compartment, took out a bottle and handed it to me.

"Sip this slowly. Drink it all. You'll need it."

I did as I was told. The liquid was cool. But when it hit my stomach, it turned warm. With each sip the nausea receded. Jack closed his eyes.

"Please tell me what is happening."

"When I told you my job involves the three C's, I meant Climatology, Computers and Anti-Cyber-Terrorism. I realize that's more like C, C, A, but I was flirting."

"What was that about Julia's and delivery?"

"I'll explain when we get there."

"Get where?"

"Arranmore."

I looked at him. "Which is where, exactly?"

"An island just off the coast of Ireland."

I sat up straight. "Are you crazy? Take me home."

Jack touched the dashboard, bringing up a monitor. He hit a few buttons. A BBC news report came on screen. I saw tanks rolling through downtown Baltimore, entire city blocks ablaze. The scene cut to New York, where international guards stood in front of Wall Street. The scene cut again to groups of rescue workers and police in HAZMAT suits sifted through the rubble, pulling bodies from underneath bricks and warped steel beams. Firemen sprayed a building engulfed in flames.

"What home?" Jack said.

The vehicle sped along in darkness. He touched a button and I reclined. I put my hand on the seat. It was warm to the touch.

"We'll stay underground and then break the surface when we can. Hopefully we'll be crossing the Atlantic in an hour. There's a blanket under your seat. If you get hungry, there's food. The bathroom's in the back," he touched his watch, bringing up a holographic map. "We should arrive in six hours." His smile was wan. "I know it's a lot to take in, but try not to be afraid, Stef. It'll do you no good, anyhow."

It was the first time I noticed his slight lilting accent. His eyes were emotionless. Jack explained we were traveling in an underground highway. There were a few different tunnels that had been constructed after Big Bomb.

Like most government initiatives after the Big Bomb, the project was incomplete. The tunnels began along the eastern coast and got as far as the Midwest before funding was cut.

Jack set our course for the southernmost tip of North Carolina.

"Wake me when we hit the surface. The car is on self-driving mode. I'll get our bearings before we hit the ocean."

He lay back on the seat.

"You'll forgive me, Stef, if this sounds like a silly thing to say considering the circumstances. But it's really a shame you didn't get to try the dessert. I'll miss those lemon sorbets."

Jack yawned and fell into a deep sleep.

I tried to sleep but couldn't. I got up and explored the vehicle. It was black on black, much larger than I expected. It reminded me of an ultra-modern take on an old hippie van, but sleeker, and more high tech.

In addition to our seats, the vehicle had room for four more people. I assumed those seats would convert to single beds as well. Further back, a table was stowed horizontally along the vehicle's side. I found a door that slid open, revealing a toilet and small stand up shower. There was a sink outside the bathroom as well as a two-burner tabletop stove and small refrigerator next to it. It was all so tidy and efficient. Perfect for a sight seeing tour.

I found sandwiches in plastic wrap and several bottles in the fridge. I took a sandwich and one of the bottles, pulled the table out and made myself at home.

Whatever Jack had given me to drink cured my travel sickness and made me downright ravenous. It didn't help that the portions were small at Julia's. I hadn't even gotten to the second course. The sandwich looked like it was tomato, basil, mozzarella and chicken. It tasted like nothing. I sipped from the bottle discovering it was white wine.

The vehicle raced along the underground tunnels, lit by sparse overhead lights. Every so often it would weave left or right through a different passage. The darkness stretched for miles ahead. We flew past a sign that read Spartanburg: 50M. I sat looking out in the space just in front of the high beams expecting something to happen. Nothing did.

The northeast was devastated. My city was in ruins. That meant no more school. No more kids. No more Mister Scott. My apartment: gone. The bank where I kept my savings: gone. All of it obliterated. The sea of dashboard readouts flashed and glowed. I lay back, letting the vehicle lull me into an uneasy sleep.

There was a stillness. An abandoned street. The lights were dim. It was a familiar street. One from childhood. I was walking. The darkness shifted. I was alone but not afraid. My feet were bare. Next thing I knew, I was standing in rushing water. A boom came from the distance. Was it thunder?

I woke with a start. The vehicle had broken to surface level. We sped along a forgotten highway. When I was ten, my parents took me to North Carolina as a young child. We visited Civil War sites in Boone and Winston-Salem. I was terrified of the reenactments in the once battlefields that were now flower-dotted meadows. Men dressed in grey and blue, the smell of gunpowder stinging my nose. How quaint it all seemed now, to think of a war where not even six hundred fifty thousand people died and almost all of them soldiers. The Big Bomb took out more than a billion. Who knows how many died last night?

We were on a long stretch of crumbling concrete, asphalt, potholes, racing past barren trees, abandoned highways and rusted skeleton cars. The sole indicator we were in North Carolina was the red clay.

I tried moving my arm. My shoulder ached. I clenched and unclenched my hand, then touched Jack's elbow. He woke like he, too, had been ripped from a dream. Without looking at me, he touched the dashboard, checked the weather, the pollution and radiation levels, and scanned some headlines.

"I could use some coffee," he said. "Would you mind making it?"

I went to the back of the vehicle, found the actual water bottles I had missed in the underground darkness, put on an electric kettle and found the packets of instant coffee.

While the water heated, Jack checked the weather pollution and radiation levels. They were no different from yesterday. While it was reassuring to know whatever happened last night wasn't a nuclear bomb, as Jack suspected, the Northeast took the brunt of the damage. D.C. and all parts south were spared. So far, no one had taken credit, which was a good sign. No one could take credit if all of them were dead.

"The scale of this destruction was a ruse," he said.

"A ruse?" I said "You mean they just killed a few hundred thousand or million people as a slight of hand?"

"That's exactly what I'm telling you," he said.

"Why?"

The dashboard beeped. Jack looked at the indicator, frowning. "I was afraid of this. Sit down and strap in tight."

Jack touched the dashboard and brought up the trunk's camera. I saw two gigantic vehicles behind us. They were black rusted semi trucks, but gigantic. They covered a lot of ground and were gaining on us.

A flash came from one of the trucks. Jack pushed a button and was now in full control of the car. He swerved just in time to avoid a missile. He tapped another button. The vehicle shot ahead. I gripped the armrests and swore under my breath.

Despite our thrust of speed, the two vehicles kept gaining. We came upon an intersection. Jack swerved left at the last second. We headed towards an above ground tunnel. The trucks unleashed a rapid burst of gunfire.

"Hang on," Jack yelled. He floored the vehicle. We were halfway through when I heard metal and glass crunching. We'd cleared the tunnel just as a fireball belched its way towards us. He sped on, eyes staring at the rearview camera. He didn't slow down for another mile.

"Self-driving patrol trucks. The highways down here are still no-go zones. They were second gen by the looks of it. Thank Jesus for out of date AI," he said.

We kept up our pace past Wilmington. I smelled the ocean before I saw it. The green waves crashed hard on the sand. It was low tide. The yellow cloud stretched all the way out to the horizon.

We drove on to the beach, coming to a rolling stop.

Jack pushed my legs back, opening the glove compartment. "Hurry up and drink two bottles of the stuff I gave you last night," Jack said.

Jack showed me how to strap into the seat using a special attachment. He checked the ocean levels on the dashboard, punched in a code, and the vehicle hummed. I felt the wheels retract underneath us. A sort of hydrofoil descended in its place. I drank the bottles down, gagging on all that liquid.

The vehicle screamed over the water. The sound was deafening. The thrust was so powerful it made last night's top speed seem like a lazy Sunday drive. Both of us were thrown against our seats as the vehicle raced across the Atlantic like a skipping stone.

After forty-five minutes, Arranmore appeared on the horizon, a faded grey lighthouse welcoming us. My body ached from holding on to the seat handles. It felt as if my ears would never stop ringing.

Jack slowed the vehicle as we reached the coast. He brought the wheels down, driving us on the beach to the lighthouse. It was late afternoon. The island looked deserted. We left the vehicle, making our way on unsteady legs to the lighthouse door. Jack knocked twice. After a long minute, a man opened it.

"Jesus," he said. "Thought we'd lost you for a moment." He turned to me. "And who might this be? Never mind. Come in out of the chill. Old man's waiting."

Once upstairs, a man greeted us. His hair was dark grey. He wore a heavy fisherman's sweater. I recognized his voice as the one who spoke to Jack through the dashboard.

"Welcome home," he said, shaking Jack's hand. "I'm sure Jack had a reason for bringing you. We'll get to that shortly. Name's Owen Jones. They call me Commander, but it's more of a nickname than a real title. We don't go for that sort of hierarchy any more." When I didn't answer, he took a closer look. "Think she's in shock, poor girl. Let's have the medic look after you."

He led me by my good arm to a man with a brown beard who wore horn-rimed glasses. The man made me sit on an operating table. He poked and prodded. I winced.

"Not shock. Just exhaustion. As for that shoulder, seen worse. Just need a sling for a week or so, is all."

"I feel nauseous," I said.

"Your body went through hyper-travel. Nausea's normal. It'll pass after you acclimate to this time zone," the medic said.

Owen cleared his throat. "We should know if the program worked in a few hours, Jack."

I looked at the two of them. "I have a right to know what's going on."

"She doesn't know, Jack?"

"We were there when it happened. Beyond that, no."

"She witnessed it?

"She was the last one to walk through."

Owen looked at me. "Were you really? In that case, you will be of great assistance to us." He paused. "But I trust you understand, everything I tell you must be kept in confidence."

I managed a nod.

"Very well," he said. "A terrorist group planned on wiping out the world yesterday. Based on Jack's intelligence, we stopped them."

"Why would they want to do that? There's nothing left to wipe out. The countries are still rebuilding. America isn't any further along."

Owen took off his glasses and polished them with a handkerchief. "Oh, it could have been America, or Japan or Brazil. We only found out they chose America three hours before it happened. It was unfortunate we couldn't stop them."

"Wait I minute." I pointed at Jack. "He said you had something to do with climatology and computer science and cyber security."

Owen said: "For the past three years, the C.C.C.'s mission to do two things: Stop global terrorism, and reverse the effects of yellow cloud. We monitored a small but very effective terrorist organization made up of eco-terrorists and the last remaining religious zealots in the Middle East who made an uneasy but very effective partnership. Both had the same goals, you see."

"First I've heard of it. No one's claimed responsibility for any attacks for years."

"Of course not," Owen said. "If they had, it would have shown their intention."

I stared at him.

"Remember the London attacks a few months ago?" Jack said.

"Of course. What little of London was left was wiped out. Only ten thousand remain. It was senseless."

"On the contrary," Owen said. "It was deliberate."

"But why, damn you." My cheeks flushed.

"They wanted to destroy the program."

Owen told me the chief architects of Big Bomb were a group of religious terrorists who believed that only the complete and total destruction of the planet would cause Armageddon. They spent years creating the Big Bomb. And while it caused the worst holocaust the world had ever known, the world persevered. The remaining zealots went underground to plot their return.

Democracies pledged this would never happen again. Out of that pledge, the C.C.C. was born. A hand-selected group whose goals were two-fold. Stop the zealots. And eradicate the yellow cloud.

The international organization took its time. A few years were spent in covert training. Then at a joint government conference, the leaders of the remaining nations announced their initiative. They showed off simulators that would test the computer programs for accuracy. They believed a program would be operational in less than two years.

The announcement was a very loud false flag meant to ferret out the terrorists' locations. It wasn't until six months ago when the London incident occurred that the C.C.C. finally got a fix on their location. That's when they learnt about the other groups involved.

"Religious fundamentalists, eco-terrorists and hackers were working together." Jack said. "The group diversified. While the religious fundamentalists worked on bomb building, the hackers and eco-terrorists worked on a program to increase the yellow cloud's toxicity"

"And prevent our own program from launching," Owen said. "That last bit certainly gave us a start. They'd been watching us, you see. Through back channels. We weren't as clever as we thought. But they still hit the wrong target."

I stood up from the operating table. My feet were unsteady. "The computer program was in London?"

"No," Jack said. "The server was in London. We'd migrated the program to a different location by then."

The London server was set away from everything, in the outskirts of the city. It was meant to look like a disused server. They even went as far as to construct the building out of rusted metal. But the hackers saw through it, of course. There was way too much energy production for a building that was supposed to be abandoned. The most rudimentary infrared scopes could detect it.

The C.C.C. knew it had to be smarter after London got hit. So they designated three servers where they could migrate the program like a shell game.

"Unlike London, we hid them all in plain sight," Jack said. "We picked three major cities, constructed three servers, and hid them in the least obvious spot.

"Ruby's is in Brazil. Julia's wass in America. And Perl's is in Japan," Owen said.

My mouth dropped. "The servers were all in restaurants."

"That's right, Jack nodded. "And they were the most attractive feature, too."

"Rain Rooms," Owen said.

I vomited in a bedpan on the nearby table. The medic rushed over and gave me another bottle to drink.

"We thought they were on to us. So we migrated to Julia's from Perl," Owen said. Then we received intelligence they planned to hit the restaurant the same day. We had no choice."

The program's migration progress had read ninety-nine percent for the past month. Sometimes it stayed that way even though it was completely migrated. Other times it meant the program failed and you'd have to restart. Jack had experienced the frustration many times before on much less important projects. When he learned the terrorist group planned to attack Julia's, he made the decision to launch the program. At the same time, Owen was ensuring the terrorist groups were taken out once and for all.

"Once the program launched, we had to disable the worldwide internet as a necessary precaution," Owen said.

"The kids," I said. "Their brain chips."

"There will be some chaos, for those who lived, I grant you. But it'll be short-lived compared to what would have happened."

Jack smiled. "Perhaps when all is said and done, you'll reconsider teaching. The world needs good teachers. And you're now the only other person who knows the truth. Moreover, the server passed along all its information to you."

I started to say something, but he held up a hand to stop them from talking.

We spent the rest of the afternoon in the lighthouse watching the international news broadcasts. The channels reported new developments as they came in. More people died than was first reported. No one took credit for the attack. The American president vowed a swift and decisive end to this carnage to ensure no lives would be lost again on such a grand scale.

"Easy enough for him to say, now," Owen snorted. "We've

fixed it for him. I'm sure he'll be only too happy to take the credit if he can."

Daylight turned to night. We drank stout and ate a thick stew for dinner. The weather was damp, almost cool for the first time in ages.

"There's a safe house a few miles inland," Owen said. "You should go there and wait for instructions," he said. "Bring the lady as well."

I listened to them talking but nothing registered. I was beyond jet lagged. My eyes were heavy. My brain felt swollen.

We left the lighthouse, got in the vehicle and drove for twenty minutes in bumpy silence until a farmhouse appeared, its small front porch light glowing in otherwise total darkness.

Jack took me inside the drafty house. A small fire died in the corner of the main room. It was warm and inviting. Jack led me to a room with a bed, table and chair. An orchard stood just outside the window. The farm had milk from genetically modified sheep. There were chickens and a vegetable garden. The farmers could always use extra help, he said. There were neighboring farmhouses with fifteen children in total. On this small remote island, it was easy to hide them when authorities came by. None had chip embeds. Though their mothers and fathers taught them as best they could, their education stopped at the American equivalent to eighth grade. The kids were good, and strong and smart. They thirsted for knowledge. Without speaking, I undressed, got under the covers and closed my eyes.

I don't know how long I slept. It looked like early morning when I woke. Grey. Silent. The blanket smelled of horses. I kept my eyes closed and lay quite still, listening for sounds of life. There was no Jack or Owen. No farmers or kids. Just silence.

Then something peculiar happened. I heard a sound coming from outside. Strange, yet familiar and comforting. With the sound came a sweet fragrance through the half open windows, and the steady beat of a song I'd known all my life, as clear as if I'd never forgotten it. I didn't even have to open my eyes to know for certain. Raindrops are unmistakable.

CHAPTER 11
I'd rather be right here

Reginald sat at the opposite end of the salesman's desk, half-heartedly flipping through a large three-ring binder of carpet swatches. Different thicknesses. Different colors. Orange for the adventurous type, beige for the neutral personality, animal patterns, abstract patterns, all kinds of patterns.

"Thing is, it's not about price. No, really," the salesman insisted. "At Carpet World, the only thing that matters is quality. Other guys, they'll sell you a Persian rug for thousands, just because it's thousands. Or they'll sell you a liability because it's on discount. They don't care about quality. But we do."

"Mm," Reginald said. He picked up another binder.

On Monday, a friendly hand on his shoulder signaled dismissal. Twenty-five years on the job. Dismissed without warning. He'd hoped to get five more years out of the place. It would have been a full decade of working to keep his mind off poor Greta, rest her soul.

She was his heart and soul. Without her, he let the job encompass him, pointless as it was. County Control Officer. It was all but a token title. There were no counties, let alone countries to control. It was all the same entity now.

The day after dismissal he decided if it was time to redecorate.

That ugly brown rug had to go. It was faded and stained by years of foot traffic. He thought if I'm spending more time at home, might as well make it look nice. So here he was at Carpet World.

The salesman kept talking. Reginald kept flipping. At last he found a plain dark green color that reminded him of pine. Seemed like a good a fit as any.

"This one," he said, pointing.

"A fine choice, sir. We've never yet had to make good on our refunds, mind you. But should you require a different rug, for whatever reason, we will replace it within sixty days."

To Reginald's surprise, Carpet World installed it the same day. He stood in his socks, staring at his forest floor. Greta would not have liked it. Not for a month or so. Then she would have claimed it was her idea to choose green. He smiled, remembering. Then a grief washed over him. To overcome the feeling, Reginald shuffled out of his apartment and moved his long thin frame down the street to the state-owned grocery store, hoping for the best and expecting the worst. It was just past nine in the evening.

Sometimes it was better at night when others had given up. He found the last ripe tomato in the store, or what passed for tomatoes these days. With enough salt and maybe some dried herbs he could fool himself into believing it belonged on a proper tomato sandwich. Greta had loved tomatoes; He used to feed slices of them to her with is fingers.

Back in his apartment, Reginald made his simple dinner. He cursed himself when he cut the tomato, and the juice spurted out along with seeds, flying through the air until they landed. Reginald did his best to clean up the mess. The carpet didn't show any stains. So at least there was that. Satisfied, Reginald ate his dinner, and turned in early.

The next morning he woke up at seven, a force of habit he

hoped would disappear with time. To his surprise, green stalks protruded from the carpet. Reginald stood there, toes curling in the carpet, deciding to ignore it for the time being. He left is apartment to eat breakfast next store.

Just after ten, he dropped by the Office Of Retirement to fill out forms in quadruplicate. The woman behind the counter looked bored. As long as she filed them correctly, he thought, it didn't matter. So much could go wrong between filling out forms and filing them.

Reginald passed by the church where he and Greta had married. It was deconsecrated three years ago, now turned into living quarters. He wondered what it was like to sleep in the room with the stained glass windows.

He shook away the ghosts of memory and went back to his apartment. He was greeted with four large green stalks growing from the carpet. The ripest tomatoes he'd ever seen were hung from the stems, their skins glossy. He was drunk from the smell.

He plucked one from the vine and sliced it with a serrated knife. Closing his eyes, half in fear, he took a bite. It was the best tomato he'd ever eaten. He spent the rest of the day snacking on tomatoes, taking a nap when he'd eaten his fill.

He woke the next morning. Reginald decided to return to Carpet World. Someone there might be able to explain what had happened. Perhaps there was a new innovation that salesman had neglected to mention.

The walk was longer than he remembered. The streets more deserted than before. He carried the crumpled receipt with the address stamped on it.

When he got to the location, Reginald saw an empty storefront. No people. No carpet displays. Dirty windows. The only sign any store had been there was the metal desk where he had sat looking at the carpet samples. It was covered with dust.

He called the number. After two rings a recording announced the number had been disconnected.

There was nothing to do but walk back home. Greta would have loved this story. "It was the damnedest thing," he imagined himself telling her. How many times he had started a sentence with "It was the damnedest thing," to her over the years.

Reginald passed by the supermarket and bought in food for the week. Milk, grapes, dwarf potatoes, the last of the seasons' cucumbers, and a bottle of Shiraz. It was Thursday. He always had wine on Thursdays after a long day at work. It seemed so much more fulfilling than waiting for the weekend.

At home, Reginald washed some grapes and sat munching them in front of the television. They had seeds. They always got stuck in his dentures. Tonight was no exception. Annoyed, he went to the bathroom and removed his dentures, plucking the seeds from his mouth, tossing them behind the couch.

The next morning, his walls were covered with grape leaves.

The grapes tasted as good as the tomatoes. If this kept up, he could open a farmer's market in his apartment. Of course, he knew this would take years to approve. Not even his fellow County Control Officers would be able to expedite the process.

"Oh Greta, what to make of this," he said.

Her name was an exclamation, a love letter, a wish and a mournful sigh. Her name punctuated everything and always would.

Reginald spent the day watching TV. Game shows. Shopping shows. Shows about genetic mutants. Soap operas. He sat through everything until the late news came on.

With a decisive snap, Reginald shut the TV off at eleven thirty, walked into his bedroom and opened the closet door. The overhead light bulb was dim. But he knew what he was looking for. He grabbed a desk chair and stood on it, holding the closet walls for support.

On top of the closet was a shelf. And on that shelf were rows of boxes. Reginald chose the small white one, now yellowed from age. He stepped down and made his way back into the living room.

He sat on the couch. In the box was another box containing two silver necklaces. One was heart shaped, one key shaped. Reginald held them for a long time. He hadn't seen them in years. Before now he couldn't bear to look at them.

Reginald thought back to when he and Greta were young and broke. Splurging on dinners they'd share. Scraping together money for months, just so they could have a good time. Buying each other cheap little gifts.

Even after they'd become well off, they never forgot those cheap necklaces. The jeweler took pity on him because it was all he could afford. Said he was doing him a favor, selling him two for one. The jeweler said he wanted them to avoid a Gift Of The Magi moment. He then spent a few minutes explaining the O Henry story to him. Reginald was polite enough to listen. But he didn't need a moral to understand what the jeweler had done for them. The most inexpensive gift meant the world to them both, because it was for them both.

Reginald poured himself a glass of wine, allowing the memories to come back. The tears didn't flow. Instead, a smile formed on his lips. He went into the kitchen, and pulled down another wine glass from the cupboard.

He filled it and set it on the table next to his own glass. Then he opened his necklace. Inside it was a lock of Greta's hair. His fingers felt it. Still soft after all these years. Still smelling of her shampoo.

Reginald thought about quality, and what the carpet salesman said. He took Greta's hair, sprinkled it on the carpet, and then he lay back on the sofa, closing his eyes. He fell into a deep sleep, hoping he would need it.

CHAPTER 12
God Loves Us

South Hills Village Mall has the greatest arcade in Western Pennsylvania. And I know this because I've been going to Fun Dave's since around 1984 when I was about eight or so. And now it's 1991 and I'm almost old enough to drive on my own and I've gone to a lot of arcades but nothing beats it.

The best thing about Fun Dave's is that it hasn't changed in all those years. Except for the games. Like, they don't sell overpriced drinks or snacks like the other places. They didn't put in a row of ski ball or basketball games not that I have anything against that. It's just a bunch of well maintained and up-to-date video games and pinball games, a couple of automated change machines, a couple of employees who will come up to players and exchange their money in between levels so as not to break their concentration or tear them away from their winning streak, and of course the owner, "Fun" Dave Janowski.

Fun Dave is in his 40's. None of us know anything about him except he isn't a pedophile. And the reason we know this is because as long as I can remember a paranoid mother or father has been waltzing in every other month or so on a fact-finding mission to see just what kind of place their kid hangs out in all day and who is running it. Some just walk right up and ask him outright if their kids are in any danger. I have witnessed this firsthand at least two dozen times, maybe more.

Fun Dave always answers the same way. Like, first he'll chuckle and say "It's because of the mustache, right?" But the truth is, he doesn't have a pedophile mustache. He has a handlebar mustache that makes him look like Lemmy from Motörhead, the band my friends and I have just started listening to. Everyone knows Lemmy isn't a pedophile.

Fun Dave then points to the ring on his finger and explains not only is he not interested in little boys or girls but he is married and has kids himself and if they happen to be in there, he'll point them out. And he understands their concern, but he runs a safe establishment.

Fun Dave then points out the four mirrors in the corners of the room. "Behind those mirrors are cameras. They are recording a 360-degree view of this place at all times even when we're closed. I've been open since 1982, and we've never had an issue. Not once."

I once told my mom about it over dinner once and she said "Good for him. I wouldn't put up with stupid parents either. They sound like PMRC types, or those old ladies in church who think AC/DC is from the Devil."

Sundays may be church day for most of our community but on Saturdays our church is Fun Dave's. There was a gang of us, numbering anywhere between six and eight every week. But once you get in there, unless you are playing side-by-side or taking turns on the same game, you go to your favorites.

Street fighter II is pretty awesome, but frustrating, too. Learning the precise sequence to do a super is annoying. Like, when I play Ken, I can do a Hurricane Kick okay, but Blanka's super combo is something I can never get right. I just mash the buttons and move the joystick and hope for the best.

As of late, I spend my allowance money on The Addams

Family pinball game as it can do no wrong by me and I get so many free games out of it I sometimes think either I'm a pinball wizard like Tommy or the game is broken.

Even though Fun Dave refreshes the games, he still keeps the breadwinners and old favorites around, which means my favorite game is still there: Gauntlet II. I always say if I can get three friends and we play as two Elves and two Valkyries, one quarter each will last a half hour. Not bad at all.

The thing about Fun Dave is he keeps those machines well oiled. If they break, he gets them repaired pretty much overnight. I guess it makes sense because he must make mad amounts of money on each of those games but still, you'd be surprised. Some owners don't care as much.

Like, two weeks ago I went to another mall with a friend of mine whose mom was driving. She had to pick something up at Sears, an appliance like a giant microwave or something, I don't know, and they had shipped it to the wrong mall, but rather than wait she just sucked it up. I was over at his house when she got the phone call and she said to me okay, look, you can either go home now, or you can come with us and you can play in the arcade while I deal with this and then we'll get pizza.

Going to a different arcade and a different pizza place in one night? Sign me up. So we go to the other mall in a different part of town that's a bit more working class, and the mall looks like it hasn't changed since the 1970's and the stores are unfamiliar and one of the kiosks in the middle sells nothing but different kinds of flavored popcorn that no one ever buys so you just know it's all kinds of stale. It's that kind of place.

But whatever, she drops us at the arcade and says she'll pick us up in a half hour, which isn't a lot of time so we get antsy at first until we see the video games. A lot of them were broken. The local kids are already on the games that are working, and

they don't look like they're going to lose any time soon. So we
scrounge for what's available.

We ended up taking turns on Galaga, which I still love,
but even that wasn't great because the fire button wasn't as
fast as I'm used to and I lost my first life at stage three which
is ridiculous because I never, and I mean never ever lose any
fighters until stage five and that is only if I get distracted. So it
is obvious the game was rigged or the owner doesn't take care
of them like he should.

It was the first time I can recall that I ever felt like leaving
an arcade early. When we got to the pizza place in the same
neighborhood it at least had Street Fighter but we couldn't even
be bothered. It made us appreciate Fun Dave's that much more.

The weird thing I've noticed though, is that there is one
game in Fun Dave's that is always unplugged. It's only by the
light of the other games can I even make out the title: Elijah. It
is written in like, some fake Biblical script. No one ever talks
about the game, so I figure it must not be a hit. At the same
time, when it occurs to me, I have to wonder why Fun Dave
keeps it.

It's not a large multiplayer game, like a Mortal Kombat
or X-Men. It's more Galaga-sized but still, you could replace
it with another moneymaker easy when space is limited. The
truth is I don't think about it that often unless I happen to pass
by it, but it's back by the driving games, the kind where you sit
to play and I don't like those games. And seeing as how loud
it is in an arcade, I've never asked anyone there. I doubt my
friends have even noticed it.

I have my learner's permit and I'm practicing driving as
much as possible so I can pass my test because I don't want
to be like some of my friends who have failed twice now. This
morning it was raining and usually my mom takes the car to
my high school to walk a few miles around the track but when

it rains, I swear three hundred other people in our suburb go to The Village Mall and walk the indoor perimeters before going to Gloria Jeans for coffee and then meet up in the food court to gab about who knows what.

All I know is, I drive her there this morning, and it's early, like eight thirty. And it's pouring. The kind of rain where you have to put the windshield wipers on the fastest setting and even then it's sheets of water so it's like you only see every other swipe. Pittsburgh gets a lot of rain, all the time, but it's this kind of rain that people really hate. Somehow I get us there and at that time it's so early I find a spot almost right up front and we race inside because we never bring umbrellas since it's one more thing to carry.

Once inside, mom is off to find her friends and I sip my McDonald's coffee because I don't like Gloria Jeans and I'm wondering what to do with my time. I assume the arcade isn't open yet. I've never seen it open that early ever. I'm usually not there until noon. Either way, I walk around the mall looking at the stores. Some have their lights on and some are still off. But the gates are closed to each one, which feels so weird to me.

I can see some hot older girl dressed all in black folding stuff in Spencer's and she's playing The Cure and I try to talk to her about that as I like The Cure too, but she just ignores me because she isn't paid to deal with customers until the gate goes up, so I keep walking.

I walk the downstairs perimeter first. The only store that is open is the cool hair salon with its first customer of the day. Helen, the older Chinese woman with the really cool skater haircut is in the back. She's the one I go to when I get my hair cut.

Upstairs, the barbershop is open. That's the one where my dad goes because it's cheaper. I used to go to that one, too. I went to a guy named Dave (not Fun Dave) who smoked while he cut my hair. Dave then had a heart attack, big surprise. And so Beatle Paul took over. We called him Beatle Paul because he looks so much like Paul McCartney it is scary. After a while I decided to go to Helen because I wanted skater hair and my dad's barbershop doesn't keep up with cool trends like that.

So I am just about to go to the post office to see if I can get some stamps when I notice Fun Dave's gate is three quarters of the way open, so I figure I'll take a look and see if I can't maybe get in a few rounds of those games I suck at or play something I've never tried when no one is watching so I don't look like I suck.

I stand at the entrance. The overhead lights aren't on but they never are. Still, there's enough light from outside, that I can see only a couple games are on. Fun Dave's is right next to the mall's eastern exit, and even though it's still pouring, the rain clouds are bright white. It's bright enough that for the first time I can actually make out the carpet in a proper light. It's burgundy with different patterns on it. I can't tell what the colors are. But I'm surprised; For some reason I thought the carpet was brown all this time.

I walk in without saying a word. Here and there, I hear familiar sounds, like the Pac Man jingle and the guy who keeps saying "Body blow! Body Blow!" from Punch-Out. Seems like Fun Dave likes to let the older games keep him company in the morning. The newest ones, the X-Mens and Captain Americas are still sleeping.

I'm walking around in the half dark and I put a hand in my pocket to grab a bill figuring I can use the coin machine, as I doubt he turns those off. I start to make my way to the machine when out of the blue I hear a video game I've never heard before.

It's funny how I can recognize games without having played them just by their sounds. They become part of the background texture most times, but I bet if you played them for me isolated, nine times out of ten I could guess what game it is and get it right. But this one is new.

What I am hearing is music. The first word that pops in my head is "beautiful." I look around in the half dark, trying to see where it is coming from.

At this point, I see a game I've never seen before. And Fun Dave is playing it. I know it's him because I see his handlebar mustache in profile. He's standing at the controller, which seems to be a combination of side buttons, like on a pinball machine, and a regular joystick/button combo.

Dave's face is glowing from the game. I get closer and then I see why. The entire game, including the side panels, is glowing. On the side panel is an illustration of a wheel of fire in the sky. I shut my eyes for a moment, because I think for a second the wheel just moved and maybe my mind is playing tricks on me. I open them again and I realize I'm right the first time. The illustration—the wheel—is moving.

I get just close enough to remain outside the glow of the game, watching Dave all the while. He looks serene, which is the opposite of how someone looks when they play video games. Sometimes his eyes even close as he plays. He doesn't seem concerned about winning the game, whatever that means. I step up behind him and my mouth drops open.

He's playing Elijah. I was right about the script looking Biblical. Next to the title is, I assume, Elijah's face, with hands stretched out to the sky like some mad prophet. I haven't even looked at the video screen but I am already bewildered by it.

"What are you doing here, Ryan? We're not open yet."

"I'm sorry, Fun Dave," I say. My voice is hoarse. "The gate was almost all the way open. I thought this game was broken."

"No," he answers. "It works just fine."

"Then why do you keep it turned off? What is wrong with it? Why do you—"?

My words trail off. I am going to try and tell you what I see on the screen, but I have a feeling it might be easier to describe what I don't see. First off, it's not like any other game I've ever played. Whatever graphics they are using are light years ahead of anything on the market today. This game makes Mortal Kombat look like Adventure. This is like a three-dimensional thing with a lot of roominess. Like I could step inside it and walk around in it if that makes sense.

I have been playing games now for ten years. Every game I've ever seen has an objective you can define within thirty seconds. Fight something. Run away from something. Rescue a princess. Come in first, if it's a sports game. I've been watching Fun Dave play for a few minutes now and I have no idea what is going on. I'm just watching a shape walk. It walks in the woods. Then a cave. Then a modern city. Then an ancient city. The shape comes into view sometimes, becomes a defined person, other times it retreats to the shadows.

A voice talks through the speakers. It sounds like scriptures to me. But it also sounds like something other than scriptures. Narration? A speech? I wish I could be more specific but at this point I'm am starting to get nervous because I am weirded out.

"I want to try."

I see Fun Dave think about it. His eyebrows kind of screw up for some reason I don't understand. I mean it's a video game. What's the problem?

"I don't know, Ryan."

It's not like I want to beg but there's something about a game I've never played that I have to try it even if it sucks. Especially this one since it's never on, like, ever. So I say: "Please. I just need change. I'll wait till you're done."

"The game doesn't work like that," Fun Dave says. And then

he steps away from the game and turns to me. The game reacts to his movements. What I mean is, it doesn't keep playing regardless without him, like if you were playing Galaga and if you didn't move, the aliens would keep bombarding you until you died. This game doesn't stop exactly. More like, it waits. I am watching it and it literally slows down somehow.

"There are only a few of these games out on the market," he tells me. "Somewhere between seven and ten all over the world that we know of. Most of us arcade owners have decided to keep them to ourselves."

I talk without taking my eyes off the screen. "I don't get it. It's a video game. Right?"

"You see Ryan, parents accuse people like me of stuff all the time. They don't see me as a small business owner. They think I want to hang out with kids."

I am torn between staring at the game and giving Fun Dave the attention he deserves. He's just admitted he has to put up with stupid stuff from parents who say horrible things. I hate that because all of us love Fun Dave. So I manage to look away from the game for just a half second to make eye contact. "But we all vouch for you, Fun Dave."

"I know that, Ryan," he smiles. "But the games are getting more violent. There's a backlash. Parents and lobbyists are starting to complain to the government about it. And it worries me. They already put warning labels on records. What do you think will happen to video games?"

I want to answer but I can't because it's like my eyes are transported through the screen. I want to play it so bad, but I don't want to be rude. Also, like any gamer, I kind of want to know what I'm getting in to. And I'm afraid if I ask there won't be an answer, because I am looking at the shapes on the screen that seem as if they are waiting for me with infinite patience to take the controls.

I decide to be a bit patient, too. "I suppose parents would argue games have gotten more violent. But this game doesn't seem violent at all."

Fun Dave agrees. "Far from it. This game is God."

I don't think I hear him right. Actually, I think I hear him one hundred percent right but there is always the chance I am wrong, so just to check I say "Sorry, what?"

Fun Dave looks at me without blinking, like stares into my soul kind of look.

"How is God in a video game?" And then it dawns on me. "Oh you mean like, it's a game that teaches you about God. Like Oregon Trail taught us about the Oregon Trail."

Fun Dave steps back from the light of the game. He puts his hands up and says, "If you really want to know, try it."

Of course I want to try it, I mean like, I believe I have made that very clear by now but I can understand the nature of this situation being weird, like me and Fun Dave having a heart-to-heart in front of a game about God at nine thirty in the morning. I shake my head. I need to know some basics before I begin.

"How do I start? What do I press?"

"Doesn't matter. You have twenty minutes. Then I gotta pull the plug before I open. Okay?"

"Yeah, sure," I mutter. And then I step into the light of the game. I don't know what to do. So I touch the joystick with my left hand and one of the side buttons with the right.

I am transported. I am in the game, while being outside of it. Like I am having an out-of-body experience while being in my body at the same time. My first thought fills me with fear. Fun Dave turned out to be sketch after all and drugged me somehow because something is happening to me. But then this thought leaves as soon as it arrives.

I am now calm. I am covered with gold light. I am not playing as the figure walking in the game. I am literally the figure in the game. Walking in a modern city like New York, or London, maybe. Everything is moving in time lapse, except me. I don't know how I know this, but I am given to understand that I am the figure. But also not me. It is also God. This is something I understand as if the game is inside my brain. The game has not spoken to me at this point.

I open my mouth to try and speak. But no words come because to be honest I don't even know what I should ask. I have never been this speechless.

I've read many books so far, way outside my literature classes at school. Like, I've read "The Idiot" and "The Dharma Bums." I tried to read religious books outside my own religion like The Bhagavad Gita but didn't understand most of it because it was so foreign to me. But what is really mindboggling to me at this point in my life is that this strange video game is not foreign to me at all.

I start free falling. What I mean is, I am falling in the three-dimensional game but I also have the literal sensation of falling, like through the carpet into a void, or portal. I panic. The game speaks and I don't know if it is speaking out loud or if it is speaking in my head, but this is what it says:

Yea though I walk through the valley of the shadow of death I will feel no evil for thou art with me.

I am no longer falling. The game is no longer falling. The scene has now changed to a forest. There are animals everywhere. I hear them. Birds chirping. Stuff like that. I don't know. I'm not sure if my hands are moving any more. They feel weightless.

I haven't taken any drugs, haven't even smoked a cigarette because I can't stand the smell. But all these classic rock musicians have talked about their experiences on acid, and how it seemed like doorways opened and whatnot. This is kind of what I'm feeling. On the surface the experience in the game is basic, even boring. So I'm in a forest, so what? But on another level it's like—everything there is a creation that holds some deeper significance. My senses are heightened. The forest has a smell. My ears are buzzing from the sounds. I am trying to look up but every time I try, I end up looking around me instead. This point feels significant to me.

Sunlight is cascading down through the trees, shimmering in yellow orange and gold as it touches my skin. It feels as if it's going through me now, becoming part of my being.

And then the power goes off.

Fun Dave puts his face in front of the game to snap me out of it, and in fact snaps his fingers a couple of times to really snap me out of it which works. "Sorry, Ryan. Time's up."

My hands are still on the controls. I blink at the now dark screen and then I turn to Fun Dave.

"What. Was. That."

Fun Dave smiles but not in a creepy or scary way, more like a smile that says he may not know what it is all about but he knows a little bit and is starting to get it.

"You tell me what it is," he says.

I laugh at that. "Me? How? I can't even begin to describe what it was I just experienced."

His voice is calm. "Try."

So I try. I describe what I saw and how I felt. I sound like an idiot.

"What did it tell you?"

I exhale once. "It quoted a scripture. About the valley of the shadow of death and not being afraid. Then it said other stuff I didn't understand. But mostly it was quiet. It felt like it was talking to me without talking. Sharing feelings rather than words." I rub my eyes for a minute trying to get them to focus. "Weren't you standing next to me? Didn't you hear it?"

Fun Dave gestures to the arcade. The games are all lit up, one hundred percent. "I was a little busy. But I just wondered if it was the same message as what I heard."

"Was it?"

"No. Mine was talking about Jonah and the whale. That was right before you showed up, I guess."

I look Fun Dave in the eyes. They are now glowing from the video games. "How does the game work?"

"Ryan, I don't rightly know. It's best not to think of it as a game. I've played it now for a couple years and it is never the same twice and it never breaks down and to be honest I've never even fed it a quarter."

I am starting to get upset. I know it's not a practical joke because I have just spent twenty minutes playing it but he has to know something. "Come on. Where did it come from? There must be a game manufacturer."

"Believe it or not young man, we did think of that. There were six of us in the arcade association who all tracked down the company as well as the phone number and the mailing address of the guy who created it. The company is called Alpha Omega Inc., and they are based in Palo Alto."

"What'd they say?"

Fun Dave puts his hands in his pockets. "Nothing. Our letters went unanswered. I must have left half a dozen messages on their phone. No one ever called back."

"What about the game's creator?"

"According to the pamphlet that came with the game, his name is A. Jacobs. No address except the company's. He's not in the phone book. Far as anyone knows, there's maybe ten or twelve of these games in existence. None ever break."

I bite my lip, lost in thought. Then a bulb goes off. "Don't you order games by the title? I thought you like, lease them or something."

Fun Dave shakes his head. "I never ordered this one. In fact, none of us did. This game just showed up one day. But we've all come to the same conclusion."

He pauses like he's waiting for me to ask and I have to ask, although I don't want to. "What?"

"The game has a power to it. Let me put it this way: I was raised Catholic. I was an alter boy at that. I've learned more from this game than I have in all my years going to Mass. I'm saying this feels like a spiritual short cut."

My head is starting to hurt from too much thinking.

"But why did it come to you?"

"I can't answer that."

"If it's so important why keep the game shut off?"

Fun Dave starts opening some quarter rolls and placing them in his coin belt. "Because in this day and age, people are outraged by everything. The so-called moral-majority thinks anything that makes our culture great like music and movies and even video games must be bad for us. Some morons call our culture Satanic. And the things that are truly evil, well, they look the other way because they don't know how to fix it. Like nuclear war. Acid rain. Poverty. Hunger. See, they can't fix that. So they pick on an easy target so they can feel good about themselves."

Fun Dave finishes putting the coins away. He escorts me to the door.

"The reason why I am keeping it unplugged is because I don't want it taken away from me. I don't want the word to get out. Understand?"

"I think so," I say. I mean, I kind of do but at the same time I don't. But at this point I figure it's easier to agree.

"Tell you what," Fun Dave says. "Here's five dollars. Come back when we're open." He points to the game. "But keep this to yourself. You're a good kid. If you ever want to play Elijah again just stop by twenty minutes before we open."

I thank him and then wait outside. Part of me doesn't feel like playing a regular video game now. I had enough stimulation for one day.

Turns out, my mom is ready to go anyway so I have to drive us home. It's still raining like balls. It's rushing in the gutters as I drive and the streets are turning into giant puddles. The news radio says there's a flood watch in effect until that evening. Everything smells like damp concrete. I get her home and dry off and ask if I can borrow the car to go back out to the arcade. She doesn't mind if I drive without her as long as I follow the limit.

She shakes her head. "You heard the radio. Flood watch. You saw how bad Washington Road was. Besides, didn't you already play today?"

I put my hand in my pocket to touch the five-dollar bill. "No," I answer. "If there was one thing I did not do today, it was play a video game."

CHAPTER 13

Space is the place

Delta flight 305 was half-full, which was kind of a surprise considering it was the day before Thanksgiving. Shelly finished closing all the storage doors, and radioed the pilot for final confirmation.

Hector bounced around as always, making sassy jokes and pouring drinks for the first-class passengers who paid two times as much for extra legroom and free drinks. Shelly could understand if they were on a cross-country or international flight. It took less than an hour to go Portland to Seattle.

Even from the middle of the plane, she could hear Hector singing. He was in an especially good mood that night as it was his last flight until Monday. He was going to have a four-day weekend with his boyfriend in Seattle. Hector was the self-described queen of the Jewish Cubans, or Jewbans as he called them.

Shelly grabbed the intercom, scanned the room and took a deep breath.

"Good afternoon, Ladies and Gentlemen. Now that everyone has finally closed their laptops and stowed their luggage underneath their seats and returned their tray tables to the upright position, I can finally inform the pilot we are ready for take off. Remember, the quicker you do as we say, the quicker we leave."

Hector popped his head through the curtains. "Sassy bitch," he whispered.

Julie also worked the main cabin. Hector called her Ms. Cunty. Julie was mean to the passengers and coworkers alike. Shelly once asked how she ended up becoming a flight attendant. "I used to be a school teacher," Julie answered. No further explanation.

The three were more or less on the same schedules, working the commuter flights up and down the west coast. It was rare Shelly traveled farther than Cabo San Lucas. Vancouver, Portland, Seattle, San Francisco, Los Angeles and San Diego were her main cities. Anchorage in summer. She hadn't spent a lot of time there, but had it on her list of places to go when she went on an actual vacation.

Shelly hoped her route might change. She looked forward to seeing more of the world. She was born in Portland. Still lived there. Though it had changed quite a lot since she was a child, Portland never lost its essence. This familiarity made it a perfect home base.

Shelly instructed passengers to watch the inflight safety video. Julie liked to do the point-to-the-exits and here's-how-you-work-your-seatbelt gestures. Since the plane was small, there was no need for a second demonstrator.

"I think she gets off on it," Hector said, "like she's some dominatrix or something. Wouldn't be surprised if the bitch wore a strap on at night."

Hector demonstrated for the first class cabin with his usual flair, swishing his hips and throwing the belt together like he was one of Madonna's backup dancers. Shelly caught the show whenever she could.

The pilot's calm voice came over the PA. "Good afternoon uh,

ladies and gentlemen, this is your captain Michael speaking. All
of us on Delta flight 305 would like to welcome you aboard. The
weather outside is light rain with uh, some fog, but it shouldn't
cause us problems once we're airborne. We are scheduled to
take off in just a minute here, and your flight to Seattle will be a
pleasant forty-five minutes from lift-off to touchdown. So, uh,
sit back and enjoy the ride, we'll uh, be leaving here shortly. "

"Uh. Uh, uh, uh," Hector said through the curtain.

The three flight attendants took their seats after one final
crosscheck. The plane hummed and whirred. Shelly studied the
passengers. She'd perfected the art of looking without looking,
more out of curiosity than any sense of security. She knew
how to recognize a situation when it arose; she'd gone through
plenty of emergency training. It was something her mother had
to bring up at every phone call.

"I hope you didn't read the papers today."

"No, mom, I didn't."

"Good. Because there was a hijacking. In Murtala
Muhammad Airport. In Nigeria."

"Mom. Can you not start this again? I don't fly international.
I don't even fly to New York. "

"But you are trained for it, right?"

A passenger stood up, folding his jacket. He reached up to
open the overhead compartment.

"Sit down, sir," she said.

"I'm just putting my jacket away. Just gimme a sec."

From her seat, Julie snapped: "Are you deaf?" She pointed to
his seat. "Sit. Down. Now."

The man protested. "But I'm just putting my jacket away."

Julie fixed her eyes on the man. "You had twenty-five
minutes since you boarded to put your jacket away. It's too late.
Do you understand? Or do you want me to report you to the
TSA when you land?"

"Okay, fine." The man sat back down. And then under his breath: "Calm down."

Julie unbuckled her belt, stood up to her full height, eyes never leaving the man. She walked with deliberate steps and kept walking until her face was right in front of his. Shelly watched the man's face change expression several times, from outrage to anger to fear.

"Don't you dare tell me to calm down. I have to deal with people like you day and night. You think the rules don't apply. You think if I make a fuss all you have to do is write a nasty review, or send a tweet to Delta and you'll get me fired and get a free ticket somewhere. Guess what? It doesn't work like that on my plane. If you reach for your mobile device, I will make your life a living hell. Understand? If I get a sense you're even thinking anything negative about me, I'll make sure when you land there will be so many federal authorities ready to cavity search that you won't be able to walk straight for a month. Get this straight—when I say buckle up, I mean it. When I say sit down, I mean it. You don't stand. You don't move. You shut up. And you sit there." Her nostrils flared. "And you shut up."

Julie sat down, a sigh of relief and happiness exiting her lips.

Shelly went back to checking out the passengers. She often played a game where she'd try to guess their life story or occupation.

The man Julie yelled had carried on two phones, a laptop, and a tablet. Only someone who worked in tech would bring that many electronic devices for a 40-minute trip. His arrogant demeanor and hipster mustache were also dead giveaways. He was the type of guy who'd get his ass kicked in the working class bars in San Francisco.

On the other side of the row was an overweight middle-aged woman. She wore a Washington Huskies sweatshirt. A proud mom visiting her son, Shelly thought. And the one sitting behind her was a businessman. One older gentleman was wearing a fishing vest and fisherman's hat. A couple looked like they were in a band together. Both wore all black.

No babies this trip. As much as she loved babies, Shelly was relieved. The last few trips had been filled with babies. Their morning flight had three screaming babies on it. So she was happy to give her own ears a rest. But at the same time, it was unusual.

Shelly frowned. The day before a holiday plane half full, no babies. What gave? Was the economy really that bad? Were more people driving longer distances to save money? How much money could you really save considering the cost of gas?

Hector poked his head through the curtains.

"Hey girl, do you have any extra Diet Coke?"

Julie sighed. "What's the matter, Hector? Trying to watch your weight? Again?"

Shelly ignored the comment. "How many you need?"

"Just like, two or three."

Shelly walked to the back of the cabin, scanning the overhead compartments and passengers out of habit. At the back she brushed by a man sitting by himself. He was wearing a black suit and white shirt. He also wore a black tie with a small tiepin. And sunglasses. Shelly thought he looked familiar.

She reached into the drinks cart and fished out three Diet Cokes. As she was walking back, the man said: "Excuse me, Miss."

"Sorry, these are for first class passengers. We'll be serving the main cabin drinks in just a minute." Shelly kept walking.

Hector grabbed the Diet Cokes from her. "Thank you, sweety."

Julie went to the back of the cabin, and moved the drinks cart to the front with the speed of a racecar driver. Shelly managed to duck into an open row at the last moment to let her pass.

Julie was mean, but at least she was efficient. Here's your drink. Here are your pretzels. Here's your napkin. In just ten minutes they were at the back of the plane. The man in the suit and sunglasses was their last customer.

Julie smiled. "And now. What may I get you?

"Bourbon and soda. Please."

"Jim Beam okay?"

The man nodded.

Julie made his drink and placed it in front of him with napkin and snack. To Shelly she pointed at the drinks cart. "You got this?"

"Sure."

Julie went back to her seat to scrutinize passengers for wrongdoing.

Shelly put the drinks cart back in its place and checked the bathrooms to make sure they were clean. The fasten seat belt sign had been turned off for just a few minutes; the bathrooms hadn't even been used.

Miss," the man said.

"Yes?"

He handed her a note.

Ever since she started working as a flight attendant, men, and even some women but mostly men, assumed she was fair game. They'd chat her up, try to buy her drinks. A man once told her he was staying for a month in a suite at The Nines and she was welcome to stay there whenever she wanted provided she continue to service him.

Her mom had told her to wear a fake wedding ring, but it was too much effort to pretend. A polite refusal was all that was needed. If it ever got out of hand, Julie would be all too happy to help.

"Look, I'm not really interested," she said.

"Miss, I think you need to read this note right now." He nodded toward a black briefcase on his lap.

Just as he said this, a woman walked by on her way to the bathroom. Shelly turned sideways to let the woman pass. Then studying the man for a moment, she took the note and unfolded it. The handwriting was neat and the letters were in all caps:

I HAVE A BOMB ON BOARD THIS PLACE. I WANT 500,000 DOLLARS BY 5PM IN CASH. PUT IT IN A KNAPSACK. WHEN WE LAND, I WANT A FUEL TRUCK READY TO REFUEL AND A SET OF PARACHUTES. NO FUNNY STUFF OR I'LL DO THE JOB.

Shelly raised her eyes to look at the man, feeling her fingers tightening around the note.

"Listen very carefully. Give that to the pilot. Explain the situation. And then come back here and tell me what he's going to do. You're going to be sitting with me, and you'll pass notes to the pilot."

He swallowed his bourbon.

"Before you go, please make me one more of these. But with less ice this time. That other woman added too much."

Shelly stood up in a daze, went to the drink compartment, and made him another bourbon and soda.

"How much is it again?"

"How much?" Shelly felt reality slipping. A woman in front coughed and it brought her back to the present. "Six dollars, but you don't have to—"

The man handed her three twenties. "This will cover the rest. Whatever's left you can keep."

He opened the briefcase a crack. She could see the jumble of wires and what looked like a clock.

"Please hurry."

Shelly strode to the front of the plane. She reached the first class curtain but Julie cut her off.

"You took a long time there. What's going on?"

Shelly shook her head. "Not now, Julie."

Hector popped his head through the curtain and saw her eyes.

"Trouble?"

"I need to see the pilot."

Hector's flamboyance belied how experienced he was in crisis situations. He had more emergency training than any flight attendant who worked for Delta. Hector started his career years before September eleventh. He'd survived two bomb threats, and an attempted hijacking that ended with an air marshal breaking the terrorists' neck. During a short stint with El Al, an incident occurred that he refused to talk about. "The only thing I'll say is, Israeli men are as sexy as they are deadly."

Hector knocked on pilot's cabin. Two knocks. One knock. Three knocks. The door opened and Shelly was pushed inside. The door shut as fast as it opened.

Despite being on the job for two years, she'd never been in the cockpit before, at least not during a flight. It was roomier than she imagined.

"What's the matter?" Captain Michael asked.

Shelly handed them the note. "He has a bomb. I saw it," she said. It's in his briefcase. He's asking me to go back out with notes on what you're going to do."

Michael radioed to Seattle. "We have a situation. Affirmative. He wants five hundred thousand. And parachutes. And a fuel truck. Uh-huh. Uh-huh. Okay. We'll stall."

Michael scribbled a note and handed it to Shelly.

She looked at it, and furrowed her brow. "I'm having trouble reading this."

"It says 'We've radioed Seattle and are waiting for confirmation of your requests. Please don't do anything.'"

The co-pilot shifted in his seat. "Twenty-five minutes."

Shelly left the cockpit. Julie's demeanor had changed. She was pale and quiet. "Whatever you do, don't breathe a word," Shelly said to her.

She reached the back of the plane. The man in the black suit glanced at his watch. She sat down and handed him the note. "Fine," he said. "Make me another drink, please." He took out another piece of paper and started writing. She handed him the drink and sat down next to him. He'd taken off his sunglasses and was rubbing his eyes. He went back to his note.

Shelly had a strange sense of déjà vu. She watched write his note. Then it hit her.

It was one of those nights where she couldn't shake the feeling of being on a plane. She still felt like she was in the air. She was exhausted but couldn't sleep. Nights like these didn't happen often but when they did, Shelly would throw back the covers, turn on the TV, pour a glass of wine, and sit on the until she felt drowsy. She'd wake the next morning on the sofa with the TV on.

On one night she gave up trying to find anything worth watching on Netflix and settled on one of those conspiracy theory shows that investigated everything from the so-called face on Mars to what the real reason was for the pyramids to the dangers of the Bermuda Triangle. Each episode was the same: set the historical context, point out a real fact, recount a strange occurrence that actually happened, and then spend the rest of the show coming up with conspiracy theories or indulging in wild speculation.

She chuckled her way through the Bermuda Triangle episode, rolled her eyes through the ancient pyramids, skipped the face on Mars all together and was about to pick something else to watch when a fourth episode promised to investigate an airplane hijacking that went unsolved. She let the episode play, expecting more of the same garbage.

In 1971, a man hijacked a plane en route to Seattle for two hundred thousand dollars. When they landed, the authorities delivered the cash. The hijacker let the passengers go, demanding he be flown to Mexico. The pilots had only been in the air for a short time when the man jumped out of the plane. He was never seen again. His body was never found. Nor was the money. There were four potential suspects. But according to interviews with police or reporters, none of the four were involved. The trail went cold.

When the episode ended, instead of going to sleep, Shelly researched as much as she could about the mysterious man who pulled off the job. It was three in the morning when she turned in, knowing nothing more than what the show had told her.

"You're D. B. Cooper."

"It's Dan Cooper," the man said without looking up. "The reporter got the name wrong."

"You are the same person who did this in 1971."

He didn't answer.

"You look exactly the same. How is this possible?" she said, her voice starting to rise.

He gripped her wrist. "Quiet." He finished writing the note, still holding on to her wrist. "Give this to the pilot. Now."

Shelly stood up once again and walked to the cockpit. Hector knocked again and they ushered her in.

"What's it say?" Michael asked.

It was only then Shelly realized she hadn't read the note. She unfolded it and read out loud:

"Please check on the status. You should then tell the cabin that there is a mechanical difficulty and the flight landing will be delayed. The length of time will be determined by how long I have to wait for my demands to be reached. Tell the authorities I mean business."

"How you holding up?" Hector whispered.

Shelly shook her head, and kept walking.

The man was wearing his sunglasses again. His drink was mostly untouched.

She sat back down.

"No note? Why?"

The intercom buzzed and Captain Michael spoke, his voice still calm. "Hi there, Ladies and Gentlemen, uh, we have a slight and very minor mechanical difficulty. On top of that the rain is getting worse. It will uh, unfortunately cause a delay in landing. We are sorry for the uh, inconvenience, but our scheduled arrival time has changed from 3:45 to closer to 5:30. Please understand at Delta your safety comes first, and we thank you for flying with us."

A collective groan echoed through the cabin. Followed by a loud retort from Julie.

The man with the sunglasses nodded in satisfaction.

"I don't know how you have come to be here now, Mr. Cooper, or why you haven't aged, but you need to understand. This is a post September eleventh world. We have high tech security. Body scanners. CCTV. The money will probably have trackers so they can geo-locate you within minutes. For all I know, they can track the parachute. I could photograph you from this plane with my cell phone and it'll be online in a matter of seconds. It's not 1971 anymore."

The man let the last of his drink linger in his mouth before swallowing. "Are you finished?"

Shelly kept quiet.

"None of it matters," he said.

"I don't understand."

"You role isn't to understand it. Your role here is to take my notes to the pilot and bring me their notes in return. And make me drinks." That last sentence was apologetic.

"Did you run out of the money? Did you spend it all to research some youth serum? You must know that people are still talking about you. I watched an entire show devoted to it not long ago. Why on Earth would you show up dressed the exact same way?"

The man put up a hand, silencing her. "If your security is as great as you say, I wouldn't have gotten the bomb on board. Now, I'd like one more drink and then we're going to pass a few more notes. Also, may I have some more pretzels? Thank you."

Shelly made the man one more drink and gave him two bags of pretzels.

"I need to check on the cabin, otherwise they'll get suspicious."

"You know what happens if you say anything."

Shelly checked on the passengers as fast as she could. When she got to the first class curtain Julie hissed "I already checked on them."

"So. Fucking. What."

Before Julie could respond, Hector popped his head through the curtain. "You can have a cat fight later. Now's not the time."

Shelly went to the back and sat down, breathing in and out to calm herself. The man was writing another note. Without looking up he said: "What was that about?"

"Julie, my co-worker is a first rate bitch. She told me she already checked on the passengers, but I'm trying not to cause alarm." Shelly wanted to stop talking. She couldn't. The words came out as if she were compelled to talk. "I have no idea how they haven't fired her by now. I guess it's because of seniority or something. Some days it takes all of my energy to not strangle her. Almost two years I've been putting up with her. I can't deal much longer."

"Look at it this way," the man offered. "After this, you'll have no problem getting a transfer."

Shelly stared at him. "You know what happened to the last woman who played personal secretary for you? She ended up in a convent. I saw it on TV. She became a recluse because of you."

The man stopped writing. He looked up, but not at her. "I couldn't help that. All I can say is, there are worse ways to live than being in a convent locked away from your people." He turned to face her, his eyes expressionless. "Besides. You're different."

'What do you mean 'your people?'" she asked. "You don't have an accent. Are you Canadian?"

He handed her the note. "Please read this before you go. I want to make sure you understand it so there is no miscommunication."

She read the note.

TWO HOURS IS A REASONABLE TIME FOR THEM TO GET WHAT I REQUESTED. THANK YOU. PLEASE RADIO AHEAD THAT THE BILLS SHOULD BE UNMARKED, UNTRACEABLE AND NOT LARGER THAN TWENTIES. PLEASE PUT THEM IN AN ATTACHE CASE. WHEN WE LAND EVERYONE WILL STAY ON BOARD. IF YOU TRY ANYTHING, I'LL USE THE BOMB. PLEASE KEEP ME ABREAST OF ANY CHANGES IN TIME.

A minute later, Shelly was back in the cockpit handing the note to Captain Michael. It now felt routine, as if it had been included in her job description. Treat passengers like children when they don't listen. Make drinks and hand out snacks. Pass notes from a terrorist to a pilot.

Was terrorism the right word? Did it count as terror if only four or five people knew and didn't feel terrorized? Hector was undaunted. Julie was her usual crabby self. Michael was calm. The co-pilot was angry. Shelly was more irritated than afraid.

Captain Michael radioed again, and then wrote her a note.

"Make sure you can read this before you go," he said.

Understood on the cash and have relayed message. Delta has agreed to your ransom and is gathering it ASAP. We should be all clear to land at 5:40. If there is anything in the meantime, please advise.

She left the cockpit to find Hector drinking a mini bottle of whisky from the drinks compartment.

"Don't judge. You never get used to these things. Trust me."

At the back of the plane once more, she handed him the note. "If you have trouble reading I can tell you what it said."

He scanned the note and then put it down.

"What did you mean 'your people'?"

The man looked out the window toward the heavy clouds beneath them.

"Every theory has been wrong," he said. "I have heard them all over the years. People said I was a paratrooper. It was an inside job. Others thought I was a daredevil. Some think it could be done, others said it couldn't and I must have died. They've been wrong for more than forty years. It's only been informed by the same incorrect sources."

"Why are you so desperate for money that you need to threaten us?"

The man sputtered, "I'm not desperate."

"Then what?"

He sighed.

Years ago. He'd been sleeping in his apartment when some presence roused him. That was the word he used. Presence. Like an unseen force swept him out of bed. He got dressed, got in the car and drove. It was three in the morning. He felt like someone else controlled his movements.

He was aware of getting into his car, fastening his seat belt, even turning on the radio as he left his apartment. He drove like he knew where he was going, never speeding. He headed south on an interstate somewhere in Northwest Washington. The rain and fog made it so he couldn't see more than five feet in front.

He drove for an hour before exiting the interstate. He took a winding back road through Mt. Baker National Forest. Without knowing why, he pulled his car off to the side, got out and walked through the dense forest until he found a clearing. That's where they met him.

He looked outside the window. There was nothing there to see.

"They said everything we knew about the world—about the universe, was a lie. But that I was different. In my subconscious I knew the truth. That's why they chose me for the job. They needed me. So two days later, I did it."

"You were chosen. They needed you. This is your job. You know the truth. You realize none of this makes sense, right?"

"Later this evening, you'll understand. Just like the last woman who helped me. But don't expect anyone to believe you."

The man continued peering out the window into the dark mass of storm clouds. After a few minutes, he returned to his pen and paper. He wrote with haste but his penmanship was still perfect.

Shelly envied it. One look at his perfect block letters and she was taken back to elementary school, and her low marks for penmanship. Her teacher, Ms. Ford, mocked her for being left-handed. She sat there crying. Why would a grown up make fun of her for something she couldn't control? It was bad enough the other kids taunted her for being new to the school. She hadn't wanted to move.

When she was seventeen, the elementary school merged with the high school. It was two months before her graduation. All of a sudden there were little kids everywhere. Elementary school teachers she hadn't seen in years now walked the hallways like ghosts from her past.

One day she walked into study hall and saw Ms. Ford. She was filling in for the regular teacher who had an unforeseen emergency. Shelly sat down and burned with anger for forty minutes.

At the end of class, she had made up her mind to speak with Ms. Ford. When she approached, Ms. Ford's face brightened. "Shelly! Almost done, eh? Excited for college? Where will you be going?"

"Parsons."

"Oh, that's fancy. For fashion or art?"

"Art."

"Splendid. But more than a bit surprising. I must say when you were younger, you didn't show that much promise," she chided.

Shelly smiled. "That's because I had a horrible teacher who made fun of me every day for being left-handed. Do you know what that does to a child? Do you have any idea what a horrible human being you are? Do you know how many scars you've left?"

Shelly turned and ran outside the classroom. Her last image of Ms. Ford was that of a light bulb head with a round black dot of a mouth open in shock.

"One more note should do it," the man said. "Read it first in case—"

Shelly snatched the piece of paper from his hands and left her seat.

She walked down the aisle. After all this time, none of the passengers knew what was going on. Julie had kept her mouth shut. Hector was still playing consummate host while sneaking mini bottles of liquor to calm his nerves.

Before she entered the cockpit, Shelly read the note:

RADIO TO HAVE A BUS WAITING FOR PASSENGERS. WHEN LANDING, ANNOUNCE THAT PASSENGERS MUST STAY ON PLANE FOR MECHANICAL REASONS. DO NOT SCARE THEM. ONCE BUS ARRIVES THEY MAY DEPLANE AT MY SIGNAL ONLY. YOU ARE TO REMAIN IN COCKPIT. HEAD TO BRIGHTLY LIT SECTION OF TARMAC. THEN TURN OFF INTERIOR LIGHTS. I WILL BE WATCHING AS TRUCK REFUELS. ANY PROBLEMS AND PLANE GOES BOOM. PLEASE LET ME KNOW IF YOU NEED MEALS. ALSO PLEASE RETURN ALL OF MY NOTES.

"Well that's weird," Captain Michael said to himself. "Why does he want the notes?"

Shelly stood looking the plane's dials and measurements. The irrational anger that had sprung up from her childhood had left.

"How you doing, Shelly?"

"Fine. He's not being physical or demanding. I'm just worn out."

"We'll be fine. You know, we were just thinking how much this reminds us of that guy from the nineteen seventies, what's his name? D B Cooper?"

"Actually it was Dan Cooper," she said. "The reporter got it wrong.'"

"Figures." Captain Michael gathered up all the man's notes and handed them to her. "I'm tired of passing notes. Just tell him we said 'Roger that.'"

"They told me tell you 'Roger that.'"

The man nodded. "We should be landing soon."

"Do you want another drink?"

"No, thank you."

After twenty minutes, Captain Michael's voice came over the intercom.

"Uh, Ladies and Gentlemen, we are finally going to make our descent into SEA-TAC, in about uh, five minutes, actually. Thing is, the mechanical problem we have, is more major than we thought. If everyone stays on board until we tell you to deplane, uh, we should have no issues."

Shelly could hear the tension in their voices.

"Again I want to reassure you uh, this is only a precautionary measure. Just sit tight and when we land, please keep your seatbelts on and remain seated until we tell you. We thank you again for your patience."

"You heard the pilot," Julie said. She glared around the cabin. "Keep those belts on and stay seated until we tell you to leave. Any questions or comments, keep them to yourself." And then as she'd forgotten: "And no electronic devices either. Not even after we land. I see you touch your phone, I'll break it."

A few minutes later, the plane was taxiing toward the waiting buses and fuel trucks. Julie shut down any commotion before it began. After ten minutes, Captain Michael's voice broke in.

"Ladies and Gentlemen, uh good news. Our mechanical issue is resolved. However, we are unable to bring you to your gate. Ground crew are currently removing luggage. Since it was a half full flight they should be done quickly."

Captain Michael shut the PA for a moment.

A passenger asked Julie: "Does that mean we can leave?"

Her eyes narrowed.

Captain Michael broke back in.

Uh, sorry for the confusion there, ladies and gentlemen, was just conferring with our ground crew. Luggage has been removed. They have brought the staircase over. You are free to leave by the front exit. The ground crew will escort you to the bus that will take you to your gate. Again my apologies for the delay and thank you for flying Delta.

The man in the black suit grabbed his briefcase and stood up. "Stay here," he told Shelly. He made his way to the front with the rest of the passengers. Despite their frustration, they were still taking their sweet time to open the overhead bins and remove their luggage, jackets and personal devices.

When the last passenger left, Dan Cooper shut the airplane door. He opened the curtains to first class. Hector let out a high pitch scream and clutched his chest.

"Turn off the interior lights."

Hector complied.

He motioned for Shelly to join them at the front.

"Okay very good," he said. He opened the briefcase a crack to show Hector, and Julie his bomb. "Open the cockpit."

He glanced out the window. The passengers were running in the rain to the buses. The ground crewmembers were wearing reflective raincoats. Men were refueling the plane.

"Now it's very simple. We all stay here until the plane's refueled. Then when the money and parachutes are on board, we leave."

"For where?" Captain Michael asked.

"Where's the money," Cooper said.

The co-pilot pointed to the cockpit. "May I ask?"

The man in the black suit nodded. "Everyone sit down in first class. Each person sits in his own row.

"You won't get away with this," Julie said. "They'll have your ass in about ten minutes. You're done for."

He walked over to Julie. By the time he was three feet away her bravado had vanished. He showed her the bomb again. She looked at the floor.

"Money is here, same with chutes," the co-pilot said.

"Open the aft staircase."

"Done and done," Hector said.

He pointed to Shelly. "Go down the stairs. Get the money and the chutes. Tell them everyone on board is unharmed but you have seen the bomb. Don't answer any other questions. Once you get the stuff, we'll close the staircase. Once fueled, we leave."

When Shelly answered it was like hearing another person's voice. "Okay."

"One last thing. Tell them if they try to use scrambler jets I'll blow us up."

The sound of torrential rain was deafening. There were three officials at the bottom of the staircase. One wore a raincoat and hat. He had a small Delta button on a lapel. He looked important. The other two had guns pointed on her. She guessed they weren't Delta employees. At the sight of the guns she stopped cold.

"She's one of ours," the Delta employee shouted. The other two lowered their guns. He climbed up one step. Then another. "Everything okay?"

"Yes. We're fine. But he does have a bomb. I saw it."

He handed her two attaché cases. "Money's in the left. Chutes in the right."

"He said if you use scrambler jets he'll—" her voice broke.

"We won't," the Delta employee said. "Tell him he has our word."

Once back on board, Shelly tried to speak but her voice wouldn't come. The man in the black suit grabbed the attaché cases. "I heard what they said. Come to the front and sit down."

Once up front, he told Captain Michael to close the aft staircase. "How's the fuel coming?"

"They need to use the second truck to finish."

"Oh God," Hector said. "Look, mister, you mind if I have a drink?"

The man went over to the drinks cart. "I'll get it."

Hector fanned his face with his hand. "I'll have whatever you grab."

The man took three mini bottles and handed them over. Hector unscrewed one, and toasted the man.

Julie glared at him. "You are toasting a terrorist, you stupid Mexican idiot."

Hector sat up. "Okay first of all, I'm Cuban, not Mexican, second of all, fuck you, cunt."

"Shut it."

When the second truck pulled away, the man in the black suit ordered Captain Michael to start the plane.

"Want to tell me where we're headed or should I just drive around?"

"Mexico City," the man said. "Take a Southeastern course. The most minimum speed you can manage. A hundred knots. Ten thousand feet maximum. I want the landing gear to remain deployed and the wing flaps should be lowered to 15 degrees. Is that clear?"

Captain Michael thought for a moment. "It's clear, but impossible. They way you want me to fly, we wouldn't even reach the border unless we stop to refuel."

"What would be the best place to stop?"

Captain Michael went into the cockpit to check his plans. "Your best options are Reno or Las Vegas."

"Reno."

"Roger that."

"Remember. Ten Thousand feet max. A hundred knots. I also want you to leave the cabin unpressurized. "

The rain had not let up and the ascent was rough. Shelly knew Captain Michael was a great pilot. His reputation was that of a professional who was grace under pressure.

Once they reached ten thousand feet, Captain Michael

turned around and shouted through the open cockpit door "What now?"

"Everyone into the cockpit but you," he said, pointing to Shelly.

"Why me?"

I'll need your help."

Hector and Julie crammed into the cockpit. The man shut the door behind them.

He opened the attaché case to verify the money was there. He didn't bother counting it. He took off his tie and laid it on one of the first class seats. Then he opened the second case.

"You're not going to make me jump out with you, right?"

He picked up a parachute and examined it. The ripcord had been cut and lightly sewn back together. He snapped the cord and threw the parachute on the ground.

The man rummaged through the case, checking the parachutes. "No. I just asked for more parachutes so they wouldn't try anything. They always do, though. Every single time."

"How many times have you done this before?"

"Every twenty years since the thirties. When you people started flying internationally."

He looked out the windows. It was completely black. In the distance Shelly thought she could see an outline. Something was moving toward them.

The man hit a switch, deploying the aft air stair. Shelly felt the rush of wind knock her back. She sat with her knees on a seat, gripping the headrest.

The man shook his head. "It's like I said to the woman back in nineteen seventy-one. You must understand—you are not alone in up here."

Through the back windows she could see the outline of something getting closer. It flew above them at a slight angle. It approached in slow steady movements, as if gravity and wind resistance had no meaning to it.

"They money isn't for me. I'm just a collector," he shouted.

Shelly could see it clearer now. Shaped like a trapezoid. Not black, but more of a murky dark green, like the bottom of an algae-covered pond. It hovered with insistence behind the airplane. It couldn't have been more than a football field length away.

The man made his way to the stairs. Shelly followed, holding on to the seats for support. She watched the man descend one step at a time, gripping the railing.

He stood on the last step, waving his hand toward the approaching craft. The outline headed closer.

He looked up at Shelly. He turned to jump. As if remembering, he looked over his shoulder. "You people really need to think about the infrastructure. Stop being freeloaders."

Dan Cooper jumped. She watched as the craft sucked him inside.

The craft backed away without a sound. Or, Shelly thought, maybe it just moved forward without having to turn around.

The cockpit door burst open. Hector and the pilots fought against the wind.

They screamed for her to close the aft stair doors. Shelly couldn't move. She stood transfixed, looking at the spacecraft as it left.

Just before it disappeared in the clouds, she saw something written on the side in yellow capital letters. The typeface reminded her of Cooper's neat penmanship. Despite the rainy evening, it was still legible, as if illuminated by a faint glow. She clung to the seats, the violent air whipping her hair, and squinted to read the word. The unwillingness to accept it came as she finished saying it out loud. "Skydot."

CHAPTER 14

Punk Rock Girl

When a lot of my friends get tickets to see a show, they aren't interested in seeing the opening band. They'll get there early enough to get a spot in front of the stage, but when the opening band comes on, they'll be at the bar.

I have never understood this behavior. Sure, a lot of opening acts are untested, or aren't as good as the headliners, unless you're dealing with two major acts. But what I love about the opening acts is you never know what you're going to get. Some might be so terrible it takes every ounce of the audience's collective being not to rush the stage. Others give such a great performance you think they're better than the headliners.

Opening bands are way more interesting to me. It's been like that ever since I saw my first show. Or to be more accurate it's been like that because of my first show.

When I was thirteen and a half, I saw a local band in Pittsburgh called the Frampton Brothers. They were kind of a punk band but filtered through the same melodic lens as The Kinks. They reminded me of a band out of Seattle called The Young Fresh Fellows. The singer of the Young Fresh Fellows would go on to sort of be a semi-official member of R.E.M. at least when they were still a touring act.

At that point while kids my age were still into G.I. Joe dolls, I'd been taking drum lessons for two years. From five to eleven, I played piano and hated every minute of it except for the piano teacher named Karen who was very sweet. Karen was the patient instructor as I struggled through Bach and Scott Joplin while her grey cat Miffy napped in my lap.

I hated the piano because I hated sight-reading music and my hands were small. After suffering through it for half a decade, my parents stopped forcing me to take lessons.

I was a fifth grader, freed from piano lessons, now trying out instruments in elementary school music class, trying to find a good fit. I couldn't make a sound when I tried the bassoon. The clarinet yielded only a bit more success. It wouldn't be unfair to say I was horrendous at it. To this day, I still cringe when I think of the feeling of that wooden reed against my teeth and that weird ventriloquist dummy face you have to make to play it. When the teacher told me there were no drummers in the school and maybe I might want to try out the drums, I jumped at the chance.

Drums were a percussion instrument, just like piano. But I didn't have to worry about scales and chords or even reading the music. I had an ear for drums and natural rhythm. I discovered I could play any rhythm by ear. If the teacher showed me how the rhythm went first, I could parrot entire songs back. It didn't do much for sight-reading but in terms of technique I managed just fine.

I had some friends who were in junior high by then. One introduced me to scores of college rock and local bands. The Frampton Brothers were just one of hundreds of bands that provided the official soundtrack to my youth.

When I asked my parents if I could see them live, I expecting them to say no. To my surprise, they agreed before I'd even finished asking.

"But only if your dad drops you off and picks you up," my mom said.

Made sense. I was nowhere near old enough to drive into the city. It's not like I expected her to let me take two buses to get there and two buses back.

The show didn't start till eight so dad would be home from work and finished dinner by then. They agreed he'd pick me up by ten thirty so he'd be home in time to go to sleep and wake up in time for work. That was all he really cared about, anyway. I could have gone to a riot and as long as he got his eight hours it didn't matter.

I have no doubt my mom did some behind-the-scenes cajoling to ensure this would take place. Once my dad was ensconced in our suburban home post-work, it was a chore to even get him to drive to the grocery store. To head back in the city like that meant she either caught him in a generous mood, or it was a slow week at work. I didn't ask and didn't care. I was going to my first show. To see The Frampton Brothers. That's all that mattered.

Graffiti was a small club. Its name was written in front of the place in neon. Though the location was in a somewhat rough section of Pittsburgh at the time, my parents either were pioneers, or naïve enough that it didn't matter to them. My mom was a product of the sixties. She'd s seen Bob Dylan and Joan Baez live at Berkeley, as well as Lenny Bruce. She knew the transformative power of a live performance. Looking back, I suspect she also had an inordinate amount of faith in me as being a responsible kid. Though this was true, I'm still surprised I was given that much leeway.

Since my dad was a local TV news reporter, I had heard and seen my fair share of stories about that part of town. For the most part, it was made up of poor college students and working class residents who knew their neighbors and tried their best to stay out of trouble. But it bordered a few neighborhoods that were rough enough that you'd think twice about walking down the wrong street, especially after dark.

Despite their progressive attitude, on the night of the show my mom still gave me a mini-lecture on keeping my wits about me. It may have had more to do with her upbringing; She'd grown up in a poor neighborhood before moving up the economic ladder.

"Just stay in the club until you see your dad out front," she said. "And if there's any trouble, ask the guy behind the bar for help, or even someone on stage if you need to." Then she slipped me a twenty and told me to have a good time.

After that lecture I felt like I'd be safe as long as I'd be safe inside that red brick club, surrounded by musicians. Like a rock and roll force field, no harm would come to me.

The sun was just setting when my dad dropped me off. "Ten-thirty. Look for me out front."

I went up the stairs to the club's entrance, showed them my ticket and had my hand stamped. I was a half hour early but I didn't care. I loved it.

There's a certain coldness you feel in an empty club before it fills with people and the house lights go down and the bands come on. It's the only time the air-conditioning works. It disappears as soon as people pile in and the music starts. To this day, I love feeling that chill. For me, it's anticipation.

As much as I liked The Frampton Brothers, I looked forward to the opening act. They were an all-girl punk band called The Pussy Kills. Their photo was on flyers stapled to the telephone poles around the university and outside the club. One girl had a mohawk, one was bald, and the other had long messy hair and a nose ring. All of them were tattooed.

I watched a roadie come out and test the guitar and drums

and bass for sound levels. The club's PA guy was fat. His large ZZ Top beard hung out over his belly. He looked bored.

It was a Monday night in summer. Most of the college students were away. The Frampton Brothers at the time weren't exactly huge stars. I thought there'd be a lot more people in the club by the time the Pussy Kills went on. There were ten people on the floor if even that.

The Pussy Kills strutted out with such presence that before they even played a note or sung a word a curious feeling came over me. I looked at them and was mesmerized. They had more than stage presence. They had power. They made me feel like anything was possible. If the band gave the nod, we could take over the world, or get rich, or become poor, or burn a building down or steal a Jaguar and drive across state lines. And no matter what we did, I was sure we would get away with it, too.

The lead singer was the one with messy hair. It was dyed blue. She was wearing a pink baby doll dress, fishnets and combat boots. She chugged an entire beer in one go and put it on an amp. The drummer counted off the first song. The lead screamed into the mike.

I heard once that some megastar performers like Bruce Springsteen always look toward the nosebleed seats during a performance, so that even those furthest away feel like he is looking right at them. In a venue as small as Graffiti, watching the lead singer of The Pussy Kills made me feel like she was putting on a concert for me alone.

She plucked her bass and looked around the room while she sang, Every so often, she'd look in my direction. She represented everything awaiting me if I could only get through my pathetic pre-pubescence. She represented sex and rock and roll before she even grabbed the microphone. And drugs too, in one sense. Because like any drug you take the first time, even a drug called music, you know that good or bad, the experience will leave you forever changed.

The first song ended. To call the applause sporadic was generous. The band didn't seem bothered. "We're The Pussy Kills. We came all the way from Austin. And we are here to rock your fucking face off," the lead singer said. With a "One-two-three-four" the drummer launched them into the second song. The rest of the audience may not have cared but I was floored.

I studied their performance like I was in acting class. The lead singer's boot rested on an amp. Face smeared with mascara. She screamed her head off. The drummer sweat through her T-shirt, playing like someone possessed. The guitarist stood immobile, looking at her instrument in blind concentration. They played in unison with brutal intensity.

To a budding musician this was vital education. To a nerdy pre-pubescent, however, this scene was better than any teenage sex comedy I watched after midnight when my parents had gone to sleep. I could care less about a bikini-clad buxom doe-eyed babe emerging from a swimming pool or a curly haired blonde rubbing suntan lotion on her cleavage. My fantasy was right in front of me: smart, accomplished players and (I imagined) semi-dangerous women who had musical talent and a fuck-off attitude.

The other people there were the club's owner, the bartender, a server, and the few beer-bellied regulars in their late thirties and early forties who showed up every night because it was their watering hole, and because they liked music of all kinds. Even though I wore my black Converse Chuck Taylors and black t-shirt and black jeans, I stood out like a skinny sore thumb whose voice hadn't yet changed.

During the third song the singer kept repeating something I couldn't really make out, except for the lyric "shooting up with malice, Mistress Alice." In between stanzas she'd whoop or holler, trying to drum up any enthusiasm from the audience.

Pittsburgh crowds can be rough. This audience wasn't throwing beer bottles but they were indifferent. That was much worse to me. She was working the crowd like a carnival barker. I was the only one bobbing my head and jerking back and forth to the ferocious beat in my spot on the dance floor.

During the fifth song, the singer jumped off the stage. She gripped her microphone with both hands, bent over, and got right in my face. She scream-serenaded. An involuntary picture popped in my head of Desiree.

My first kiss of any kind had only been a few years before. Desiree decided one day that she wanted to kiss every boy in our class. So one afternoon after school let out, we all lined up, and took our turn behind the tree. I'd been one of the first to line up. Not because I was so keen on kissing her, but because my last class was physical education. Since it was it summer, the class was outside, not far from the tree. She kissed thirty boys that day. Small ones, tall ones, skinny ones, fat ones, even the ones in remedial class. Somehow this wasn't sexual so much as something on Desiree's to-do list.

When it was my turn I walked towards the tree, and held my breath. There she was, smiling, waiting. I looked at her, closed my eyes, felt her lips against mine, and exhaled. It was such a small kiss, like a butterfly had touched me. It was over before it began. Candy-scented perfume lingered on my lips. A boy behind yelled "Hurry up, I got soccer practice."

Seeing this woman so close to my face was a much more profound experience. I didn't want it to ever end. I wanted to join her road tour and play back up drums or help them break down their equipment every night. I was very good at breaking down drum equipment. I could pack up my snare drum, and trap stand in less than a minute. How much longer could a whole drum kit take? And extra drumsticks? I had a bagful, baby. What size did you want? I had 2b's 5a's, 7a's even thick, hard marching sticks. They could have them all, every night. I wouldn't even mind if they broke them. They'd high five me every night. And when I got my license, I could save them time by driving them to gigs. I'd be the best roadie ever.

The lead singer stared into my eyes, winning me over as if I needed to be won over any more. I couldn't make out the lyrics. My ears were ringing. She wasn't trying to be sexual, which made it highly sexual. I'd had zero experience in that department. Aside from Desiree's kiss, I'd had two health classes under my belt and that was it. I knew more about playing the piano.

Thoughts of sex were there all right, but all I really wanted at the age was to be part of a gang. The rest would follow in its own time, I knew. Still, it was undeniable that I was becoming a man.

Before the singer leapt back on stage, she mussed my hair, making me feel like her thirteen year-old kid brother, but even more awkward because I now had a thirteen-and-a-half year-old'd rock hard erection poking in my jeans. I was glad I wore a longer t-shirt.

Like most boys in their early teens, it didn't take much to get me going. I was a walking erection. But this was different. I'd just discovered punk. And now, I was at a show, looking at hot trashy punk rock girls in baby doll dresses who could play their asses off. The only way I could have gotten more aroused is if the bartender had spiked my Diet Coke with Viagra.

After forty minutes, their set ended. I applauded and shouted "yeah!" I didn't know what else to shout. The Pussy Kills did manage to win over a few more audience members before it ended so at least I wasn't the only one making noise.

The singer shouted "you've been fucking great," And with

that they swaggered off the stage. Thirty seconds later, they came back on to help the roadie move their instruments and make way for The Frampton Brothers.

I stood there thinking I should help because I could totally make their exit a smoother one. I had considered getting on stage, but I had to pee from the Diet Coke and there's nothing more awkward that I know of than being thirteen with an erection and a fierce need to pee. Self-preservation won out.

The Frampton Brothers weren't due to come on for another half hour. I knew this even without looking at my watch because they were eating hoagies and drinking beer at the other end of the bar. I had time. I would wait until I was at half-mast to relieve myself so it wouldn't go sideways and end up all over the place.

When I exited the bathroom I saw The Pussy Kills hanging out by the bar, chatting with The Frampton Brothers. They made a beeline for me with the lead singer leading the charge. I resisted the urge to run back in the bathroom and stood my ground. The lead singer handed me a drink with ice in it. It was club soda.

"Thirsty?"

"Always," I said, having no idea why I said that.

It was hard to tell what was going on at first as the band were still talking to teach other as well as people at the bar. I heard snatches of conversation about people they knew in town. Someone named Curious Craig, whoever that was, hadn't shown up. They seemed glad about that. They also talked about the shitty PA system and how they at least made enough to pay for gas, not like last night in Cincinnati. And how late they could leave before they made their next show. To my ringing ears it was all a blur of words, and I contributed none. I just stood there trying and failing not to stare.

After a while the bassist and drummer drifted off, leaving

me alone with the lead singer. In her combat boots she must have been six foot three. She shook her long unkempt hair away from her face, smiled down at me and said "Hey, man."

We were alone. Oh god. I sipped my drink and almost missed the straw. My hands were shaking. "Your show rocked."

"Thanks."

"What's your name?"

I'm Stitch," she said. You?"

"Evan." My name sounded stupid. I wish I had a cooler name. Something more punk. Like Sid. Or Iggy. Or something. Anything. Up until that point I'd spent my life telling people "It's not Kevin, it's Evan." They always got my name wrong.

"Nice to meet you, Evan. This is our first time here."

"No shit?" I said.

"We're playing Baltimore tomorrow and then Philly and then New York. After that we're finally done. We've been on the road for nine months."

"That's cool," I said. "I've never been to New York."

"You really liked us?"

"Absolutely. I didn't know your stuff before. Seeing you live though, you guys were awesome." The sound coming out of my mouth was so high-pitched I might as well have been sucking helium.

"I'm glad, man. 'Cause I have something for you." She handed me a CD. "There may be some songs on there you don't get. But that's okay. Just keep listening. A lot of our audience doesn't at first."

"Why?"

"Because most of our stuff is political. About being a woman in this modern world."

"Well. I think you're doing a good job. Being a woman. I mean—"

Stitch laughed. I felt my face flush. She pointed to the CD.

"Our address is in there. If there are lyrics you don't get, or something you want to talk about, write me. Promise you will, ok?"

"I promise. Thanks," I said. "And for the drink, too. I guess you have to take off, right? I won't keep you."

Somewhere along the line I picked up that phrase from adults. I won't keep you. It sounded so polite and at the same time aloof, like perhaps I wanted her to leave even though that was precisely the last thing I wanted to happen. If I could've hopped on their beat up van and gone all over the world with them I would have done so in a heartbeat. Everything I learned about not getting into vans with strangers went out the door.

Her laugh was like gravel in a glass. It was only then I noticed she'd been smoking. She'd been holding the cigarette behind her and exhaling above my head.

"You're not keeping me at all. Shit, dude, you're a fan. We're trying to slay them every night but it's hard. Someone like you means a lot. Especially to me."

"I do?"

"Uh-huh. You hadn't heard of us before now. And I could see it in your eyes, man. We converted you tonight. That feeling is why we keep playing every night."

She bent over and looked at me. I hated it when tall people would bend over to talk to me. It made me embarrassed the same way I felt embarrassed by having an erection appear at the drop of a hat or show of a thigh or the sight of combat boots or proximity to girls in general.

I could smell beer and cigarettes. And two kinds of sweat, The "I played my heart out," kind of sweat. And the "I've been living in a van for months," kind of sweat. She didn't smell anything like Desiree.

"I need to ask you something, ok?"

"Go ahead." I said, swallowing hard.

"Are you with anybody?"

My heart beat so hard it felt like the amps were pounding out the bass again. Can a thirteen and a half year old be nonchalant? I gave it my best try. I sipped my soda and walked over to the bar to put it down on the counter.

"If you're asking me if I'm going with anyone, I'm not," I said. "I'm single."

The laughter came out before she could put her hand over her mouth. Even though my face turned red, I still had to laugh. I was a teenaged idiot.

"I'm sorry." She sucked on her cigarette and blew it just above my head again. She dropped ash on my shirt by accident, but brushed it off. "I meant like, I know it's an all ages show, but we're not used to people like you coming out to see us. I appreciate it like hell. I just meant like how are you going to get home." She paused for a minute. "Do you have a home?"

I felt a sinking in the pit of my stomach. The bond was broken. We were no longer relating like common musicians. Even though I hadn't told her I was studying the drums. She should have known it, though. I looked the part. My forearms were drummer-sized. I'd been moving in time to her music all night long. It should have been obvious.

For an irrational second, I hated her. She had screamed in my face and blew smoke around me and gotten me aroused and now she was treating me like—

"I've got someone picking me up at ten-thirty." I pointed. "My dad's gonna wait for me outside."

She dropped the subject with her cigarette, stubbing both out with her boot. "Fuck yeah, man."

We stood there looking at each other. I dug in to my wallet. I didn't have a piece of paper for an autograph. All I had was left over change from the Diet Coke. I handed her a five-dollar bill "Could you sign this?"

She asked the bartender for a something to write with and he gave her a red marker. She held the bill to my chest using it as a makeshift desk. The marker went over a nipple and it was instant boner once again.

She folded the bill and handed it to me. "There you go, little dude."

The house lights were dimming. The Frampton Brothers were about to come on. The sound guy was talking into the microphone Check one. Check two. Check, check, check."

Stitch lit up a fresh cigarette, and blew the smoke right in my face this time. She got really close to me. I could see the running mascara and lipstick smears. And somewhere beneath the smoke and beer, and sweat and more sweat, the faint smell of sweet. "Be careful tonight. The world's a fucked up place. And The Pussy Kills like to take care of their fans."

Before I could react, she closed her eyes and kissed me on the cheek.

She stood up straight and smoothed her dress, took a drag of her smoke and blew it out the corner of her mouth. "See you next time. Don't forget to write."

Stich went past the bar and out the side exit where the van was waiting for them. The kiss burned my cheek.

The Frampton Brothers launched into their first song, one called "Leonard Zelig," where all they did the entire song was shout "Leonard Zelig." Kind of like that song "Tequila" that Pee-Wee Herman danced to. Except at the end of the song, The Framptons would paraphrase a Modern Lovers song and say, "Nobody ever called Leonard Zelig an asshole." I didn't know until later about the Modern Lovers reference. It took a few years to realize there are so many connections in music, as in life.

The club was more energized now. I could feel people dancing all around me. It was only at that moment that I realized a ton of people showed up after all. The floor was packed.

I unfolded the five-dollar bill and squinted to read what she had written. She'd left the five on the bill alone but added a bunch of zeros after it, along with a message: To our number one fan in Pittsburgh. 5,000,000,000. Spend it in one place. XOXO Stitch.

I made my way to the bathroom to check my face. Sure enough there was a smear of dirty red lipstick on my cheek. I wanted to leave it there and show everyone I knew at school. I wanted to find Desiree and tell her. "You may have kissed every boy in school, but a grown woman kissed me."

Instead I washed it off, drying my face with a paper towel that felt like sandpaper. It didn't matter. I'd been kissed by rock and roll. There was power in that kiss. I was pretty sure I'd retain it well into high school.

Acknowledgements

A heartfelt thanks to the bands and musicians who have over the years been a source of inspiration:

Ween, Mercury Rev, The Woolen Men, Guided By Voices, Tricky, Luna, Camper Van Beethoven, The Church, Funkadelic, Robyn Hitchcock, Adrian Belew, Sun Ra, and The Dead Milkmen.

Thanks also to my brother Jason for being a friend, supporter, litmus test and moral compass.